STEPHEN DANDO-COLLINS

the war dog

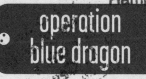

operation
blue dragon

RANDOM HOUSE AUSTRALIA

A Random House book
Published by Random House Australia Pty Ltd
Level 3, 100 Pacific Highway, North Sydney NSW 2060
www.randomhouse.com.au

First published by Random House Australia in 2013

Addresses for companies within the Random House Group can be found at
www.randomhouse.com.au/offices

National Library of Australia
Cataloguing-in-Publication Entry

Author: Dando-Collins, Stephen, 1950–
Title: Caesar the war dog: operation blue dragon / Stephen Dando-Collins
ISBN: 978 0 85798 053 3 (pbk.)
Series: Caesar the war dog; 2
Target Audience: For primary school age.
Subjects: Dogs – Juvenile fiction.
Detector dogs – Afghanistan – Juvenile fiction.
Detector dogs – New South Wales – Sydney – Juvenile fiction.
Dogs – War use – Juvenile fiction.
Dewey Number: A823.3

Cover photographs: skydivers © iStockphoto.com/vadimmmus; landscape of
Band-e-Amir lakes, Afghanistan © iStockphoto.com/cristophe_cerisier;
camouflage pattern © italianphoto/Shutterstock.com
Cover design by Astred Hicks, designcherry
Typeset by Midland Typesetters, Australia
Printed in Australia by Griffin Press, an accredited ISO AS/NZS 14001:2004
Environmental Management System printer

Random House Australia uses papers that are natural, renewable and recyclable
products and made from wood grown in sustainable forests. The logging and
manufacturing processes are expected to conform to the environmental regulations of
the country of origin.

For Louise, who has trained me well.
With grateful thanks to Richard and Zoe.
And for the many fans of Caesar the War Dog *who*
couldn't wait for the next adventure to begin: Seek on!

CHAPTER 1

In the golden glow of dawn, an Australian Army Black Hawk helicopter swept in low over Sydney Harbour. Below, ferries, water taxis, speedboats and yachts were already out on the water, leaving foaming white trails behind them. Inside the helicopter's passenger compartment, Sergeant Ben Fulton of the Special Operations Engineer Regiment (SOER) sat in full combat rig of bulletproof vest, camouflage jacket and trousers. A holstered Browning Hi Power 9 mm automatic pistol was strapped low on his right thigh, and a rappelling harness covered his torso. Leather combat gloves moulded to his hands so precisely they were like a second skin. On the belt around his waist were a full water canteen, a sheathed combat knife, spare Browning magazines and two pouches – the larger one empty, the smaller one containing dog biscuits.

The helicopter's side doors were open, and the combined noise of the aircraft's engines, spinning rotors and slipstream was almost deafening. Headphones covering Ben's ears protected him from the noise and allowed him to listen to the exchanges between the Black Hawk's four-man crew.

'Two minutes to insertion, Sergeant Fulton,' the pilot's voice crackled in Ben's ears.

A small microphone attached to the end of a stalk that projected from Ben's headset permitted him to talk to pilot and crew. 'Copy that, skipper,' he replied.

Between Ben's legs sat a brown labrador – Caesar, the most celebrated and decorated explosive detection dog, or EDD, in Australian military history. Caesar was calm and content despite the noisy, windy ride. He wore an operational harness, doggles (the custom-made goggles used by Special Forces dogs on airborne missions) and puppy Peltors, which are ear-protectors for dogs.

Briefly lifting the puppy Peltor from Caesar's right ear, Ben yelled above the din of engines and rotors, 'Here we go again, mate.'

By way of reply, Caesar turned and licked his handler on the cheek. Ben ruffled Caesar's neck, smiling, then sat up and began to check his equipment one last time. Everything about Caesar's demeanour told Ben that his EDD was thrilled to be with him and back on operations. What a road they had travelled since they'd last been in action together. That had been in Afghanistan when EDD and handler were separated during a gruelling firefight with the Taliban. Ben had been seriously wounded and his best friend, Sergeant Charlie Grover of the Special Air Service Regiment, had lost his legs in a rocket-propelled grenade blast.

For thirteen long months Caesar went missing in Afghanistan while Ben and his family back home had tried desperately to track him down. And then one day Sergeant Tim McHenry of the US Rangers spotted Caesar performing in a two-man travelling circus at a remote forward operating base in Uruzgan Province and had commenced the process to reunite Ben and Caesar. Six months later, upon Caesar's return to Australia, Ben had done what many had considered a strange thing. Knowing that Charlie was struggling with his recovery, and with the agreement of his children, Ben had given his beloved Caesar to Charlie to serve as his care dog.

Charlie and Caesar had been a great pairing, with Charlie teaching Caesar more than a hundred hand signal commands. Though Caesar had been loyal to Charlie, Ben had known that deep down Caesar was missing him and his explosives detection work, just as Ben and his family were missing Caesar. During that time Ben worked with another EDD, Soapy. But Soapy was no Caesar. And, sadly, Soapy was later found to be suffering from a hearing defect. Deafness is a problem developed by some labradors as they grow older, and what Ben had thought to be disobedience was in fact the result of Soapy's failing hearing.

A deaf or partially deaf EDD is not a dog that can be used for military field work. Soapy was a danger to himself, to his handler and to the troops around them. Learning of Soapy's condition, the Special Operations Engineer Regiment had decided that he was to be immediately retired.

Just as Ben was arranging for Soapy to live with a kind family in Holsworthy, he'd received a call from Charlie. After the two old friends caught up on each other's news, Ben was intrigued to hear how Charlie was finding his brand-new prosthetic legs.

'They fit like a glove, mate,' Charlie had replied. 'So much so, I'm planning to go back on SAS ops.'

'Really?' Ben had said, incredulous. 'No one's ever done that before.'

'I know. General Jones wants me to take the SAS selection course on the new legs. When I pass, I get to go back on ops.' Charlie had taken that course years before to get into the SAS and had passed with flying colours. But that had been on two good legs.

'Ah,' Ben had responded, 'I guess the general expects you to flunk the course this time because of your prosthetics.'

'I'm sure he does, and I'm going to prove him wrong, Ben,' Charlie had defiantly declared.

Charlie had been so confident he would pass the test he'd promptly returned Caesar to Ben. And here they were – Ben and Caesar, a team once more, to the delight of both. Prior to this they'd undertaken a two-week EDD refresher course at the Holsworthy Army Barracks, with Caesar showing that he'd lost none of his incredible ability to sniff out even the faintest hint of explosives. But that had only been practice. Today, Ben and Caesar were on a live op, tasked with helping to protect one of the most important people on the planet – the secretary-general of the United Nations, who was scheduled to open the World Peace Conference at the Sydney Opera House later in the day.

'Thirty seconds,' came the pilot's voice.

'Copy that,' Ben replied, before removing his headset and strapping on his Kevlar combat helmet. From now on he would receive and transmit messages with the crew via hand signals. Ben slid goggles from the helmet down over his eyes, clipped a line to Caesar's harness, gave him a reassuring pat then rose to his feet.

His tail wagging, Caesar looked up. The expectant expression on his face seemed to say, *Ready to have fun when you are, boss.* To Caesar, EDD work was all fun.

Ben hooked his own harness to the rappelling line, then looked out of the heelo's open door. The day's first rays of sunlight glinted off the tiles of the sweep-ing, curved sails of the Sydney Opera House. Ben never

5

ceased to marvel at the beauty of this world-famous harbourside structure, but today he had no time to admire the architecture. As Ben stood in one doorway, a crewman manoeuvred Caesar to the other. Taking up the slack on the line attached to the labrador's harness, the crewman knelt beside him with one hand gripping Caesar.

Caesar was completely at ease. Standing in the doorway, he poked his snout out into the early morning air and revelled in the slipstream rushing over his face. To him, it was just like sticking his nose out a speeding car's window – but better!

The Black Hawk pulled up abruptly, its nose rising a little before levelling out to hover fifty metres above a courtyard on the northern, harbour side of the Opera House. The Black Hawk crewman nearest to him sent Ben's rappelling line snaking down to the brick paving of the courtyard below.

'Line down,' the crewman informed the pilot.

'It's a "go" for insertion,' the pilot instructed.

The crewman gave Ben the thumbs up. With a nod, Ben launched himself out the door. In a matter of seconds, he rappelled down the line, sliding expertly to the ground. After unhitching his harness, Ben looked up at the Black Hawk and gave a thumbs up to the aircrew. Caesar was then eased out the second door and quickly lowered. All the way down, Caesar looked straight ahead. While Ben knew that Caesar didn't consider being lowered from choppers to be the best fun, he knew that Caesar didn't hate it either. His faithful EDD simply accepted it as part of the job of helping Ben.

As soon as Caesar's paws touched the ground, Ben released the clip that attached the dangling line to Caesar's harness and clipped a short, two-metre metal operational leash to his collar. Ben, again, signalled to the heelo. Trailing the two rappelling lines that were being electronically winched in, the Black Hawk lifted away. Climbing rapidly, the heelo turned back the way it had come, and soon disappeared from sight. The insertion had taken less than two minutes.

After sliding his goggles up so that they sat on the front of his helmet, Ben dropped to one knee and removed Caesar's doggles and Peltors, then slipped them into the empty pouch on his belt. Looking around, he saw a group of blue-uniformed police officers standing at the edge of the forecourt. Rising to his feet, he urged Caesar forward and strode toward them. Coming to attention in front of a grey-haired police officer wearing the insignia of a superintendent, Ben saluted.

'Sergeant Ben Fulton and EDD Caesar reporting for duty, sir,' Ben announced.

Superintendent Ryan Strong returned Ben's salute then said, with a friendly smile in Caesar's direction, 'Glad to have the army's best EDD team working with us today, Sergeant. This combined services op is of vital importance.'

'Yes, sir.' Ben had been thoroughly briefed back at SOER headquarters on what was expected of Caesar and himself that day.

'Fulton, Sergeant Leon Kovic and his police detection dog, Rubi, will be working with you.' Superintendent Strong turned to a police dog handler standing nearby with a black kelpie on a leash. 'Good hunting. Don't miss a thing. I'm not having anything happen to the secretary-general of the United Nations on *my* watch. My reputation is on the line – and so is yours.'

'Yes, sir,' Ben returned. 'You can rely on us, sir.'

While Ben was receiving his orders, Caesar was eyeing off Rubi. His tail wagged slowly, signalling that he wanted to be friends with the keplie, while the expression on his face seemed to suggest he was thinking to himself, *You look interesting. What are you doing here?* Rubi, for her part, looked the other way, almost as if she was embarrassed by Caesar's attention.

As the superintendent hastily led the rest of his men away, Ben and Caesar approached Sergeant Kovic and Rubi. 'Ben Fulton,' he said in introduction, offering a gloved hand. 'Good to be working with you, Kovic.'

Sergeant Kovic gave Ben's extended hand a cursory shake. At the same time, Caesar went to say hello to Rubi by sniffing her rear end – the way that dogs do –

but Rubi let out a wary yelp and backed away. 'So,' Kovic said with a sneer, 'the rock stars have arrived. Going to show us how it's done, are you, Fulton?'

'What do you mean?' Ben returned.

Sergeant Kovic waved a hand at the sky. 'Flitting in by heelo. Cars aren't good enough for you famous Afghanistan veterans? Just because your dog has been on TV and in the papers and got medals.'

Ben was surprised by the policeman's antagonistic attitude. 'Mate, we had to come all the way up from Holsworthy,' he said, trying to keep it friendly. 'If we hadn't hitched a ride with an army Black Hawk, we'd still be stuck in traffic. We're here to protect the secretary-general of the UN, aren't we? Let's do our jobs.'

'Just don't let your big head get in the way,' Kovic replied. 'I'm in charge.'

Even though they were of the same rank, this was a New South Wales Police op, so Kovic would be in charge of the EDD sweep. Ben, contrary to Kovic's belief, had no problem with that and was determined not to argue. 'Gotcha. Where do we start?'

'The Concert Hall. That's where the secretary-general will be speaking.'

'Okay. Lead on.'

Even before Ben had finished, Kovic had turned his back to him. With Rubi on a tight leash, Kovic led the way into the Opera House via an emergency door.

Ben and Caesar followed. They walked along a lengthy concrete corridor that ran beneath the building, their footsteps echoing dully. There were no windows, just bright white ceiling lights. Up a set of concrete stairs, the dogs taking the steps in bounds, they passed through a metal fire door to emerge inside the vast Concert Hall, close to the front of the stage.

For a moment, Ben and Caesar stopped to take in the impressive hall, its ceiling soaring more than twenty metres above their heads. The world's leading singers, dancers and musicians had performed on the stage here, to millions of adoring fans. But this evening, the auditorium would be filled by important delegates from around the globe, and the stage would be occupied by speech-making dignitaries.

At the moment, the only people in the hall with the EDD teams were local police officers and a plain-clothed Federal Police security detail with earphones in their ears. With no curtains or stage scenery in place, the stage was bare. Above it hung eighteen large clear perspex reflectors known as 'the clouds'. As Ben knew, these had been introduced to improve the quality of sound for the audience. Ben also knew, from his earlier briefing at Holsworthy Army Barracks, that the stage, sitting just over a metre above the auditorium floor, was about twenty metres wide downstage and eleven metres deep.

'We start with the stage – that's where the secretary-general and the VIPs will be for the opening speeches tonight,' directed Kovic. 'You take the back half and I'll sweep from the front.' With that, he stalked downstage with Rubi on a close leash.

'Roger that.' Ben, in contrast, unclipped Caesar's leash and released him. Kneeling beside his canine partner, he said with affectionate pride and a double pat, 'Time to go to work, Caesar. Seek on, boy. Start at the back.'

With his nose close to the timber floor, Caesar quickly trotted to the back of the stage. To him, this was no different to any bridge, bazaar or farm compound that he'd searched in war-torn Afghanistan. The background aromas were different, but Caesar's obsessive focus was on using his incredibly powerful sense of smell to detect the telltale scent of explosives chemicals. When Caesar had passed his basic training several years back, becoming Australian Army EDD 556, he'd been rated by the chief instructor, Sergeant Angelo, as one of the most outstanding explosive detection dogs to have ever passed the course.

Sniffing every rope, every girder, every winch and lighting switchboard, Caesar went in search of explosives that might have been planted by terrorists. Ben, at times, would whistle directions to his EDD, and each time Caesar would respond by immediately turning left or right to continue his search. Caesar completed checking his allocated part of the stage in half the time it took Kovic and Rubi to check the front section.

'Your dog was fast,' Kovic snapped, but he wasn't being complimentary. '*Too* fast for my liking. He could have missed something.'

'Caesar miss something?' Ben shook his head. 'Highly unlikely.'

'I hear your dog hasn't been on a live op in quite a while,' said Kovic, looking Ben square in the face. 'Maybe he's rusty. Rubi and me, we'll check the back half of the stage, too. Just in case.'

'That would be a waste of time,' Ben declared. 'Caesar has checked it and, believe me, it's clear.'

Kovic glared at him. 'As I understand it, Fulton, your dog's last job was looking after some bloke in a wheelchair. Isn't that right?' A supercilious smirk tugged at the corners of his mouth.

'Caesar is as sharp as he ever was,' Ben countered, defending his four-legged friend, who was sitting attentively by his side. 'The back half of the stage is clear. End of story.'

Sergeant Kovic ignored him and proceeded to lead Rubi to the back of the stage.

'Listen,' Ben said, 'if you're going to double-check every metre that Caesar checks it's pointless having us here. This place has to be cleared by four o'clock. It'll take two dogs to do that. Either you trust Caesar, or we head back to base and leave you to it.'

'You can't leave!' exclaimed Kovic, a note of panic in his voice. 'You're under orders.'

Ben shrugged. 'Then let us do our job, mate, and back off!'

Their confrontation was brought to an end by a voice from the back of the hall. 'Sergeant Kovic, what's the hold-up?' demanded Superintendent Strong, who stood with his hands on his hips, silhouetted in a distant doorway.

'Er, no hold-up, sir,' Kovic quickly replied, shooting Ben a nervous look.

'Then I suggest you get a move on,' Strong bellowed. 'We don't have all day!'

'Yes, sir.'

'How about we split up and each search half the complex?' Ben suggested to Kovic. 'We'll never get the job done in time, otherwise.'

'Yeah, yeah, all right,' Kovic begrudgingly agreed.

The two EDD teams went their separate ways.

Several hours later, Ben and Caesar emerged into the main forecourt. Caesar gladly welcolmed the breeze, with its hint of ocean saltiness, after being inside for so long. Although, the mixture of sounds from passing boats, helicopters and chattering tourists did take a little getting used to after the thick concrete silence of the empty Concert Hall.

After Ben and Caesar methodically checked the forecourt and the flight of broad steps that led to the main doors of the Opera House, Ben satisfied himself that all was clear, and gave Caesar a break. Even though Caesar had more stamina than most EDDs and would work for hours on end, Ben wasn't taking any chances – especially on a job as crucial as protecting the secretary-general of the United Nations. It was important for handlers to remember that even the best EDDs could become bored and lose interest if worked for long stretches of time. Sitting on the main steps, Ben gave Caesar a dog biscuit, which was washed down by a few gulps of water from his canteen.

'You're doing a great job, mate,' said Ben, ruffling his labrador's ears.

Caesar's tail wagged happily.

It wasn't long before Superintendent Strong came striding up to the pair. 'Where's Sergeant Kovic?' he asked Ben, looking frazzled.

'Still working inside, sir,' Ben replied, quickly coming to attention.

'Have you checked the forecourt?'

'Yes, sir. All clear.'

'I want you to check the secretary-general's arrival route.'

Ben hesitated. 'With respect, sir, Sergeant Kovic is in charge of the sweep, as he keeps telling me.'

An irritated scowl came over the superintendent's face. 'You take your orders from *me*.'

'Yes, sir,' replied Ben. 'Which way will the secretary-general be coming, sir?'

'He's arriving by water,' said Strong, turning to look across Sydney Harbour.

Ben followed his gaze. 'By water?'

'He's staying across the harbour at Admiralty House, the Sydney residence of the Governor-General. A Navy boat will bring the secretary-general over here this afternoon – it's much easier to guarantee his safety that way.' Superintendent Strong produced a faint smile. 'That way, the secretary-general also gets to have a nice little cruise on Sydney Harbour.'

'Exactly where will the secretary-general land, sir?'

'At the Man O'War Jetty.' Strong pointed to the jetty, to the right of the forecourt. 'Check it out, Sergeant.'

'Yes, sir.' Ben saluted then moved off toward the harbour's edge with Caesar. The Man O'War Jetty was an old structure that dated back almost 200 years. Originally, there'd been a colonial gun battery on Bennelong Point, where the Opera House now stood. In days gone by, crews from warships had come ashore there.

Nowadays, the jetty was only occasionally used by VIPs and tour groups coming to the Opera House by water.

Methodically, Ben and Caesar checked the T-shaped jetty. Caesar scoured it with his nose down but found nothing of interest. Having just completed the check, Ben was reattaching the metal leash to Caesar's collar when Sergeant Kovic and Rubi arrived on the scene.

'Who told you to check that jetty?' Kovic demanded.

'Superintendent Strong did,' Ben replied.

'You should have told me what you were doing.' When Ben remained silent, refusing to take the bait and argue with him, Kovic looked toward the water and said, 'Well then, is Man O'War Jetty clear?'

'Yes, it's clear.' As Ben spoke, he felt Caesar straining on his leash. Frowning, Ben looked down. 'Caesar, what's up, boy?'

Caesar let out a little whimper, as if to say, *I'm not sure, boss, but I want to check it out.*

Ben let Caesar drag him toward the water's edge, where low waves were breaking up against the sandstone seawall beside the Man O'War Jetty.

'Looks like your labrador wants to go for a swim, Fulton,' Kovic said sarcastically.

'Maybe he does,' Ben murmured distractedly, intrigued by his EDD's behaviour. He let Caesar tug him all the way to the wall, where the labrador put his front legs on the sandstone ridge and looked obsessively at the water. Ben, dropping to one knee beside him, unclipped Caesar's leash. 'What's up, mate?' Ben asked quietly. 'Something bothering you? Something in the water?'

Caesar looked at Ben and let out a little whine, as if to say, *There's something here, boss*. Then he returned his gaze to the water lapping beneath the jetty.

'Okay, Caesar, seek on!' Ben instructed.

With that, Caesar sprang elegantly over the wall and dived into the harbour, hitting the water with a splash.

'What the heck is that dog up to?' said the bemused Kovic, bringing Rubi to stand beside Ben.

'You'll see,' said Ben.

Paddling strongly through the waves, Caesar headed toward the underside of the Man O'War Jetty. Despite his strength, his progress was slow in the rough water as incoming waves washed back off the wall. Caesar gradually worked his way under the jetty and out of sight. Meanwhile, the sight of two dog handlers peering into the harbour attracted the attention of several of the policemen on duty, who gathered around Ben and Sergeant Kovic.

With Caesar out of his sight, Ben was beginning to worry. 'Caesar, where are you, mate?' he called.

Superintendent Strong bustled up to them. 'What's happening?' he demanded, nudging policemen aside.

'The army dog has gone fishing, sir.' Kovic chortled.

'And you might be surprised with what he catches,'

added Ben, defending his EDD. Again he called, 'Caesar, where are you, mate?'

But there was no sign of Caesar.

'Your dog's down *there*?' Strong said, with a mixture of concern and puzzlement. 'Will he be all right?'

'I think so, sir,' Ben returned, sounding a little uncertain now that there was still no response. 'Caesar! Come back, mate.'

A chocolate-brown head appeared from beneath the jetty. Swimming toward Ben, Caesar had a black plastic parcel between his teeth. Normally, when Caesar found something suspicious, he would immediately sit and look at it intently. In the EDD business, this was known as his 'signature', and Ben had learned long ago to recognise what it meant when Caesar did this. But here in the water, Caesar couldn't do that. So, being both a very clever and conscientious dog, he had made a decision – to take the package to Ben.

'Caesar!' Ben yelled, trying not to sound too alarmed. 'Let go of the package. Let go of the package, mate!'

'What's he found?' Strong asked, squinting into the waves below.

'Looks like we might have an IED, sir,' Ben replied.

Superintendent Strong paled and turned to Sergeant Kovic. 'Have we by any chance planted a fake bomb for exercise purposes?'

'Er . . . no, sir,' Kovic answered, looking sheepish.

'I thought the water police had checked that jetty.' The superintendent clicked his two-way radio on. 'This is Strong. Clear the area!' he commanded urgently. 'Clear the area! And send in the Rescue and Bomb Disposal Unit. We have a potential live IED. And they'll need a boat. I repeat, clear the area of all non-essential personnel!'

Ben, his heart pounding in his chest, called to his EDD. 'Let go of the package, Caesar. Let go!' Ben was worried that Caesar could puncture it with his teeth and set off the bomb.

Caesar got the message. He released the parcel, which, to Ben's great relief, floated free. Then, as Kovic and Superintendent Strong kept an eye on the parcel bobbing beside the seawall, Ben directed Caesar around to the steps at the foot of the Man O'War Jetty. There, on his knees, he grabbed Caesar's front legs and helped him scramble from the water.

'Well done, mate! You haven't lost your touch,' Ben said proudly. But for Caesar it was first things first – he vigorously shook himself from head to tail, giving Ben a face full of spray. Laughing, Ben pulled Caesar close. 'Well done, boy. Well done!'

Caesar, pleased that Ben approved of what he'd done, licked him on the face and nuzzled into him.

'But we won't be picking up any more packages in future,' Ben added affectionately.

Superintendent Strong scowled at Sergeant Kovic. 'Your dog didn't pick up any trace of that IED, Kovic?'

Kovic looked as if he were about to protest, but seemed to think better of it. 'No, sir.'

'A good thing we had Sergeant Fulton and Caesar with us here today then.' The superintendent shot Kovic a severe look. 'Wouldn't you say, Sergeant Kovic?'

Kovic smiled weakly. 'Yes, sir.'

CHAPTER 2

Hand over hand, Sergeant Charlie Grover VC hauled himself up the rope, then brought himself to his feet on top of the sea cliff. Behind him, nine other men were struggling to climb fifty-metre ropes. On the rocks below, where waves were crashing with angry explosions of spray, another thirty men waited their turn. Like Charlie, every man had a heavy pack on his back. Unlike Charlie, they were not yet members of the SAS. From each arm of the Australian Army, they had come on this selection course to try to gain entry into the most elite unit in the Australian military – some say the most elite, respected and feared Special Forces unit in the world. Four out of ten candidates had already failed the first test. Little more than one in three of those who remained would pass this final back-breaking, mind-bending three-week selection course and be inducted into the SAS.

Charlie, dripping perspiration, was the first man to top the cliff. He had dragged himself up using only his powerful arms. Even when confined to a wheel-chair, Charlie had continued to lift weights to keep up his impressive upper body strength. As he surveyed the soldiers below, Charlie stood on two new prosthetic legs clad in camouflage trousers. He'd shown them to Ben's children, Josh and Maddie, and they had been amazed at how lifelike they were. Made of Kevlar, they were hollow and covered with a plastic 'skin' that looked incredibly real – they even had fake hairs on them.

Charlie had spent several weeks becoming accus-tomed to these new legs. The stumps of his own amputated legs sat snugly in them. One prosthetic fitted below his right knee, but because his left leg had been amputated above the knee, the prosthetic for that leg included a false knee that bent just like the real thing would. These prosthetics had soon become so comfort-able that Charlie almost forgot he was wearing them.

To see Charlie walk now, it was hard to tell he had false legs. It was only when he ran that it became appar-ent. As the mechanical knee on the left leg was a little stiffer than the real thing, Charlie appeared to limp a little. Not that he had let that slow him down. In a flat-out 100-metre race with others on the SAS selection course, the super-determined Charlie hadn't been the fastest but he hadn't come last, either. That had been a big surprise for the instructors running the course. They had expected Charlie to struggle on his prosthetic legs.

If Charlie had been anyone else, he wouldn't even have been here. But he was a Victoria Cross awardee, and that counted for a lot. He also had friends in high places. His former commanding officer in Afghanistan, Major General Michael Jones, had recently been made the Australian Army's Special Operations Commander, in charge of Australia's Special Forces units. This included the SAS Regiment, the 1st and 2nd Commando Regiments, and the Special Operations Engineer Regiment – Ben and Caesar's unit. A lot of junior officers at Special Operations Command had been sceptical about Charlie retaking the SAS selection course. Even General Jones feared that Charlie would fail it, and he'd told Charlie so to his face.

Charlie could hear Jones in his head now. 'I'm only doing this for old time's sake, Grover,' the general had said the day he'd given Charlie the okay to take the course. 'And to prove to *you* that you'll have to settle for a desk job and forget about going out on ops again.'

'Thank you, sir,' Charlie had responded. 'I'll be pleased to prove you wrong.'

A harsh voice interrupted Charlie's thoughts. 'What do you think you're doing, soldier? Having a little bludge, are we?'

Charlie jerked back to reality. Grey-haired SAS Sergeant Major Cliff Howard, the chief instructor running the course, had his gnarled face right in Charlie's. 'No, Sergeant Major,' Charlie snapped back.

'Then get your backside out of here! You may be first man up the cliff face, Grover, but there's a jungle out there waiting for you. Let's see how you and your plastic legs cope with that!'

Charlie quickly unclipped himself from the rope-climbing harness, stepped around the chief instructor and set off at a jog along a dirt track that stretched into a forest of trees.

The sergeant major watched him go and shook his head at the sight of Charlie's awkward run as he disappeared beyond the tree line. For twenty years, Howard had served on secret SAS operations around the world and had fought alongside Charlie on some of those missions. But that was back when Charlie had two good legs. As far as the sergeant major was concerned, Victoria Cross or no Victoria Cross, Charlie Grover's career in active service was over and he had no business being on the course. It took men of extraordinary physical and mental toughness to survive SAS missions – anyone could see that a legless man didn't fit that criterion. Sergeant Major Howard was convinced that, sooner or later, Charlie's prosthetics would fail him, and the VC awardee's hopes and plans would come crashing down in a heap.

As Charlie ran determinedly along the bush track, pace by pace he pushed the words of the negative chief instructor from his mind. He thought, instead, of Caesar and Ben. He missed his four-legged friend and felt sad about giving Caesar up. He knew, of course, that Caesar was over the moon about being reunited with Ben, and that Ben and his family were equally pleased with the arrangement.

Caesar's loyalty and devotion had astonished even Charlie. Ben had once told Charlie that Caesar never forgot what he was told and never forgot the people in his life. And, most importantly, Caesar never gave up. Charlie couldn't think of better qualities for a care dog.

'Never forget, never give up,' Charlie began to chant to himself, in time to his pounding steps. He was determined to block out Sergeant Major Howard's disdain and to push through the pain of running on nothing but adrenaline for hours on end. 'Never forget, never give up. Never forget, never give up. Never forget, never give up!'

* * *

Charlie was covered from head to toe in mud. All around him, the other men on the selection course were on their stomachs, struggling through the red-brown mud, trying to crawl toward a ridge up ahead.

'Come on, Grover!' bellowed Sergeant Major Howard,

standing beside the patch of mud and glaring down at Charlie. 'Get a move on! You're slowing everybody down!'

Charlie, exhausted, looked up at the sergeant major through eyes that had not closed for sleep in fifty hours spent running, swimming and climbing.

'Or should we treat you as a special case?' the sergeant major continued. 'Is the weight of that Victoria Cross of yours too much for you to bear?'

Charlie had come to think that the chief instructor had it in for him and was trying to bully him into giving up. Well, tough luck, thought Charlie. He was determined to complete the course and prove all his critics wrong. For inspiration, Charlie thought of a boyhood hero of his, British fighter pilot Douglas Bader, who had lost both his legs after crashing his plane. Bader had been fitted with prosthetic legs that were much more primitive than the ones Charlie was wearing. Yet Bader not only got into a Spitfire fighter plane to fly it with superb skill despite his prosthetic legs, he'd become one of the greatest air aces of the Second World War. If Douglas Bader could return to active duty with prosthetic legs, so, Charlie told himself, could he.

'Never forget, never give up,' Charlie mumbled, dragging himself through the mud.

'What's that, Grover?' the sergeant major barked. 'Got something to say? Want to drop out, do we?'

'No, Sergeant Major,' Charlie yelled in response.

'Then get a wriggle on, man!'

'Roger to that, Sergeant Major!' Charlie returned through gritted teeth, dragging himself forward on his bleeding forearms.

Charlie would not admit it to anyone, but his prosthetic legs were slowing him down. He could live with the fact that after many hours on them without a rest they were beginning to chafe his skin and make the stumps of his legs bleed. But the worst thing about them was that they gave him no propulsion in the mud. They dragged behind him like lead weights, forcing Charlie to use his arms and upper body for much of the strenuous physical work the instructors were putting him through. But Charlie would rather drop dead before he quit voluntarily. Pulling himself to his feet, he drove his plastic legs toward the top of the ridge.

Once there, he could see that the rocky ground ahead dropped down to a fast-moving stream. Dense bush spread beyond the brown water. Another soldier on the course was already swimming across to the other side. An instructor standing by the stream looked up and urgently waved for Charlie to come down to him, then pointed to another instructor waiting on the far bank. Charlie dropped onto his backside and slid down the slope, then plunged into the water. His legs trailed behind him as he swam across. With a supreme effort, he dragged himself up onto the bank.

'Enjoying this, soldier?' the second instructor asked with a leering smile.

'Haven't had so much fun in years,' Charlie quipped. He was determined to wipe the smile off the face of this young instructor, an SAS trooper who Charlie recognised to be a former recruit in a squad that Charlie had once commanded. Back then Charlie had been the one giving the orders. Now, no matter the rank of the aspiring SAS recruits, these instructors were in total command.

The instructor's smile disappeared. 'Move it, clever clogs! Run!'

Gathering all his strength, Charlie ran on, into the bush, following a rough path made muddy by recent rain. On and on he loped with his awkward gait. Behind him, other exhausted soldiers were pulling themselves from the stream and, dripping wet, followed him at a staggering run.

Charlie could see that several trees had fallen across the path ahead. As he came to them, he noticed that the ground fell away sharply beyond their trunks. While Charlie's prosthetics had given him the ability to walk and run again, they could not offer the agility he'd once possessed with his powerful legs of skin, bone and muscle. Rather than try to vault the fallen trees, Charlie was forced to clamber over them.

As he was awkwardly making his way across the

horizontal trunks, another SAS candidate overtook him. Taking a flying leap to clear the trees, the soldier roughly shouldered Charlie aside. In the SAS, every man helped his mates, but on this course to gain entry into the elite unit it was every man for himself.

Charlie was knocked off balance and sent toppling over the tree trunk. Feeling a strange sensation in his left leg, he tumbled over and over, down the muddy slope beyond the fallen trees. When he came to a stop at the bottom, he found that he'd landed on top of the man who had bowled him over. Without an apology, the soldier pushed Charlie away, got to his feet and continued on. But when Charlie went to get up, he couldn't. Looking down, he saw that his left leg was missing. He looked around and saw that the prosthetic had become caught between two fallen trees at the top of the rise. It jutted skyward up there, as if it had taken root.

With a loud curse, Charlie hauled himself back up the rise to retrieve it. Just as he reached the top, the chief instructor arrived. Smiling, Sergeant Major Howard took a seat on one of the fallen trunks and reached for Charlie's prosthetic. 'Lost something, Grover?' he said, holding it up.

Without a word, Charlie grabbed the prosthetic from Howard, seated himself on another tree trunk and set about refitting the leg. All the while, other men on the course went huffing and puffing past. One of the prosthetic's attachments had broken, but Charlie didn't let that stop him. Once the left leg was in place, Charlie stood up.

'Face it, Grover,' said the sergeant major. 'You're not going to finish this selection course. Quit now. No one will blame you.'

Charlie didn't reply. Climbing over the trees, he slid down the muddy slope. But when he went to run, he found that the mechanism of his left knee had seized up and jammed. The entire leg now hung stiff and useless. Charlie kept going, dragging his left prosthetic along like deadwood.

'Give up, Grover! Give up!' Howard bellowed.

But Charlie pushed on. Over the next half hour, all the men who'd been behind him on the course caught up and passed him. Undaunted, Charlie laboured on at the back of the pack, which, before long, disappeared out of sight.

It was after dark when Charlie, the last to arrive, reached a clearing where lamps hung from trees. A stop for the night had been scheduled, the first break for the men in days. Candidates were sitting and lying on the ground, done in and hardly able to move. Charlie noticed several green Army Land Rovers and a Unimog truck parked nearby, and could smell food cooking. The food was for the instructors, who would deliberately eat in full view of the hungry candidates. No candidate was permitted food until he either gave up or completed the course, which was all part of the process of breaking down the mental strength of the course participants. For the mentally tough Charlie, food was the least of his concerns.

With folded arms, chief instructor Sergeant Major Howard stood waiting for Charlie. Like the other instructors, Howard had caught a ride to the camp site in a Land Rover. The sergeant major called Charlie over, then looked very deliberately at his watch. 'You know there was a time limit on this section of the course?' he asked, a faint smile crossing his lips.

Determined to remain on his feet, Charlie stood before the sergeant major, physically shattered but mentally indomitable. He jammed his hands in his pockets. 'Yes, Sergeant Major,' he replied.

'Anyone who didn't arrive by the cut-off time is ejected from the selection course.'

Charlie nodded slowly. 'Yes, Sergeant Major.'

'The cut-off time was twenty-seven minutes ago. You weren't even close, Grover. You and your fake legs are not up to SAS standard. Take the Land Rover back to base. You're off the course.'

Charlie lay his head back and closed his eyes. It was the first time in his life that he'd been beaten. And today he'd been beaten by his own legs.

CHAPTER 3

'Look at that view!' Nan Fulton exclaimed as she stood with her family on the rolling green lawn of Admiralty House, gazing out over Sydney Harbour on a gloriously sunny winter's day.

It just so happened that the very same weekend that Ben and Caesar were in Sydney on EDD duty at the Opera House, Ben's family was also in the harbour city. Nan had brought Josh and Maddie to attend a Childen's Spectacular at the Entertainment Centre that night. So, when Ben received a last-minute invitation from none other than the secretary-general of the United Nations, he was pleased to bring his family along. And here they all were, with Ben in dress uniform and Caesar beside him wearing his emerald-green SOER dog jacket.

'There are so many people!' said Maddie, pressing shyly against her father and taking his hand.

In front of them, hundreds of guests were enjoying a Sunday afternoon garden party hosted by the governor-general of Australia.

'But not many kids,' observed Josh, sounding disappointed. Nan had told him this outing was a great honour, but he'd rather have gone to the movies.

'What a location!' Nan went on, taking in the mansion and its grounds. 'I could live here in a flash!'

Historic Admiralty House was one of the most scenic locations in the world. As the Fulton family looked out, to their right the latticework of iron girders that form the Sydney Harbour Bridge rose majestically into the sky, and directly across the harbour stood the Sydney Opera House.

Guests were seated around tables under umbrellas on the immaculately tended lawn, chattering, drinking tea and munching on sandwiches as they waited to meet the party's guest of honour, Dr Park Chun Ho, the Korean-born secretary-general of the United Nations. The secretary-general and his family were staying at Admiralty House during the World Peace Conference, which Dr Park had opened the night before.

Politicians and civic leaders from all over the country were in attendance, as well as selected journalists and foreign diplomats. At the specific request of the secretary-general himself, several last-minute names had been added to the guest list. After learning of the discovery of the package beneath the Man O'War Jetty, Dr Park had wanted to meet Caesar and his handler. Uniformed attendants guided the Fulton family to one of the outdoor tables, where they all took a seat. Caesar settled contentedly beside Ben in the shade, with his tongue hanging out.

'Daddy, what's a secretary-general do?' Maddie asked. 'Is he like a general in the army?'

'The secretary-general runs the entire United Nations, sweetheart,' Ben replied, giving Caesar a pat as he spoke.

'Oh.' Maddie thought for a moment, then asked, 'What does the United Notions do?'

'Everyone knows what the United *Nations* does,' said Josh. 'It runs the world.'

'Not quite, son,' Ben said with a smile. 'It's the world's peacekeeper, and the largest humanitarian agency on the planet.'

'That's what I meant,' said Josh.

Maddie wanted to ask what 'humanitarian' meant but didn't want Josh to make fun of her.

Nan must have read her mind. Leaning close, she said to Maddie, '"Humanitarian" means looking after people, Maddie darling.'

'Oh. Okay.' Maddie stored the piece of information away for later use.

As Ben looked at his family, his thoughts drifted to his late wife, Marie, and how she would have enjoyed a day like today. She'd died from breast cancer when the children were younger. Raising his eyes to the sky, Ben felt sure Marie was here with them all.

While the crowd mingled, the Governor-General's secretary conducted Dr Park and his family around the garden, introducing them to the guests at every table. When they finally approached the Fultons, everyone came to their feet. Except for Maddie, who had settled on the grass beside Caesar, her arms draped around his neck.

Dr Park was an elegant man, tall and slim with short dark hair. He had lively eyes and a smile that lit up his face. 'Hello, it is a great pleasure to meet you,' he said, shaking each of them by the hand. He even bent down and shook Maddie's hand. 'And this must be the famous Caesar,' he said, looking at the labrador with a smile. He turned to Ben. 'May I pat him?'

'Of course you can, sir,' Ben replied. 'Don't worry, he might be a war dog, but he doesn't bite.'

Clearly fond of dogs, Dr Park reached out to the chocolate-brown labrador. 'Hello, Caesar.' To his surprise Caesar sat up like a soldier coming to attention, and held out a raised paw – a trick Charlie had taught him. Laughing, Dr Park shook Caesar's extended paw. 'It is a pleasure to meet you,' he said. 'Thank you for your good work yesterday.'

'He likes you!' Maddie exclaimed with delight.

'And I like him,' said Dr Park, straightening. 'I imagine he is a brave and intelligent friend to you all.'

'He sure is,' Josh agreed. 'Caesar's the best!'

As seats were brought over for them, Dr Park introduced his wife and daughter. Mrs Park was a pretty, petite woman with thick, shiny black hair, while Hanna Park was a dark-haired girl of about the same age and height as Josh. Hanna spoke confidently, sounding very grown-up. Her English was excellent, though she had a faint American accent that puzzled Josh, because neither Dr Park nor Mrs Park had American accents.

The adults talked for a time about the World Peace Conference, before Dr Park looked around the table and said, 'Would you all forgive me if I had a private word with Sergeant Fulton?'

'Of course,' said Nan, speaking for them all.

Rising and taking Ben's arm, Dr Park guided him away from the table.

Caesar's head came up as he saw Ben being led away. His eyes followed his handler, and there was a questioning expression on his face that seemed to say, *Do you need me, boss*?

Ben, anticipating Caesar's reaction to his departure, turned back to him and called firmly, 'Caesar, stay! Stay with Maddie.'

Caesar looked at him intently, tilting his head.

Ben smiled. 'It's okay, mate, I'm not going far.'

That seemed to satisfy Caesar, who dropped his head back onto Maddie's lap.

Ben and Dr Park were joined by a member of the

secretary-general's staff, a fit-looking woman in her twenties with very short hair.

'Sergeant,' said Dr Park, 'I would like you to meet Miss Liberty Lee, my personal security adviser.'

Ben shook hands with Liberty Lee. 'Personal security adviser?' he said. 'Am I right in thinking that would make you the secretary-general's personal bodyguard?'

'Yes, that is so,' she replied blankly. She looked at Ben intently, as if ready to spring into action at any moment.

'I find "personal security adviser" sounds a little less intimidating than "bodyguard",' Dr Park said with a chuckle. 'Miss Lee was seconded to my service from the army of the Republic of Korea, my native country. She accompanies me wherever I go, to protect me.' Then he added, with a playful twinkle in his eye, 'And she owes you an apology, Sergeant.'

'Me?' Ben responded, surprised. 'Why's that?'

Dr Park looked a little embarrassed. 'Miss Lee is very zealous in the performance of her duties. She also has an independent and unorthodox streak. Unbeknown to me yesterday morning, Miss Lee planted a fake bomb beneath the jetty leading to the Sydney Opera House. This was the bomb so cleverly located by your dog, Caesar.'

'What!' Ben, astonished, looked from Dr Park to

Liberty Lee. '*You* planted that IED? I don't understand. Why would you?'

'Miss Lee, perhaps *you* will explain to Sergeant Fulton,' said the secretary-general.

'Of course, Dr Park.' Liberty turned to Ben. 'I swam from here to the Opera House and secured the package beneath the jetty. I did this to test the Australian security measures for Dr Park's visit,' she said matter-of-factly. 'Congratulations. You and your EDD passed the test.' She flashed him a warm smile and, if Ben wasn't mistaken, winked at him.

Ben was stunned by the revelation. 'Did my superiors know you were doing this?'

'It seems that no one knew, Sergeant,' said Dr Park, patting him reassuringly on the shoulder. 'Not even myself. It was Miss Lee's lone initiative. I have reprimanded her for it, and she has since explained to the police what she did and why.'

'I did clear it first with Australia's chief of security,' Liberty explained. 'He said I could go ahead. He was confident my pretend bomb would be found, boasting that Australia has the best explosive detection experts in the world.' She smiled faintly at Ben. 'You and Caesar proved him right, Sergeant.'

'So what was in the package?' Ben queried.

'Only chemicals,' said Liberty Lee. 'The kind used in IEDs. That was what your Caesar sniffed out.'

'Okay, but . . .' Ben lifted his Army slouch hat and scratched his head. 'You say you swam from here to the Opera House?' He looked at the choppy water. 'This is one of the busiest harbours in the world! How come you weren't seen out there?'

'I swam underwater most of the way,' Liberty replied, like it was no big deal, 'surfacing only occasionally.'

'Underwater?'

'I am a martial arts master. I can hold my breath for six minutes.'

'Six minutes?' Ben let out a low whistle. 'That's impressive.'

Liberty shook her head. 'Not really. I'm told the world record for holding one's breath is more than twenty minutes.'

Ben raised his eyebrows. 'Wow. Anyway, I'm just glad we passed your test.'

She nodded. 'You and Caesar are very good at what you do.'

'As my son said, Caesar's the best,' Ben returned modestly.

'And I am the very best at what I do . . . when the secretary-general will permit me to do my job to the best of my ability.' She directed a pointed look Dr Park's way.

'There are limits to all things, Miss Lee,' Dr Park said in a fatherly tone, 'including the lengths to which I will permit you to go in the name of my protection.' He took

Ben's arm once more. 'Now that we have shared our little secret, come, let us rejoin the others.'

While Ben had been conferring with the secretary-general, Mrs Park had been deep in conversation with Nan Fulton. And to Josh's surprise, Hanna began talking to him. They discovered they were the same age.

'How come your name is Hanna? That doesn't sound very Korean to me.' Josh groaned inwardly as he heard the words come out of his mouth. Why did he say that?

'You obviously don't know much about Korea,' she replied with a teasing look. 'Hanna is a very popular name in my country. It means flower.'

'Oh.' Josh felt like an idiot. 'Josh is short for Joshua,' he babbled, hurrying to cover his ignorance. 'My mum chose that name for me.'

'Where is your mum today?' Hanna asked.

'She died a few years ago.'

'Oh.' A genuine look of sympathy came over Hanna's face. 'I'm sorry.' They sat there in silence, looking out at the busy harbour. 'Sydney is such a cool place, Josh. It's not like Korea. More like Hong Kong.'

'Really? I've never been there.' Josh was impressed by how well-travelled she was. 'Why do you have an American accent?'

'Because I go to school in America,' Hanna replied. 'We live in New York City now because my father works at the United Nations headquarters.'

'Cool.' Josh made a note to Google it when he got home.

'Do you have Facebook?' Hanna asked.

Josh looked a little sheepish. 'I'm not allowed on Facebook. Dad and Nan say I'm too young.'

'Oh.' Hanna sounded disappointed. She thought for a moment, then looked at Josh triumphantly. 'We could email each other – you're allowed to do that, right?'

'Sure I am,' he replied, a little defensively.

'Good.' Hanna reached into her bag and took out a pen. 'Here, give me your arm.'

Josh shot her a quizzical look but offered her his left arm.

Hanna wrote on the underside of Josh's forearm. 'That's my email address,' she said, smiling at him. 'What's yours? I'll remember it. I go to the Stuyvesant School and I'm a member of Mensa.'

'Cool.' Josh had no idea what Mensa was other than it was another thing for him to Google. He reeled off his email address just as Ben, Dr Park and Liberty Lee returned to their table.

'What were you talking about, Daddy?' Maddie asked from where she sat on the ground with Caesar, whose tail began to wag at Ben's return.

Ben, uncertain of what to say, glanced at the secretary-general.

'We were talking about perceptions and deceptions,

my dear,' said Dr Park, as he and Ben took seats with the group. Liberty hung back, keeping watch nearby.

'Oh,' said Maddie, none the wiser. 'Caesar wanted to know, that's all.'

'You know, I think that Caesar is a very good name for a military dog,' Dr Park said. 'The same name as a famous and very clever general of ancient Rome.'

Even Caesar was paying attention to the secretary-general as he spoke, sensing that there was something special about this man.

Ben nodded. 'I have told Josh and Maddie the same thing, sir, about Julius Caesar.'

Dr Park grinned. 'Very good. Then, Josh, Maddie, permit me to tell you a story about a Korean general from long, long ago who was as clever as Julius Caesar.'

'Oh, no, not *that* story again!' said Hanna, raising her eyebrows. 'I've heard it a hundred times, Father.'

Hanna's mother glared at her. 'Hanna! Do not be disrespectful to your father.'

'Sorry, Mother,' Hanna responded with a sigh.

Everyone at the table leaned in to hear Dr Park's story. 'Long ago, in ancient times,' he began, 'a famous Korean general led his soldiers to fight a foreign army that had invaded our land. Unfortunately, our army was forced to retreat all the way up a hill. They were surrounded by the enemy below, who decided to wait and starve our soldiers into submission. It was a very hot summer, and both armies soon ran out of water. But the Korean general had plenty of rice for his men, and this gave him an idea. He had his cavalrymen bring their horses to the hilltop, where the enemy at the bottom of the hill could see them, and ordered the troopers to wash them.'

'Wash them?' Maddie poked her head up from where she was sitting on the grass. 'But you said they'd run out of water.'

Dr Park smiled and nodded. 'And so they had, my dear Maddie. So they had. Our general had his cavalry troopers pour buckets of rice over the horses' backs and pretend to scrub them down. You see, from a distance, the pouring rice looked like water.'

'I suppose it would,' Nan Fulton remarked. 'An optical illusion.'

'Wow!' Josh marvelled. 'What a great trick.'

'Then what happened, sir?' Ben asked.

'Well,' said Dr Park, 'the thirsty soldiers of the invading army said, "Our commanders told us that the Korean army had no more water than we do. But, look, the Koreans have so much water that they can waste it on washing their horses." This caused a mutiny in the invading army, whose soldiers departed to find water. And they never returned. Our general won the war without spilling a single drop of blood.'

'If only all wars could end as peacefully as that,' said Nan.

'Quite so, Mrs Fulton,' agreed Mrs Park. 'Quite so!'

'I myself look for a peaceful solution to every conflict,' said Secretary-General Park. 'That is one of the roles of the United Nations, and to demonstrate this, we do not have an army of our own.' As he spoke, his secretary, a portly Englishman named Jeremy Brown, arrived on the scene. After apologising for the interruption, he bent down and whispered in Dr Park's ear.

'Ah, you must excuse me,' Dr Park said to the Fultons. 'Your Governor-General wishes us to attend to other matters. It has been a great pleasure to meet you all.'

Dr and Mrs Park bade the Fultons farewell, taking the precocious Hanna with them. Shadowed by Liberty Lee, they followed Jeremy Brown toward the house. As they went, Hanna turned back to Josh and mimed typing on a keyboard. Josh smiled and nodded vigorously.

'Josh, what was all that about?' Nan asked.

'Nothing, Nan,' Josh answered. 'Hanna and I are going to email each other, that's all.'

'How lovely,' said Nan, clearly delighted. 'I had a penfriend when I was a girl. I think Hanna would make a lovely friend for you.'

Josh wasn't so sure about that. Hanna was the daughter of one of the most important people in the world. He reckoned she would have heaps of equally clever friends, and he doubted that he'd hear from her.

Ben, in the meantime, was about to take another bite of his sandwich when he felt a light tap on his shoulder. Looking around, he broke into a smile of recognition. 'Amanda!'

'Hello, stranger,' said a beaming blonde, putting her hands on Ben's broad shoulders.

'Fancy seeing you here,' said Ben. Amanda Ritchie was the newspaper reporter who had helped Ben and his family in the search for Caesar when he was lost in Afghanistan.

'I didn't see your name on the guest list, Ben,' she said.

'We were last-minute additions,' explained Ben. 'Amanda, you've met my mother, Josh and Maddie before. And, of course, Caesar.'

'Hello there, everyone,' said Amanda. 'And hello, Caesar.' She gave Caesar an affectionate pat, and his tail wagged.

'Please join us, dear,' said Nan, offering the chair beside her.

'Thank you, I will,' said Amanda, taking a seat.

'You're the reporter who helped us find Caesar, aren't you?' said Josh.

'Oh, I only did what I could,' Amanda said humbly. 'You helped your dad a great deal, too.'

Josh nodded proudly.

'I did too!' Maddie spoke up. 'Josh and me, we were doggie detectives. Weren't we, Daddy?'

'You sure were, Princess,' Ben agreed.

Amanda smiled. 'Sounds like Maddie is a big help to you, Ben,' she said.

Ben grinned. 'Oh, yes. Maddie's got a very active and detailed imagination. She takes after her mother that way. You know, Maddie's already worked out that she's going to have seven children one day.'

Amanda chuckled. 'Seven? Really?'

'Yes,' said Maddie. 'And I'm going to name them after the days of the week – Monday, Tuesday, Wednesday, Thursday, Friday, Saturday and Sunday.' Most of the adults at the table laughed at this. 'That way,' Maddie continued seriously, 'it doesn't matter whether they're boys or girls.' It made perfect sense to her.

'Maddie has plans for her seven children to move in with Josh, Nan and myself,' Ben told Amanda, giving her a wry smile.

'Is that right?' said Amanda, highly amused. 'Where will they all fit, Maddie?'

'Oh, that's easy,' Maddie replied. 'Monday, Tuesday and Wednesday can sleep in my room with me, on double bunks. And we can turn the garage into an extra bedroom for Thursday, Friday, Saturday and Sunday.'

'But what about your husband?' asked Amanda. 'Where would he sleep?'

'Oh, he can visit sometimes,' Maddie returned. Again, the adults laughed, though Maddie had no idea why.

'You've been to Afghanistan, haven't you, Amanda?' said Josh, joining in the conversation. 'Like my dad and Caesar.'

Amanda nodded. 'I have. Yes, Josh.'

'So, it's not such a scary place, if girls are allowed to go there?' Ben had recently told Josh there was a possibility that he and Caesar would be sent back to Afghanistan on military operations. The fact that his father had been wounded and Caesar had gone missing the last time they were in Afghanistan had been playing on Josh's mind ever since.

Amanda was astute enough to realise this and carefully framed her answer. 'You know, Josh, much of Afghanistan is perfectly safe. And most of the people are really lovely. And, one day, with the help of men like your father, there will be no war in that country at all.'

Josh gave Amanda a weak smile. 'Yeah, I guess.'

'Oh, more food!' Nan exclaimed, as waiters in smart uniforms brought around barbecued snacks.

'Compliments of the Governor-General,' announced a waiter, as he placed a large raw bone in front of Caesar.

Caesar picked up the bone, lay down at Ben's feet with the bone between his paws and gnawed contentedly away at it, his tail wagging.

Amanda turned to Ben. 'What did you think of the secretary-general?' she asked.

'He seems very wise and full of charm,' Ben replied.

47

'His wife is lovely,' added Nan. 'And you liked their daughter, Hanna, too, didn't you, Josh?'

'I guess,' Josh said with a shrug. 'What's Mensa, Nan?'

'Mensa is an international society whose members are really bright,' Nan replied. 'They all have very high IQs. Why do you ask?'

Josh shrugged. 'No reason.' So, now he knew that Hanna was really smart. That was daunting.

'Caesar liked the secarty-general, too,' said Maddie, climbing onto Ben's lap.

'It's a pity Dr Park and his family couldn't spend longer in Australia,' said Nan. 'They could have come down to visit us at Holsworthy.'

'I don't think so, Nan,' said Josh with a laugh. 'They've got more important things to do.'

Ben nodded. 'By this time tomorrow, the secretary-general will probably be in one world trouble spot or another, trying to convince people to settle their differences without going to war.'

'And this time tomorrow we'll be back at our routine jobs,' said Amanda. 'You've got to admit that Dr Park's job is exciting.'

'Yes, but dangerous,' said Ben.

'No more dangerous than yours, dear,' Nan said pointedly, then regretted saying so in front of the children.

Ben looked at his watch. 'Caesar and I will have to leave soon,' he said with a sigh. 'We have to be back at base by 2000 hours. We have a training exercise starting at 0500 tomorrow.'

Ben had no idea that before long his job would link him once again with Dr Park. Only next time, the secretary-general's life would genuinely be in his hands.

CHAPTER 4

'Yo, Dog Boy!'

Josh's heart sank. Kelvin Corbett, a boy at his school, was a misfit. Repeating a year, he was older, taller and heavier than anyone else in their class. When Kelvin got something wrong or was told off by a teacher, he would get extremely angry and take it out on his classmates. For a while now, Kelvin had been harassing Josh on the walk home and sending Josh emails calling him names.

'Want some dog food, Dog Boy?' Kelvin taunted him. 'I've got a can in my bag if you're hungry.'

Josh had a pretty good idea what this was all about. When Caesar was in the media after word spread of his adventures in Afghanistan, Josh and Maddie had been minor celebrities at school for a while. Though their celebrity status had faded, Kelvin hadn't forgotten how everyone had wanted to talk to Josh about Caesar.

Walking faster, Josh tried to ignore him, playing games on his phone as he went. But he could hear Kelvin's shuffling tread behind him. Kelvin was speeding up. Bit by bit, Kelvin caught up with Josh until he was walking just a pace behind.

'Come on, Dog Boy, do some tricks for me,' Kelvin sneered. 'Roll over! Fetch!'

Just a block away from Kokoda Crescent, Josh resisted the urge to run home.

'Hey, I'm talking to you.' Kelvin kicked the bottom of Josh's backpack.

Josh flinched but kept walking.

'Come on, Dog Boy, show me what you're made of!' Kelvin kicked Josh's backpack again. When Josh still didn't react, Kelvin kicked the backpack a third time. 'Come on, Dog Boy! Or are you a coward?'

Josh had had enough. Slipping his mobile phone into a trouser pocket, he tensed, preparing to spin around and confront Kelvin the next time he kicked his backpack. Josh waited to feel the bully's boot connect. But the kick never came. When he finally reached the corner, Josh stopped and looked back. There was no sign of Kelvin.

🐾🐾

When Josh arrived home, he found Maddie running around the house with an Australian flag on a stick.

'What's going on?' Josh asked, dropping his backpack in the hall.

'Charlie's coming for the weekend,' Maddie answered gleefully, zooming past him with the flag Charlie had given her a while back. 'Yayyyy!'

'Cool!' Josh raced to his room, thinking about which computer games he'd challenge Charlie to play. All thoughts of Kelvin the bully quickly faded away.

Sure enough, Ben arrived home with Charlie and Caesar, just in time for dinner. But to Josh's surprise, Charlie was back in a wheelchair.

'How come you're in a wheelchair again?' Josh asked, as Charlie wheeled himself into the living room.

'Yeah. You said you would never need that again, Charlie,' said Maddie, sounding disappointed. 'Where are your prophetic legs?'

'*Prosthetic* legs, Maddie,' Nan corrected her with a chuckle. 'Not "prophetic" legs.'

Maddie frowned. 'What's a prophetic leg, then?'

'That's a leg that can tell the future,' said Josh, 'except there's no such thing.'

'Oh.'

'My left prosthetic leg has gone back to the manu-facturer for repairs,' Charlie explained. 'The knee joint seized up when I was in the middle of the bush.'

'That's not very good,' said Maddie.

'No, it's not, Maddie,' Charlie agreed glumly. 'And it means I can't go back on SAS operations.'

'It was a big blow to Charlie's plans,' said Ben, as he and the children took their seats at the dining table.

Caesar trotted in with one of Ben's slippers in his mouth, which he dropped beside Charlie.

Charlie laughed. 'No, Caesar, mate, I can't throw the slipper for you to chase. It's dinnertime.' He winked at Maddie. 'We used to play "chase the slipper" before dinner.' Pulling Caesar's head onto his lap, he gave the labrador a vigorous pat.

'Under the table, Caesar,' Ben commanded, and Caesar quickly complied, settling at Ben's feet.

'You should get blades instead, Charlie,' Josh suggested. 'You know, the kind the paralympians use.'

'But they don't look like real legs,' Maddie spoke up.

'They don't have to *look* like real legs,' said Charlie, 'just *work* like real legs.'

'Those guys with blades can run at a zillion miles an hour,' Josh declared.

'Are blades worth considering, Charlie?' asked Ben.

'Mate, anything is worth considering at this point.' Charlie turned back to Josh. 'Who makes blades, Josh?'

'I'm not sure, but it'll be easy to find out,' Josh said. Jumping up from his seat, he ran to fetch his laptop.

Josh returned and cleared a space on the dining

table. As the others gathered around, Nan arrived with a steaming casserole dish in her gloved hands.

'What's going on here?' she demanded. 'My beef casserole is ready to eat.'

'Very important business, Nan,' answered Josh, his eyes focused on the screen in front of him.

'More important even than eating,' added Maddie. 'We have to find new legs for Charlie.'

Nan let out an exasperated sound, then looked at Ben.

'Slip it back in the oven, Mum?' Ben suggested. 'Let the kids help Charlie. It won't take long.'

'Ten minutes, no more,' Nan declared, turning on her heel and marching back to the kitchen.

Josh, meanwhile, had discovered a website for a Sydney company called Ozzie Prosthetics. It sold Zoomers, and a photograph depicted them as slender, curved black running blades that looked a little like snow skis. A well-known Australian athlete who had won gold at the most recent Paralympics was pictured wearing them.

Charlie had manoeuvred his wheelchair beside Josh's seat, and was looking intently at the laptop screen. 'I wonder how they work in mud,' he murmured, half to himself.

'Whoa, look at the price,' Josh said in alarm.

'Money isn't a big issue for me, Josh,' Charlie said thoughtfully. 'I've got plenty saved up.'

'So, you're seriously considering these blade things,

Charlie?' Nan asked when she rejoined them with the hot casserole dish.

He looked up at her with a solemn expression. 'Nan, if these Zoomers can get me back on operations, I'll be the happiest man alive. To me, right now, mobility is as important as the ability to breathe.'

Charlie stood looking at himself in the full-length mirror. This was weird, he thought, but exciting. He was wearing Zoomer blades on his legs, while a short, stubby red-headed man stood beside him, smiling approvingly. A badge on the man's shirt read 'Ozzie Prosthetics'.

'They're so light,' Charlie marvelled, grinning like a boy who had just received his first bike. 'I can't even feel them.'

'That's carbon fibre for you,' said the man, the boss of Ozzie Prosthetics. 'Light but super strong.'

'They're so much better than my old prosthetics, Mr Breen. They don't look like legs but if they can perform like legs . . .'

'They will outperform your old legs, that I can guarantee. Think of your old prosthetics as the first Ford Model A, Sergeant Grover. This is the Rolls Royce of the prosthetic leg. The very latest model. The most advanced in the world.' Mr Breen bent down and tapped Charlie's left Zoomer. 'That knee joint is made from titanium. It contains a microprocessor that is so advanced, it thinks faster than the human brain.'

'Wow! How much for a pair of these?'

'To custom-make a set exactly to your requirements? Twelve thousand dollars.'

'Twelve thousand?' Charlie ran a hand through his short-cropped hair. 'For one pair?'

'It's the left leg – with the knee joint and microprocessor, it bumps up the cost.'

Charlie nodded. 'I'll have them. Make me two pairs, please.'

Mr Breen smiled. 'It will be our pleasure, Sergeant. As you're our first customer with a Victoria Cross medal, we'll move you to the top of the waiting list. Once we have taken your measurements, we can have a set ready for you to try out in a week's time.'

'Just one week?' Charlie exclaimed. 'You beauty!'

'The manufacturing process is computer-controlled and laser-guided. It provides perfect precision and is super-quick.' Mr Breen grinned. 'After all, speed is what these Zoomers are all about.'

CHAPTER 5

Standing tall in the living room of 3 Kokoda Crescent, Charlie looked like his old self in army uniform, his sandy-coloured SAS Regiment beret sitting at a jaunty angle. It was right after breakfast on a Saturday morning, just days after Charlie took delivery of his new blades. These Zoomers, attached to military boots, were undetectable beneath his khaki trousers.

As the Fulton family clustered around to bid him farewell, Caesar, sitting beside Ben, looked sad. Like many dogs, Caesar had a sixth sense; he knew that his friend Charlie was going away. Charlie had been ordered to take up an administrative job at SAS headquarters at Campbell Barracks in Perth, Western Australia.

Charlie was happy to do so for now. Major General Jones had reluctantly agreed to let him attempt the next SAS selection course, but emphasised that this would be Charlie's absolute final chance. Charlie had agreed that, should he fail the course this time, he would never again talk about going into the field on active service and would buckle down to working behind the scenes at SAS headquarters, putting his experience to use planning missions that would be carried out by other SAS operators. But Charlie was confident that, in his new Zoomers, he'd pass the course and be permitted back on ops.

'No one would know you were wearing Zoomers, Charlie,' said Nan. 'How do they feel on?'

'Amazing!' Charlie replied. Hoisting a trouser leg, he showed off an elegantly curved black blade. 'They're so light I can run like the wind in them.'

Ben noticed that Caesar was looking at the Zoomers with his head cocked to one side, as if to say, *What are those things where your legs should be, Charlie?* 'I think our Caesar's a bit mystified by the Zoomers,' said Ben, giving Caesar a pat.

Smiling, Charlie gave Caesar a farewell cuddle. 'Bye, mate. You and Ben are a great team. Do good work together and keep safe, do you hear?'

Caesar, tail wagging, licked him on the cheek.

Charlie gave Nan and Maddie cuddles, and gave Josh a firm, manly handshake.

'You'll let us know how you go on the selection course?' said Josh, handing Charlie his khaki travel bag.

'Don't worry, Josh, you'll all be the first to know when I pass,' replied Charlie.

Josh and Maddie watched from the window, waving

as the pair drove off to Richmond air base. Caesar was at the window, too, with his front paws up on the glass, watching the car depart.

'Once Charlie passes the test,' Maddie said to Josh, 'will the army send him to do more humungatarian stuff, do you think?'

Josh frowned at her. 'Do what?'

'Humungatarian. You know – helping people. That's what Nan said humungatarian means.'

It dawned on Josh what his little sister was talking about. '*Humanitarian*, Maddie,' corrected Josh, rolling his eyes. 'You can be so silly sometimes.'

'Yes, but will he? Help people, I mean. Like Daddy and Caesar do.'

'Well, Charlie's a soldier. He goes where he's needed.'

That seemed to satisfy Maddie. 'Good. Then Charlie is a humungatarian.'

Ping! Josh looked over at his computer. To his surprise, he'd just received a message from Hanna Park.

Hi from New York City, Josh,
How are things with you? Is there anything exciting happening in your world? Has your dog, Caesar, saved any more lives lately? I'm back at school, which now seems

really boring after our trip. What's school like there? I wish
I was back in Australia. Hope to hear from you soon!
Your friend, Hanna

'Woop!' Josh exclaimed. He'd wanted to contact Hanna ever since they'd exchanged email addresses, but he could never think what to say to the daughter of the UN secretary-general. He replied immediately.

Hi Hanna,
It's great to hear from you. Caesar is good. He and Dad are stationed nearby at Holsworthy, so Caesar gets to come home at weekends.
My school is at Holsworthy, too. It's cool. I really like it there. But there's this kid in my class called Kelvin Corbett who's been making my life hard. Nan says I should ignore bullies. She doesn't know about Kelvin, though. Otherwise, not much is happening here.
Oh, and Dad's best friend, Charlie, has cool new Zoomers instead of prosthetic legs that will help him get back into the Special Forces – I'll send you a link to check them out! That's it for now.
Your Aussie friend, Josh

Minutes after he had sent the message, there was a reply. Curious, Josh looked up the time in New York. It was early Friday evening on Hanna's side of the world.

I Googled Zoomers. OMG, they look awesome!!! That Kelvin guy sounds like a loser. I'm here to talk if you need . . .

Josh smiled and started typing.

Thanks, Hanna. I know I've got to do something about Kelvin but I'm not sure what just yet . . .

He sat looking at Hanna's message for a long time, reading and rereading the last line.

🐾🐾

'On your marks!'

On the running track at Campbell Barracks, six men hunched over their hands in the starting position. All wore shorts and khaki T-shirts. Charlie Grover, in his Zoomers, was one of the six. Tensing every muscle in his body, Charlie was ready to launch himself forward and run like he had never run before. This was his chance to really test his Zoomers.

'Get set!' the lieutenant called. 'GO!'

The six men rose up in unison. Down the 100-metre track they sprinted, toward a group of SAS men waiting at the finishing line. Charlie started a little slower than the others and, ten metres into the race, was coming last. But as he ran, Charlie's slender black Zoomer blades flashed through the air. Pace by pace, he steadily gained on the others. A taller, more powerfully built runner was in the lead. Metres from the line, Charlie drew level with him, the other four runners trailing behind, and finished in front by half a metre.

'Charlie won!' yelled his good friend Corporal Lucky Mertz, punching the air.

'Told you he would,' said a short trooper who was known to everyone in the SAS simply as Bendigo Baz. 'Those blades did the trick.'

Lucky and Baz were Charlie's best mates in the SAS. In Afghanistan, the three of them served in the same unit, and all three had been wounded in the Taliban ambush from which Charlie had earned his Victoria Cross. Charlie jogged over to the pair, beaming.

'Nice work, mate,' said Lucky, giving him a high five.

'Pretty good, huh?' said Charlie, pleased with himself and his Zoomers. 'What are you two blokes doing here?'

'General Jones sent us over with this,' said Lucky, handing Charlie a letter.

Charlie quickly opened the envelope, took out the single sheet of paper and read its contents. Then, nodding to himself, he returned the letter to its envelope.

'Well?' Lucky demanded. 'What'd he say?'

'A new SAS selection course starts next week, and I'm on it. He says it's my last chance.'

'Good for you, cobber,' said Baz, clapping him on the back. 'You'll romp it in now. I wouldn't mind having a pair of them magic Zoomers myself!'

Two weeks later, Ben, perspiring heavily, was locking the gate to Caesar's kennel at Holsworthy Army Barracks after the pair had been out on a long training run. Caesar, equally spent, was already busy eating his dinner when Ben answered a call from Charlie.

'Mate,' said Charlie matter-of-factly, 'just wanted to let you know that I've completed the latest selection course.'

'And?' Ben prompted impatiently, nervous for his friend. 'How'd you go?'

'Passed.'

'You passed selection?!'

'Yep. I'm getting my wish, Ben. I'm going back on ops. On Zoomers.'

'You little ripper!' Ben exclaimed. 'I knew you'd come through, mate.'

'You'll let Josh and Maddie know? And Nan?'

Ben smiled, imagining their reactions to Charlie's news. 'You bet I will.'

CHAPTER 6

Josh and Maddie, sitting with their father on the sofa, stared at the TV screen in disbelief.

A female newsreader was delivering the leading item on the nightly news. 'A helicopter carrying the secretary-general of the United Nations, Dr Park Chun Ho, has gone down in the far west of Uruzgan Province in Afghanistan, at the foot of the Hindu Kush mountain range. Late yesterday afternoon, the pilot of the helicopter sent out an emergency message saying his aircraft had been hit by ground fire. Dr Park was in Afghanistan as part of a UN attempt to bring the Taliban and other militias to the peace table with the government of the war-torn country. Nothing was heard from the helicopter following the pilot's brief radio message.

'Australian and US forces stationed in Uruzgan rushed to the area by air and located the downed helicopter, but no trace has been found of its crew or passengers. Grave fears are held for the safety of Secretary-General Park and the six UN officials travelling with him, who some sources suggest may have been taken prisoner by the Taliban.'

Josh jumped up from the sofa and headed for his bedroom.

Ben looked up. 'Josh, where are you going?'

'There's something I have to do,' Josh called back.

Closing his bedroom door, Josh went straight to his computer to send an urgent message.

Hanna,
I just heard that your dad has gone missing in Afghanistan. I'm so sorry. Are you okay?

He paused for a moment then added:

Don't worry, I'll ask Dad and Caesar to go over there and find him.
Your friend, Josh

When Josh returned to the living room, Ben was on the phone.

'Yes, sir. On my way.' Ben ended the call and stuffed the phone back in his pocket.

'Dad,' Josh said tentatively, 'can you do me a big favour?'

'What's that, son?' Ben replied, his mind still on the phone call.

'Can you and Caesar go over to Afghanistan and find Dr Park?'

'Yes!' Maddie cried in agreement. 'You have to, Daddy!'

Ben broke into a gentle, reassuring smile. 'It just so happens,' he said, putting an arm around each of them, 'that I've been called into a meeting with the generals, to discuss doing that very thing.'

'Yay!' Maddie cheered, jumping up on the couch.

'Awesome!' Josh couldn't wait to tell Hanna.

'Where's Caesar, Mum?' Ben called to Nan, who was busy in the kitchen. 'We have to fly to Sydney.'

Nan stuck her head around the corner. 'Maddie left him out in the garden,' she said, then paused. 'Actually, he's been out there for quite a while. I hope he hasn't been digging up my roses again!'

A Black Hawk roared through the night sky, heading for Sydney from the airstrip at Holsworthy army base. Ben was aboard, with Caesar asleep at his feet. Other soldiers sitting around Ben were also nodding off to sleep as, under the dull red glow of the cabin's interior lights, Ben surveyed a white shoebox that sat on his lap. It had a hand-drawn red cross on the front, together with the words 'Daddy's Survival Pack'. Maddie had made this for him at school and had pushed it into his hands as he was leaving home just a few hours earlier.

Ben lifted the lid of the box and took out the contents one item at a time. A packet of bandaids. A roll of bandages. A packet of headache tablets. A travel pack of tissues. Maddie's latest school photograph, with the words 'In case you forget what I look like' scrawled on the back in felt pen. A street map of Holsworthy, with 3 Kokoda Crescent circled in red. A packet of dog biscuits for Caesar. And half a dozen bags of jelly beans.

Maddie knew that her father was about to go off on another mission, perhaps for a few months. Like Josh, she had learned not to complain when Ben went away. But Maddie had wanted Ben to know that she would be missing him. Ben opened one of the bags of sweets and popped a jellybean into his mouth, then lay his head back against the cabin wall.

In his mind's eye he could see Josh running with a kite and Maddie in the arms of their mother. Maddie would have been about three then. It was only shortly after that day when they had received the news that Marie had breast cancer. Marie, the love of Ben's life and mother of his children, had died before two more years had passed. Jellybeans had been Marie's favourite sweets. Maddie hadn't forgotten.

Ben cleared his throat and took another jellybean from the bag.

Behind the facades of ordinary-looking office buildings, Australian Special Operations Command worked from a Sydney facility in Potts Point. It was there that a top-secret, late night meeting was convened by Major General Jones to discuss the missing secretary-general of the United Nations. On a large electronic screen behind a conference table, a map of Afghanistan was on display, with a pulsing red dot indicating where the secretary-general's helicopter had gone down.

Apart from Major General Jones, the meeting was attended by Australian Army and Air Force officers, as well as US Army officers from the American Embassy in Canberra. Although Ben was just a sergeant, the lowest-ranked man present, General Jones introduced him right off the bat.

'Gentlemen, I've invited Sergeant Fulton here for several reasons. First, he and Caesar are our best EDD team, and they have experience operating in Uruzgan against the Taliban. Second, Fulton and Caesar have met Secretary-General Park. They will be part of any rescue mission we mount in Afghanistan.'

'And I do believe, General,' said an American colonel, 'Caesar has spent time with the Taliban. That should uniquely qualify him for a rescue mission in Afghanistan if, as we believe, the Taliban have snatched the secretary-general.'

'Yes, if only dogs could talk,' General Jones returned with a chortle. 'Caesar could tell us a lot about the Taliban in that case.' There was a round of good-natured laughter from the room before the general continued. 'So, gentlemen, this is the situation. Because Australian and US forces are supporting the Afghan National Army in Uruzgan Province, it falls to us to locate and, if necessary, rescue Secretary-General Park and his colleagues.' There were nodding heads around the table. 'Our forces on the ground are searching for them in very difficult terrain, but we feel there's a strong possibility Dr Park and his party are being held by the Taliban in the mountains of the Hindu Kush.' He pointed to the area on the map. 'Once we locate the secretary-general, we will need to mount a Special Forces mission to extract him.'

'You got that right,' said the American colonel. 'As we speak, the US is putting together a Special Forces team with that very objective.'

'With respect, Colonel, my Prime Minister has instructed *me* to organise an *Australian* Special Forces team for the job. After all, ISAF command in Uruzgan Province is held by the Australian military.'

The colonel nodded slowly, thoughtfully. 'Seems to me like we better join forces.'

'I was hoping you'd say that,' General Jones returned. 'So, it will be a joint operation, like many others we've conducted before in Uruzgan.'

'You got it. I suggest you get your people ready to move just as soon as we know where the Taliban are holding Dr Park. That is, *if* they are holding him.'

'Then, let the planning begin!'

As the officers filed out of the room, General Jones took Ben aside. 'Fulton, I want you and Caesar over there in Uruzgan right away, ready to go into action the moment we locate the secretary-general.'

Bed nodded solemnly. 'Very good, sir.'

'I'm sending a three-man SAS team with you. Anyone in particular you'd like to work with on this?'

'Yes, sir.' Ben then mentioned the names of Lucky Mertz and Bendigo Baz, before adding, 'Charlie Grover should be the team leader.'

The general frowned. 'Grover?'

'Charlie has passed the selection course, sir. He rang me last night with the good news. His Zoomers performed amazingly well, apparently.'

'Yes, I know he's passed the course. But to send him back to Afghanistan so soon, in charge of such a delicate and important mission?' General Jones looked doubtful. 'If we stuff this up, Fulton, and the secretary-general is killed, we will never live it down.'

'Sir, Charlie's physically ready for this, and I know he's

mentally up for it,' Ben insisted. 'I trust him with my life. And, with respect, sir, *you* should trust him with the secretary-general's life.'

General Jones sighed. 'Okay, Grover will lead the team. But neither he nor you had better let me down.' He prodded Ben in the chest with a bony index finger. 'If you do, believe me, Fulton, both your careers will be down the toilet.'

'We won't let you down, sir,' Ben assured him. 'Trust me.'

CHAPTER 7

The huge International Security Assistance Force (ISAF) base in Tarin Kowt (pronounced 'Tarin Kot'), the capital of Afghanistan's Uruzgan Province, was just as Ben remembered it. Dry and dusty, it was surrounded by distant, barren yellow hills, with camp compounds and low buildings spread out as far as the eye could see. There was an endless stream of military vehicles coming and going, as well as flocks of fixed-wing aircraft and helicopters taking off and landing at the base's airfield. This was the heart of ISAF operations in Uruzgan.

As soon as Ben and Caesar stepped off the plane and into the blazing heat of the northern summer, Ben led his four-legged mate on a walk. They worked their way through the camp streets to re-familiarise Caesar with the sights, sounds and smells of the base, and of Afghanistan and the Afghan people. Caesar was visibly happy in the fresh air and free of the cramped aircraft. His tail wagged as he received pats of greeting from Australian and American soldiers. He seemed curious about the

Afghan National Army (ANA) troops they passed, as if they triggered memories of the last time he'd been in Afghanistan, but nothing seemed to dull Caesar's joy at being back at work with Ben.

And just like the old days, Caesar slept in the base kennels. He shared these quarters with other Australian explosive detection dogs and US Army dogs. The kennels had their own attendants and veterinary surgeons to care for the war dogs, and the base cooks looked after their diet. Here, Caesar had dog friends, plenty of attention and the best food. It was like a five-star hotel for dogs! Caesar recognised the kennels from his last tour of duty in Afghanistan and knew that Ben would be back the next morning to take him out for a fun day looking for explosives.

Ben was just heading back to his own quarters when he saw three familiar figures walking toward him – Charlie, Lucky and Baz.

'Good to see you, Charlie,' said a grinning Ben, shaking his best friend's hand then pulling him into a hug. 'When did you blokes land?'

'An hour ago,' replied Charlie, patting Ben on the back.

'Looks like the old firm is back together again,' said Lucky, shaking Ben's hand.

'Yeah, Caesar and Company,' quipped Baz. 'Our bite is worse than our bark!'

The others laughed.

'How's Caesar settling in?' Charlie asked as they all walked toward the mess. Charlie remembered that Caesar had taken a while to become accustomed to Afghanistan on his first tour. 'No culture shock this time?'

Ben shook his head cheerfully. 'No, he's taken to it much better. I did worry that the time he spent in the hands of the Taliban might have made him tetchy toward Afghans. But so far he's taking things in his stride.'

'Glad to hear it, especially since we could be going into action sooner rather than later.' Charlie leaned closer to Ben as they walked, and lowered his voice. 'I've been told that a video of the secretary-general was just released on the internet. The Taliban are definitely holding him.'

'Okay. At least that's settled,' said Ben.

Charlie nodded. 'We have a briefing with the Yanks at 2000 hours.'

🐾🐾

At eight o'clock that evening the four newly arrived Australian Special Forces soldiers joined the briefing in the Tarin Kowt Special Operations Headquarters. The briefing room was set up as a small theatre, with rows of hard seats facing a low stage. A large LCD screen hung on the back wall. As Ben and his three mates seated themselves at the back of the room, Ben, looking around, noted that there were a number of other Australian and American soldiers present.

'Attention!' barked a senior NCO, and everyone jumped to their feet.

The commander of ISAF forces in Uruzgan was the Australian Army's Brigadier Ken Quiggly. A tall but slight man with short ginger hair and a bony nose, he walked quickly into the room via a side door, followed by the US Army's Lieutenant General Mitch McAvoy and Australian Major Alex Jinko. As the officers passed Charlie, Brigadier Quiggly and Major Jinko saluted him.

'What was that about, Quiggly?' McAvoy asked in a low voice as the officers reached the stage. 'Officers saluting a sergeant?'

'Sergeant Grover was awarded the Victoria Cross, sir,' the brigadier informed him. 'In our army all officers, generals included, salute a VC.'

'That so?' said McAvoy, impressed.

'Okay, as you were, people,' Brigadier Quiggly called, and the men in front of them resumed their seats. 'Lieutenant General McAvoy here is 2IC at US Special Forces Command. He's just stepped off a plane from Washington DC. The fact that an officer of his high rank has been assigned command of this op should give you an indication of how important it is to our governments that this mission should succeed. So, without further ado, I'll hand over to him.'

'Thank you, Brigadier,' said Lieutenant General McAvoy, stepping to the front of the stage and moving his eyes around the faces in the room, taking in each one. He was well built, blond and handsome. 'A couple of hours ago,' he began in a gravelly voice, 'the Taliban posted a video on the internet. It shows Secretary-General Park talking to camera. I want you guys to take a look.'

Everyone turned to watch a grainy video play on the screen. Shot in poor light, it showed Dr Park sitting in front of a green curtain. He looked pale and shaken. With his eyes aimed at the camera, he said, 'This is Dr Park Chun Ho, secretary-general of the United Nations. My colleagues and I are safe and in the custody of the Taliban. The Taliban have asked me to read a statement in English.'

He lifted a piece of paper and began to read from it.

'We have the secretary-general of the United Nations. He and the six infidels with him will be killed unless all occupying foreign forces withdraw from Afghanistan at once. The Americans and their allies have one week to withdraw from our country. For every day that follows, one of the infidels will be killed. On the seventh day, the secretary-general will be killed. You have been warned. Begin your withdrawal at once.

You have seven days until the fourteenth of the month, before we start eliminating hostages.'

Dr Park lowered the piece of paper and, looking at the camera, went on. 'I am assured that if any attempt is made to rescue us a bomb will be detonated without hesitation. I urge my friends and colleagues of the international community not to risk any lives on my account. And I urge you to accede to the wishes of my captors. In the meantime, I will pray that Cheong-Ryong will look after me and those close to me. Thank you.'

The video ended, leaving those in the room in sombre silence. Ben was already replaying the video in his head, looking for clues about the condition and location of Dr Park and his fellow hostages.

'We got a problem,' declared General McAvoy. 'Obviously, our governments are not going to withdraw their forces from this country in a week. Even if they wanted to leave in a hurry it would take months, not days. We don't doubt that the Taliban will keep their threat to kill these hostages. So, we have a week to find the secretary-general and extract him and his people, despite what he said on the video about not trying to rescue them. We are not going to sit on our butts and let these people be murdered.'

'Sir,' Charlie spoke up, 'have we any clues as to where the secretary-general is being held?'

'To answer that, Sergeant, I'll ask Major Jinko from the Australian SAS to brief us on all available intel. Major?'

Alex Jinko, a senior intelligence officer with the SAS Regiment – a 'bear' in military slang – now took centre stage. 'Bring the video up again,' Jinko directed, 'with the audio muted.' The major continued as the video of Dr Park was re-run. 'We've analysed this video from every possible angle. We can say it was shot indoors in a place without natural light. The audio boys say the sound quality suggests it was recorded in a cave.'

'A cave?' said Charlie, nodding thoughtfully. 'Are they in the mountains, sir? In the Hindu Kush?'

'That's our best bet, Sergeant,' the major replied. 'They didn't have enough time to move the hostages far before shooting that video. Dr Park was probably taken by a Uruzgan brigade of the Taliban, so they'd be keeping him in or near Uruzgan. Make no mistake, capturing the secretary-general of the UN is a big deal for these people.'

'In baseball terminology, the bad guys have hit a home run,' McAvoy interrupted. 'And they know it!'

'Where exactly are we looking for the sec-gen, sir?' asked one of the American servicemen.

Major Jinko swept his hand across the Hindu Kush on the map. 'We have satellites and drones looking at every nook and cranny of those mountains.'

'But the Taliban will know that,' said Lieutenant General McAvoy, 'and they'll be lying low. If we're gonna find the secretary-general, we're gonna have to get lucky. And in the next seven days! Meanwhile, I want the extraction team ready to roll. They will be led by Sergeant Hazard, one of the most experienced Special Ops people we have. Sergeant, tell us about your team.'

The bearded Sergeant 'Duke' Hazard came to his feet and turned to face the other Special Forces men in the room. Ben, Charlie, Lucky and Baz all knew Hazard from their previous tour of Afghanistan. A Green Beret, Sergeant Hazard had been in command of their Special Ops mission when they were ambushed by the Taliban.

'We got ourselves a complication,' Hazard began, speaking slowly and deliberately. 'The extraction team was supposed to be exclusively comprised of Americans and Aussies. But the sec-gen's got other nationals in his party – British, Danish, French, Japanese and German. All their governments are insisting they have at least one man on the extraction team so they can tell their media back home they participated in the rescue of their own people. So, we're trying to get those governments to supply specialists to the team, which will be headed up by four US and four Australian Special Forces operatives, including two EDD handlers.'

'Somehow, Sergeant Hazard,' Lieutenant General McAvoy interjected unhappily, 'you and your people gotta meld a unit overnight from all these foreigners and make it work.' He screwed up his face. McAvoy clearly didn't like the idea of using such a multinational force. But his orders came from above.

'Will these foreigners all speak English, sir?' asked a worried US Ranger, Sergeant Tim McHenry, from the front row.

'They will all speak fluent English,' McAvoy assured him. 'That is the first requirement we set. The other is that they be the best in the business at what they do. It's not an ideal arrangement, but this is all about international diplomacy and cooperation. So, let's get to work, people. Major Jinko, find the secretary-general – fast! And extraction team, you go in and get those people out. You got seven days. Don't mess up! Lives are depending on you men. And one very important life in particular!'

In another room, Ben and his three Australian colleagues met with their American Special Forces counterparts for the first time. One of the Americans included in the op was Sergeant Tim McHenry – the same Tim McHenry who had identified and retrieved Caesar in Uruzgan

Province after he'd been missing for months. Ben had met McHenry when Caesar was officially returned to him here at Tarin Kowt, and they now shared a hearty handshake.

The other two Americans were both corporals – EDD handler Mars Lazar and signaller Brian Cisco. Lazar, a cheerful New Yorker with a perpetual smile on his face, told Ben that his dog, Alabama, was a Belgian sheepdog, a breed popular with the US military.

'Grover,' said Hazard, 'you will be my second-in-command on this op.'

'Okay,' Charlie returned. He wasn't thrilled to be working with Hazard again. As far as Charlie was concerned, Sergeant Hazard had been partly responsible for them being ambushed by the Taliban the day he lost his legs. In Charlie's mind, Hazard was too inclined to rush into things. But he had to accept that the US Army was leading this op and had put Hazard in charge. Charlie would have to make the best of it.

'Let's get one thing straight,' said Hazard, looking intently at Charlie. 'As far as I'm concerned, us eight guys will be handling this extraction. Those foreign "specialists", they're just window-dressing. Got that, Grover?'

'You're the boss,' Charlie responded.

'Sure as heck I am,' Hazard said firmly.

'Chances are,' said Sergeant McHenry, 'we might not even get the chance to go looking for the sec-gen. The bears need to find him first. And that, my friends, will not be easy. It'll be like looking for the proverbial needle in a haystack.'

'The guy should have tried to tip us off about where the Taliban are holding him,' said Hazard unhappily.

'How?' Lucky Mertz countered. 'He couldn't exactly say, "By the way, the grid reference for where they're holding us is such-and-such". Give me a break, mate!'

Hazard scowled at Lucky. 'This Park guy is supposed to be clever, *pal*.'

'If he was clever,' Bendigo Baz chimed in, 'he wouldn't have been flying around Afghan back country in a heelo. It was no place for the head of the UN.'

'I have a lot of respect for Dr Park,' said Ben. 'He came here to try to end this war instead of sitting on his backside in an office in New York. That takes guts. He's one brave bloke, if you ask me.'

Baz shrugged. 'He'll soon be one dead bloke if the bears don't hurry up and track him down for us.'

The gates to the Tarin Kowt base swung open. Ben, in full combat gear and sunglasses, and with an automatic rifle on his shoulder, led Caesar out through the open gateway as guards in the towers either side of the gate covered them with heavy machineguns.

Australian and Afghan infantrymen were walking along both sides of the narrow street ahead of Ben and Caesar, their rifles at the ready. Even though Tarin Kowt was home to a huge ISAF military base, there was always the risk of the Taliban and other insurgents lurking in the nearby town. It paid to always be on the alert. Caesar was on the alert, too, sniffing the early morning air as he trotted alongside Ben, assessing the many new aromas that flooded his nostrils.

As part of the plan to re-familiarise Caesar with the conditions in Afghanistan as quickly as possible, Ben had decided that the two of them should join the security operation covering Tarin Kowt's biggest bazaar of the year. Tarin Kowt held a market every week, with farmers from kilometres around bringing their locally grown produce in to sell. Once a year, a super-sized bazaar was held. This giant bazaar attracted farmers from all over the province, and also brought sellers of new and second-hand trucks and tractors, farming equipment and mobile phones – one of the few pieces of modern technology that has been widely adopted in Afghanistan.

It wasn't long after sunrise when Ben and Caesar arrived, yet hundreds of Afghan men were already crowding around the bazaar's temporary stalls. Groups of women were occasionally seen among the crowd, their heads and faces covered with the *burka*, the traditional Muslim headdress and veil that only permitted the wearer's eyes to be seen. None of the Afghans in the market paid any attention to the patrolling soldiers or the brown labrador. None of the locals gave the Australian dog a second glance, let alone stopped to give him a friendly pat. Very few Afghans kept dogs as pets, and most had no affection for the guard dogs seen at many kals, or farm compounds, in the countryside.

'Seek on, Caesar,' said Ben in a low voice, lengthening his leash.

Caesar walked slowly by Ben's side, sniffing the legs and belongings of men he passed, looking for traces of explosives. But as they walked, Ben noticed that Caesar's tail was not wagging as it frequently did when they were working together. Caesar's tail was low, indicating he was tense, and his eyes flashed suspiciously from one Afghan man to another. To dogs, each person has a distinct smell, and that smell is based on what they eat. The diet of most Afghans differs from the diets of Westerners, so, for example, Afghans give off a very different scent to Australians. That difference had surprised and disconcerted Caesar when he had first arrived, but he quickly grew accustomed to it after spending over a year in Afghanistan.

Ben stopped beside parked vehicles and let Caesar circle them. All the while, Caesar sought the scent of the chemicals that were associated with IEDs. But today, he found no bombs, and the bazaar took place without any threats to the security of the people in attendance.

When it was approaching midday, and the crowd in the bazaar was beginning to thin, Caesar suddenly froze in his tracks. He let out a low, menacing growl, quite unlike anything Ben had heard from Caesar before. Ben quickly brought his rifle down from his shoulder and cradled it, at the ready.

'What is it, mate?' Ben asked, following Caesar's gaze.

Caesar continued to growl, his stare unwavering.

One Afghan man in particular had caught Caesar's attention. Ben signalled to the lieutenant in charge of the Australian platoon, then pointed to Caesar and the Afghan who was the object of his EDD's attention. The lieutenant nodded, then, clicking his fingers and pointing Ben's way, detailed four of his men and an Afghan interpreter to join the EDD team at the jog.

'Okay, Caesar,' said Ben, 'let's take a look at this bloke.'

With the interpreter and four infantrymen on their heels, Ben and Caesar strode toward a group of men and boys who were walking away from them.

Ben looked around to the interpreter. 'Tell them to stop right there.'

The interpreter, a short, dark and clean-shaven Afghan man in his thirties called loudly in Pashto, the local language, for the group to stop. The men and boys halted in their tracks, then turned, looking suddenly fearful at the sight of the soldiers and their guns at the ready. Other Afghans nearby anxiously scooted away.

'Which one of them is it, Caesar?' said Ben, bending and unclipping the leash. 'Seek on, boy!'

Caesar trotted forward then came to a stop in front of a young man with a wispy beard and who was wearing a long white robe. There the labrador stood, looking up at the youth with a penetrating gaze, a growl gurgling deep in his throat.

The Australian lieutenant came hurrying up to Ben. 'Has your dog found explosives on this man, Fulton?'

'Well, to be honest, sir, I'm not sure,' Ben confessed. 'That's not Caesar's usual explosives signature. I'm a little baffled by what he's trying to tell us, Lieutenant.'

'Well, the dog is clearly disturbed by this bloke,' said the lieutenant. 'Knowing Caesar's reputation, that's enough for me. We'll take the man back to the base for questioning.'

The lieutenant ordered his men to arrest the young man, and they hauled him away to be searched for weapons and explosives. Although they came up empty-handed, they still bound his hands behind his back. All the while, an older Afghan with a thick black beard and greying hair was speaking heatedly with the interpreter.

'What's the old man saying?' the lieutenant asked impatiently.

The interpreter shrugged. 'He says that this is his son Nasir, sir. He claims that Nasir has done nothing wrong.'

'We'll be the judge of that,' said the lieutenant.

'Hold on,' Ben called. He had noticed that Caesar's demeanour had suddenly changed. His tail was wagging and he was no longer looking at Nasir. A young boy at the back of the group who was calling out to Caesar in Pashto seemed to have his attention. In response, Caesar nosed through the Afghan men and began jumping up at the boy, trying to lick his face. The boy laughed with delight and hugged him. Meanwhile, the men in the group were all talking at once and pointing at Caesar.

'Sergeant Fulton, would you like to tell me what the heck is going on here?' the exasperated lieutenant asked. 'One minute your dog is growling, the next he's these people's best friend. Has your EDD gone nuts?'

'I hope not, sir,' Ben returned. Perplexed, he turned to the interpreter. 'What are these people saying?'

'The boy is calling your animal "Soldier Dog", Sergeant,' said the interpreter. 'He seems to know your dog, and it looks like your dog knows him.'

'How could he . . .?' Ben began. Then, suddenly, it dawned on him. 'Unless he got to know that kid while he was lost here in Afghanistan.' Ben whistled his usual 'return' summons to Caesar, and Caesar instantly turned away from the boy, trotted back to his master and obediently sat beside him. But Caesar's tail wagged in the dust as he sat. 'You and that kid are old mates, are you, boy?' said Ben, ruffling his EDD's ears.

In reply, Caesar let out a whine of acknowledgement.

The man claiming to be Nasir's father began to plead with the interpreter again.

'This man says that he is Mohammad Haidari, and these boys are his sons, Nasir and Hajera,' the interpreter explained. 'He says that, one day in the past, your brown dog wandered into his kal. Your dog was injured and Hajera and his sister, Meena, took care of him. But then a Taliban commander took him away, saying that it was an infidel soldier dog.'

Ben nodded, smiling. He beckoned the man's younger son, Hajera, who looked to be about the same age as Josh. 'Come closer, mate,' he said.

Hajera, whose nickname was Haji, looked to his father. Mohammad Haidari nodded his consent and told his son not to be afraid. Haji slowly made his way to stand in front of Ben and Caesar, whose tail was wagging furiously.

'You looked after Caesar?' Ben asked Haji, pointing to his labrador. 'You looked after my dog?'

After the interpreter had translated this, Haji nodded. 'He is Soldier Dog,' he said, waiting for the interpreter to translate for Ben before continuing. 'He is a good dog. I trained him to be a guard dog. I will show you.' Looking intently at Caesar, Haji raised his right hand and clicked his fingers.

Caesar cocked his head to one side, clearly a little mystified, as if to say, *What's that, young friend?*

'Woof, Soldier Dog,' Haji commanded. 'Woof!'

This triggered a memory in Caesar's mind, of the weeks he had spent in the Haidari family's kal, where Haji had taught him to bark for food. Caesar let out a single bark. Haji beamed, and the men in his group – Haji's father, uncles, brothers and cousins – all laughed at Haji's ability to make the Australian dog bark.

Ben still seemed troubled. 'But why did Caesar growl at your brother?'

'My brother Nasir did not like Soldier Dog,' Haji replied. 'I think he may have kicked Soldier Dog when I was not looking.'

'I did not kick the dog, Haji!' Nasir spoke up in his own defence. 'You are making that up.'

'Well, you did not like him,' Haji countered. 'And Soldier Dog knows it.' He looked pleadingly at Ben. 'Please, Soldier Australia, my brother Nasir is not a bad person, really. He is not Taliban. My father will not allow the Taliban to take any of his sons.'

'Fulton, is this Nasir worth taking in for questioning or not?' Interrupted the lieutenant in charge. He was beginning to think that perhaps Nasir was not a threat after all. 'Your dog picked him out. It's your call, Sergeant.'

Ben looked at Nasir, then at Caesar. 'You know what, sir? That was not Caesar's usual EDD signature. I think this young bloke gave Caesar a hard time when he was with this family, and Caesar remembered.'

'So?' the lieutenant demanded. 'What do we do with Nasir?'

Ben came to a decision 'Let him go, sir. Caesar reckons he's harmless.'

'Okay, untie him,' the lieutenant instructed.

Mohammad Haidari now came forward and vigorously shook Ben by the hand. 'Thank you, thank you, Soldier Australia,' he said in heavily accented English.

'I should be thanking you, Mr Haidari,' Ben replied. 'For looking after my dog.'

Haji's father spoke again, this time in Pashto, after which the interpreter told Ben, 'Mohammad Haidari says that his son Hajera and daughter Meena should be the ones to receive your gratitude, Sergeant.'

Ben now reached into a trouser pocket and took out one of the little bags of jellybeans that Maddie had given him. He held them out to Haji. 'For you, mate,' he said. 'I wish there was a lot more I could do to thank you for looking after Caesar.'

Grinning, Haji accepted the sweets, glancing at his father to make sure he approved.

'And I'll ask local officials if there is something more

the Australian Government can do to help your family,' Ben went on. 'Please, give me your address.'

Haji's father hesitated.

'Why do you not wish to give your address, Mohammad Haidari?' questioned the interpreter, suspiciously. 'What do you have to hide?'

For years, Haji's father had been trying to walk a middle course between the government and the Taliban and other anti-government militias. He had become a *malek*, a neutral go-between trusted by both sides in the war, and was fearful of being seen to be too friendly with these foreign soldiers. It could get him into trouble with the Taliban. But, at the same time, he didn't want to antagonise the Westerners. Reluctantly, Mohammad Haidari gave the location of his compound, which lay in the northeast of the province. The Haidari family were then permitted to go on their way.

As they walked away, young Haji turned back to wave goodbye to Caesar. 'It was good to see you, Soldier Dog,' he called.

Caesar looked at his old friend, his tail wagging.

Ben, bending down beside him, ruffled Caesar's neck. 'So, you had a young friend here in Uruzgan, did you?'

Caesar let out a little whine. Then he turned and licked Ben's cheek, as if to say, *You're still my best friend, boss.*

Josh, Nan and Maddie sat facing Josh's laptop, which was perched on the coffee table in front of them. On the screen were Hanna and Mrs Park, sitting on a sofa in their Manhattan apartment.

'Mrs Park,' Nan began, 'Josh, Maddie and I wanted to tell you that our thoughts and prayers are with you both. We just know that Dr Park will be found safe and well.'

Mrs Park sniffed, a tissue clenched in her hand. 'Thank you, Mrs Fulton. We appreciate your kind wishes. It has been very difficult for us. There is much media attention, and we cannot leave our apartment. But to have contact with kind friends such as yourselves warms our hearts.'

'And we wanted to let you know that Caesar and our dad are over there in Afghanistan right now, helping in the search for Dr Park,' Josh added.

Hanna, teary-eyed, smiled in surprise. 'Just like you said they would, Josh.'

'We saw the video of Dr Park on the internet,' said Nan. 'At least he looked unharmed. I think we can all take comfort in that.'

'Yes,' Mrs Park replied gratefully, though her expression remained solemn. 'But my husband and the members of his party are in grave danger.'

'Daddy and Caesar will save them,' Maddie chimed in with supreme confidence.

This made Mrs Park smile a little. 'We are thankful that Sergeant Fulton and Caesar are there in Afghanistan.'

'We know a little of what it is like to have someone missing over there,' said Nan. 'Caesar was lost for thirteen months in Afghanistan.'

'I cried and cried for days,' added Maddie.

'I take it that Dr Park is a spiritual man,' said Nan. As someone who attended church every Sunday, she understood the comfort that religion could provide during times like this.

Mrs Park frowned. 'A spiritual man?'

'He said that with the help of, er . . .' Nan began to flounder.

'Oh, because he prayed that Cheong-Ryong would look after him and those close to him?' offered Hanna.

'That's it,' said Nan. 'I assumed that Cheong-Ryong is a Korean deity of some sort.'

Mrs Park shook her head. 'No, we do not have a god called Cheong-Ryong. Like many people in South Korea, my husband, Hanna and I are Christians. We are members of the Korean Baptist Church.'

'Oh.' Nan looked confused. 'Then why did Dr Park . . .?'

'Why did he mention Cheong-Ryong?' Hanna shrugged. 'That has really mystified Mother and me.'

'Well, what is Cheong-Ryong?' Josh asked, intrigued.

'It is a Korean term meaning "Blue Dragon",' Mrs Park replied.

'Blue Dragon?' Nan, Josh and Maddie echoed in unison.

'We have no idea why my father mentioned Blue Dragon,' said Hanna.

'It means nothing to us or to anyone I have spoken to at the United Nations,' Mrs Park added. 'My husband's doctor has suggested that my husband could be suffering from the stress of his capture by the Taliban.'

'That's quite likely,' Nan agreed.

The two families continued to puzzle over the mystery for a while before ending their Skype session by pledging to talk again as soon as there was more information.

Josh's mind raced as he walked back to his room. Setting the laptop on his bed, he lay down in front of it and Googled three words: Afghanistan Blue Dragon. The second result listed was for Band-e-Amir, accompanied by a picture of a beautiful blue lake. Josh clicked through to the site. The home page read:

Band-e-Amir is Afghanistan's first national park. It is a series of six deep blue lakes located in the Hindu Kush mountains in central Afghanistan, west of the famous Buddhas of Bamiyan.

Josh remembered that Dr Park's helicopter had been found at the foot of the Hindu Kush mountain range. With his heart pounding, Josh read on, hoping to find some reference to a dragon or, preferably, to a blue dragon. But there were no dragons in the Band-e-Amir National Park. All that Josh discovered was that Band-e-Amir had once been the second most visited tourist destination in Afghanistan, after the Bamiyan Buddhas, though the latest war in the country had ended the area's tourist trade. Disappointed, Josh was about to close the tab when his eye caught a note at the bottom of the page.

Band-e-Azhdahar is another lake in the region, located several kilometres southeast of the town of Bamiyan. Like the lakes in Band-e-Amir, it is famous for its stunning sapphire-blue water. In English, the lake's name translates to 'Dragon Lake'.

Josh looked at the words in amazement. Getting up, he paced around the room. And just in case he'd misread the entry, he read it again. There was no mistake – Dragon Lake, blue water, Hindu Kush! Unable to contain his excitement, Josh rushed into the living room with his laptop. He found Nan sitting on the sofa, her thoughts and sympathies still with Mrs Park and Hanna in New York.

'Nan, you've got to read this!' Josh exclaimed, setting the laptop down on the coffee table.

'Not now, Josh, dear,' she said softly. 'I'm too sad to be looking at computer games.'

'You don't understand, you *have* to look at this, Nan. Look, there's a Dragon Lake in the Hindu Kush mountains of Afghanistan. And it's famous for its blue water. Dragon Lake. Blue water. Blue Dragon! Get it?'

Nan looked at Josh blankly for a moment until she realised what he was saying. She sat up with a jerk. 'What!'

'Don't you see, Nan – Dr Park was trying to tell us where he was!'

Nan read the entry, then looked at Josh.

Josh was almost bursting out of his skin. 'Well, what do you think?'

A smile spread across Nan's face. 'I think we should send your father an email.'

In the early hours of the morning at the Fulton residence, the house phone rang. Waking from a light sleep, Nan turned on the bedside light and picked up the receiver.

'Hello?'

'Mum, it's Ben.' He sounded worried. 'What's so urgent?'

'Ben, darling, what time is it over there?' Nan squinted at the clock by her bed.

'It's late. Are Maddie and Josh okay?'

'The children are fine. But your very clever son has stumbled onto something. I told him the authorities would have worked it out for themselves, but –'

'What is it?'

'You remember how Dr Park mentioned a Cheong-Ryong?'

'Sure,' Ben said hesitantly, still trying to work out where this was all heading. 'Must be something to do with his religion.'

'Ah, but it has nothing to do with his religion, Ben. It means "Blue Dragon".'

'How do you know that?' Ben sounded sceptical.

'Mrs Park told us – we all spoke via Skype today. Apparently Dr Park is a Baptist, and I don't think there are many blue dragons in the Baptist Church, dear.'

'Not one,' Ben agreed, now sounding very interested.

'But that's not all. Josh went on the internet and discovered that there is a lake in the Hindu Kush called Dragon Lake. A lake famous for its *blue* water.'

'Dragon Lake?' There was a pause on the other end of the line as Ben's mind filled with the possibilities. 'Okay. Not a word to anyone outside the family about this, Mum,' he said, finally allowing himself to sound a little excited. 'This is sensational stuff.'

'So, your army people hadn't worked that out yet?'

'That's precisely what I mean,' said Ben.

'Goodness! I thought governments had all sorts of technology to work out things like this.'

'Nothing beats the human brain for creative thinking, Mum.'

Nan chuckled. 'Yet it's taken a Holsworthy schoolboy to work it out?'

'Yep. Looks like Josh might have a career ahead of him as a security analyst!' Ben said proudly. 'Got to go, Mum. Thanks for this. Tell Josh he's a genius. But don't let this get out. The Taliban will move Dr Park if they find out we're on to their hiding place. It's top-secret. Got to go.'

'Of course, dear. Bye. And good luck, Ben!' Nan hung up, then sat staring into space, stunned. 'Incredible!'

CHAPTER 8

Fifteen men sat in the Special Operations briefing room at the Tarin Kowt base, listening intently as they were briefed by Lieutenant General McAvoy and Major Jinko about their VIP rescue mission. Apart from the four Australians and four Americans already assigned to the mission, another seven had been added to the team by insistent foreign governments.

'As I call your name, you new guys stand up and state your specialty,' General McAvoy instructed. Consulting a sheet of paper, he read the first of the names. 'Angus Bruce.'

A short, slight man with close-cropped fair hair came to his feet. 'Sergeant Angus Bruce, British Royal Marine Commandos,' he said in a broad Scottish accent. 'Explosives are my specialty. I also have a wee bit of experience in hostage rescues, spanning four continents over fifteen years.'

'Christopher Banner,' the general called as Sergeant Bruce resumed his seat.

A tall, muscular man now stood up and looked around at his new comrades. 'How are you folks all doing? Corporal Chris Banner, British Royal Navy Special Boat Service, at your disposal,' he said in a strong West Indian accent. 'If it floats, I'm your man. I grew up on my father's fishing boats in Jamaica before I moved to England and joined the SBS. I'm your boat specialist.' He grinned, showing a mouth full of gleaming white teeth. 'And I'm pretty.'

Several of the others laughed.

'Jean-Claude Lyon,' the general continued, ignoring Banner's cheek.

A well-built, long-nosed man slowly came to his feet. 'Bonjour, I am Sergeant Jean-Claude Lyon of the French Foreign Legion's 2nd Foreign Parachute Regiment. Before I joined the Legion I was an electrician. The Legion, they taught me how to look after myself anywhere, anytime.'

'Casper Mortenson.'

A man of average height with dark hair stood up. 'Corporal Casper Mortenson, Danish Army Hunter Corps,' he said with a wry smile. He spoke his perfect English in a flat monotone. 'My specialisation is as an underwater diver.'

'Wilhelm Wolf.'

A square-faced private with thick blond hair came to his feet. 'Willy Wolf of the Kommando

Spezialkräfte, the German KSK Special Forces unit. I am a combat medic.'

'Toushi Harada.'

A man in his twenties and very slim, Harada looked like a teenager when he bobbed up to introduce himself. 'Yes, here is Corporal Toushi Harada. I am an expert in computer hardware and software with the Aki Haru, the top-secret technical warfare unit of the Japanese Self-Defence Force.'

'The Haki Karu?' said Duke Hazard with a frown. 'Never heard of it.'

'With respect, Sergeant,' said Harada, 'if you *had* heard of it, the Aki Haru would not be secret, would it?' This brought laughter from some of those present. 'Thank you,' said Harada, and with a bow to the others in the room, sat down.

The general consulted his sheet of paper. 'And finally, Ali Moon.'

'My name is Ali Moon,' said a small man in his forties. 'My father is Korean, my mother was born a Pashtun here in southern Afghanistan. I speak many languages fluently, including Pashto. I will be your interpreter.' Pashto was the language spoken in much of Afghanistan and was the language of the Taliban.

'Okay, people, there you have it,' said General McAvoy. 'You now have fifteen personnel, two dogs and all the technical expertise you are going to need to extract Secretary-General Park. Any questions?'

'Yes, General,' said Sergeant Bruce. 'We've been told that you have good reason to believe that the secretary-general is being held near a lake in the Hindu Kush. Can I ask how you came by that information? Was it from a satellite? Or drones? Or did it come from the NDS, the Afghan secret service?'

General McAvoy looked a little sheepish. He cleared his throat. 'We, er, are not at liberty to divulge the source of our information, Sergeant.'

Ben, sitting with Charlie, Lucky and Baz, smiled to himself but said nothing. As soon as he had spoken with Nan, Ben had gone to General McAvoy with the information Josh had discovered. At first, the general had been dismissive. But when research proved that Dr Park was in fact a Baptist, and once the general was shown Band-e-Azhdahar existed, he had taken Josh's information seriously. At this point, only Ben, the general and Major Jinko knew what the world's best security analysts in America, Australia, Britain and other countries had failed to realise – that Dr Park had cleverly identified where he and his UN colleagues were being held captive. And that it had taken a bright Australian schoolboy to work out his coded message.

'We now have satellites watching Dragon Lake around

the clock for signs of Taliban activity, the general went on. 'Major Jinko will fill you in on the area.'

'Thank you, sir.' The Australian intelligence officer stepped forward and pointed to the screen behind him, where there was an image of a stunningly picturesque blue lake surrounded by naked white cliffs. 'That is Band-e-Azhdahar, or Dragon Lake. Beautiful, isn't it? The lake sits in a bed of white travertine marble. As you can see, there are no trees, no vegetation. This is 1000 metres up in a valley between the Hindu Kush and Koh-i-Baba mountains.'

'Is there a town or city nearby, sir?' Charlie asked.

'Yes, Sergeant, the lake is a few clicks southeast of the city of Bamiyan. This is in the province of Bamiyan, which is adjacent to the province of Uruzgan, where the secretary-general's heelo went down. Bamiyan is an ancient city. It sits on the old Silk Road.'

'How big is this Bamiyan?' Duke Hazard asked while, as always, chewing gum.

'The city is home to 62,000 people, but has no gas, no electricity, no running water, no sanitation. Going there is like travelling hundreds of years back in time. Before the current war, it was famous for the Bamiyan Buddhas.'

'The what?' Sergeant Hazard queried.

'The Buddhas of Bamiyan. Giant 1200-year-old statues of Buddha that were cut into the rock. They were Afghanistan's greatest tourist attraction. You'll probably remember that in 2001 the Taliban blew those statues to pieces.'

'Freaking vandals!' General McAvoy muttered, half to himself.

'Why wouldn't the Taliban keep the secretary-general and his party in Bamiyan?' Sergeant Tim McHenry pondered out loud. 'It would be easier to disappear in a ramshackle city like that.'

'Ah.' A faint smile crossed Major Jinko's lips. 'Here's the thing. Bamiyan is home to the Hazara people, an ethnic minority. The Hazara and the Pashtun people of the rest of Afghanistan don't get on. When the Taliban was in power in Afghanistan, they persecuted the Hazaras. They hate one another, so there's no way the Taliban would get away with hiding in that Hazara city. There are 800 Hazara soldiers stationed there, along with 150 New Zealand ISAF troops. Too much activity by Pashtuns in Bamiyan is going to attract their attention. But hiding in caves near Dragon Lake is another thing. It's a clever move by the Taliban. Because of the bad blood between the Taliban and the Hazaras, we would never have thought to search Bamiyan Province for the secretary-general.'

'What's the terrain like, sir?' Ben asked.

'Difficult. Few sealed roads.'

'You mentioned caves, sir,' said Charlie.

Major Jinko nodded. 'I did. Let me bring someone into the conversation who knows Dragon Lake a lot better than I do.' He gestured to a soldier standing by the door at the back of the room. 'Ask Dr Jordan to come in.'

The door opened and a woman in a sandy-coloured shirt and trousers entered the room and joined the major and the general on stage. The slouching men in the room straightened a little in their chairs.

'This is Dr Emma Jordan,' Major Jinko went on, 'an Australian geologist from Brisbane, my home town. She's in Afghanistan serving with the United Nations Educational, Scientific and Cultural Organisation – UNESCO. Dr Jordan has in the past conducted extensive geological surveys of the Dragon Lake area for the Afghan Government. Dr Jordan, would you like to fill the boys in?'

'Er, thank you.' Clearly unnerved by all the faces staring at her, Emma Jordan cleared her throat. 'Band-e-Azhdahar is etched into travertine cliffs, as you can see,' she began, pointing to the image on the screen. 'The cliffs on the eastern side of the lake are riddled with caves. Before this war, one of them was popular with foreign cavers. The cave has no local name but cavers used to call it Deep Cave. It's large and hundreds of metres deep. A channel from the lake feeds into it and almost fills half of it with water, creating a large pool inside the cave. If I were going to hide someone at Band-e-Azhdahar, I would do it in Deep Cave.'

'How in God's name are we supposed to find these people in *that* cave system?' Duke Hazard demanded.

'That's where the EDDs will come in,' General McAvoy spoke up. 'In the video Dr Park mentioned that the Taliban had threatened to blow up the hostages. So, the dogs will track the explosives the Taliban hostage-takers will have on them.'

Dr Jordan moved to a whiteboard at one side of the stage. With a felt marker, she drew a simple diagram of Dragon Lake, with Deep Cave in the cliffs to one side of it. 'This is Deep Cave,' she said. 'In the main cavern, there is an extensive area with a high roof, 50 metres high in some places. It surrounds the vast freshwater pool I spoke of. Here.' She tapped the diagram. 'That pool is 500 metres wide at its broadest point and is 100 metres deep. The pool is fed by the lake via this connecting channel, 100 metres down.' She pointed to the channel.

'How many entrances to the cave?' asked Hazard.

'Just one. Here.' Dr Jordan marked it with a cross on the diagram.

'Only one entrance!' Hazard exclaimed.

'Yes, on the eastern side of Deep Cave,' Dr Jordan continued. 'It gives access to a long, slightly sloping corridor in the rock, which opens up to the cavern and the pool.'

'This ain't gonna work,' said Duke Hazard, shaking his head. 'The Taliban will have that entrance barricaded. Sure, we could fight our way in, but by the time we did that the Taliban guarding the hostages would have detonated their explosives and blown the sec-gen and everyone with him sky high.'

A long, tense silence gripped the room.

'That's a good point, Hazard,' said General McAvoy. 'And we can't risk the lives of the hostages.'

'Do you need another entrance to the cave?' asked Dr Jordan.

'At least one other entrance,' the general replied glumly. 'If we could distract the Taliban at one entrance, we might be able to use the other.'

'But that second entrance would also be guarded,' said Major Jinko.

'You're right,' McAvoy agreed with a sigh.

'Well, there is a second entrance,' said Dr Jordan. 'One that the Taliban would find impossible to guard. They wouldn't even know it existed – it took modern science to discover it.'

'Really?' said Major Jinko, perking up. 'Where is it?'

'As I mentioned before, this channel down here.' Dr Jordan again pointed to the channel on the diagram. 'There's a large opening a hundred metres down in the side wall of the lake, feeding into Deep Cave.'

'Hell's bells, lady!' Hazard exclaimed. 'A hundred metres beneath the surface of the lake? How do you expect us to get down there?'

'Could an underwater diver use that entrance?' General McAvoy asked, thinking aloud. 'Mortenson, you're our diving expert. Do you think you could you get in through the channel?'

Casper Mortenson stood up. 'Yes, I could, General, using a pressure suit.'

'But getting one man in wouldn't be enough, sir,' Charlie piped up. 'We'd need at least half-a-dozen men coming up through that second underwater entrance to effect the rescue while the rest of the team kept the Taliban busy at the main entrance up top. And Mortenson is the only one here trained for deepwater work.'

'This is true,' said Mortenson, nodding. 'I could not do it alone.'

'And what about the EDDs?' Ben added. 'My Caesar can do heelo drops and he can make HALO jumps from 20,000 feet, but he's not trained for underwater work.'

'And no one has yet made an underwater pressure suit for dogs,' Mortenson added with a smile as he sat back down.

'We gotta make use of that underwater entrance,' said General McAvoy, sounding frustrated.

'The Taliban certainly wouldn't be expecting us to come in that way, that's for sure!' Major Jinko commented. 'If we could keep them busy at the cave's front door, we could enter through the back door, so to speak, via the pool behind them.'

Again the room was silent. Brains could almost be heard whirring as the Special Forces men tried to think of a way to exploit the underwater entrance to Deep Cave.

'Okay, I got it!' exclaimed Chris Banner, the British SBS man. 'What about a submarine? Could a mini-sub use that underwater entrance and then surface in the pool inside the cavern and unload our people?'

Major Jinko turned to Dr Jordan. 'In your opinion, would the channel be large enough for a mini-submarine to pass through?'

Dr Jordan hesitated. 'How wide and deep would a mini-submarine be? The underwater entrance is twenty metres at its narrowest.'

'More than large enough for a small submarine to pass through,' remarked Major Jinko. 'You have no doubts about the size of the opening and of the channel?'

'None,' Dr Jordan said firmly. 'That entrance has been mapped by sonar.'

'Okay, so how do we get a sub into the lake in the first place?' General McAvoy asked, sounding sceptical.

'You drop it in,' Banner suggested.

'By parachute?' said Major Jinko.

Corporal Banner nodded. 'You got it.'

'Could an aircraft carry a sub?' McAvoy pondered.

'A mini-sub, sure,' said Sergeant Bruce, the Royal Marine Commando. 'The Special Boat lads use them.'

'That's right, man,' Banner agreed. 'We sure do.'

General McAvoy looked intrigued. 'How big a mini-sub do you guys use, Corporal?'

'S Squadron uses mini-subs that operate with four divers,' Banner advised.

'Okay, but as Sergeant Grover suggested,' said Major Jinko, 'our operation would require a mini-sub large enough to take at least six of our men.'

'Big enough for six men plus crew, but small enough to fit into a transport aircraft,' said McAvoy. 'A Globemaster or Galaxy.' The massive C-17 Globemaster was operated by several air forces, including Australia's. The even larger C-5 Super Galaxy was the largest transport aircraft in military service, and only the US Air Force could afford them.

'Doesn't the sub need to be large enough to carry the hostages as well?' Ben suggested. 'That way we could take them out through the underwater entrance.'

'Good thinking, Fulton,' said Jinko. 'But who's got a mini-sub large enough for the job?'

'The SBS's boats are too small,' said Sergeant Bruce.

'Wait a minute, man,' said Banner. 'I've been reading up on mini-subs. The Yanks retired the right boat for the job a few years back. I think it was called the *Pencil*.'

'The *Pencil*?' General McAvoy frowned.

'The US Navy built it to rescue crews of big subs trapped on the ocean floor,' Banner explained. 'Later, the Navy came up with a different design for submarine rescues, so the *Pencil* was handed over to the Navy SEALs for special ops. But they never used it, and as far as I know it was retired. The British Government tried to buy the *Pencil* from the US Government for the SBS, but they wouldn't sell it.'

'Was the *Pencil* scrapped?' Major Jinko queried.

'No, man, *retired*,' Banner emphasised. 'With something as useful as that, you don't throw it out with the trash. It must be lying around a US naval base someplace, gathering dust.'

'You don't say.' General McAvoy had heard enough. He picked up the telephone. 'This is McAvoy. Give me everything you've got on a US Navy mini-sub called the *Pencil*. Put it up on the Special Ops briefing room screen.'

Two minutes later, patched in from an IT room deep within the headquarters, an image came up on the screen of a long, thin submarine with a low conning tower two-thirds of the way from its bow. The sub truly looked like its name. Officially, it was the DSRV-801X. Beneath the picture, the sub's specifications were listed.

'Might fit into a Galaxy or a Globemaster,' General McAvoy said approvingly.

Pointing to the screen, Major Jinko read out a line from the specifications. '"The Deep Submersible Rescue Vessel 801X requires a crew of two and is capable of accommodating up to sixteen submarine crewmen or six fully equipped divers." Banner's right. This vessel is ideal for our needs – it can accommodate sixteen personnel, more than enough room to embark part of the extraction team, including an EDD, and the seven.'

'Now we're cooking with gas!' Banner exclaimed, rubbing his hands together.

'Is the sub pressurised, Major?' Ben asked. 'I'll go anywhere you send me, but I can't take Caesar into an unpressurised submarine.'

'Let me see, Fulton.' Major Jinko scanned the specifications on the screen, then nodded to himself and turned to Ben. 'Its hull is pressurised to four times the strength of a normal submarine to allow it to go to extraordinary depths. That suit you, Sergeant?'

Ben smiled. 'Thank you, sir. Caesar thanks you, too.'

'Four times the strength of a normal sub?' General McAvoy mused to himself. 'Okay. That means it should stand the shock of being parachuted into Dragon Lake. Jinko, where is this sub?'

'It says here that it was decommissioned in 2010 and that its current location is unknown,' replied the major.

'Well, locate it, for God's sake!' ordered an exasperated General McAvoy. 'This sub is the answer to our prayers. Find that sub and confirm that we can get it into the belly of a C-5 or C-17.'

'Yes, sir,' said Jinko. 'But, with respect, first we have

to confirm that the secretary-general and the others are being held in Deep Cave.'

'We go forward on the basis that they are in that cave until and unless it's proven otherwise!' McAvoy barked, heading for the door. 'Thank you, men. And thank you, Dr Jordan, ma'am.'

'Atten-shun!' called Major Jinko.

All the men in the room rapidly came to their feet and stood stiffly at attention.

Dr Jordan looked at Major Jinko, blinking with surprise. 'Was I any help to you, Major?'

'Indeed you were, Doctor, thank you,' he said, shaking her hand.

'One more thing, everyone!' McAvoy called, turning from the door. 'We need a name for this mission.' He thought for a moment. 'Operation Blue Dragon. We'll call it Operation Blue Dragon, Jinko. And the team will be known as Strike Force Blue Dragon.'

'Roger that, sir,' Jinko returned.

'And,' McAvoy added, 'from this point forward, we do not refer to the secretary-general as the secretary-general, or use his name. From now on, we call him "the Big Cheese". We can't risk the Taliban catching on to this operation. So he's the Big Cheese. No Afghan will have a clue about who or what we're talking about.'

'Roger that, sir,' Jinko acknowledged. 'The Big Cheese he is.'

It was hard for Josh and Maddie to keep the information about Dragon Lake secret. Josh wanted to tell everyone at his school how clever he was, and Maddie wanted to tell everyone that she had the smartest brother in the world. But they knew they would have to keep the secret to themselves if Dr Park was to be saved.

As Josh ate breakfast the day after Nan shared his discovery with his father, Nan asked him to do her a favour. 'Josh, would you walk Maddie home from school this afternoon? I have to go for my annual mammogram, and the only appointment I could get is just when you two are getting out of school.'

'Okay, Nan,' said Josh, spooning the last mouthful of cereal.

'What's a nannogram?' asked Maddie, wiping her mouth with the back of her hand.

'A *mammogram*,' said Nan, rubbing Maddie's face with a napkin, 'is a test for breast cancer. And we all know how important it is to detect that early.'

Maddie, associating breast cancer with their mother, looked over at Josh, alarmed.

Reading her mind, Josh smiled reassuringly. 'It's just a check-up, Maddie. Come on, we'll be late for school.'

'I hope Nan's all right,' said Maddie worriedly as she and Josh walked home from school. 'Those nannograms must be scary.'

'She'll be fine, Maddie, don't worry,' Josh assured her, as they came to an intersection. After looking each way to be sure the street was clear, he took Maddie's hand. 'Come on, let's go.'

They had just crossed the street when a voice boomed from behind them. 'Is she your girlfriend, Dog Boy?'

Josh's stomach filled with dread. He quickly let go of Maddie's hand and glanced around, already knowing who he would find. 'No, she's my little sister.'

'Who's he, Josh?' Maddie asked.

'No one,' Josh mumbled. Speeding up, he put a hand on his sister's back, urging her to do the same. 'Get a move on, Maddie!'

'He can't be no one,' Maddie countered, struggling to keep up with Josh's stride. 'He has to have a name. Everyone has a name. Even dogs have names. Houses have names sometimes. People give their cars names –'

'So, Dog Boy has a sister,' Kelvin Corbett said loudly. 'Dog Girl.' He laughed to himself.

'Who *is* he?' Maddie hissed.

'He's in my class,' said Josh. 'His name is Kelvin.'

'Why is he following us?' whispered Maddie.

Josh shrugged and walked even faster. 'Because he's creepy.'

'What'd you say?' Kelvin demanded.

'He said you're creepy,' Maddie said matter-of-factly.

Josh groaned. 'Shh, Maddie!'

'Creepy, am I? You don't know a thing about me, Josh Fulton,' Kelvin called. 'I know a million more things than you do. You think you're so smart, with your dumb exploding dog.'

'Caesar's not dumb,' Josh called back.

'And Josh knows way more than you do!' said Maddie, sticking up for her brother.

'Oh yeah? Like what?' Kelvin retorted.

Maddie stopped in her tracks and turned around. With her hands on her hips, she declared, 'My brother knows where the Tabilan are keeping the sceraty-general of the United Notions.'

'Maddie!' Josh grabbed her hand and pulled her along.

'Oh yeah?' said Kelvin. 'Where are they keeping him? In your backyard?' He laughed darkly.

'No, silly,' Maddie retorted. 'They've got him inside a big blue dragon. So there! You never knew that, smarty pants, and Josh did!'

'In a blue dragon?' Kelvin laughed again. 'Your sister is loony, Dog Boy.'

Josh was tugging Maddie away when a car pulled up beside them. Nan Fulton leaned over and wound down the passenger window. 'Hop in, you two,' she called. 'I was able to get out of the clinic earlier than I'd expected.'

Josh didn't have to be invited a second time. He had never been so grateful in all his life to climb into his grandmother's battered orange Ford Fiesta. He and Maddie slipped onto the back seat and closed the door.

'Who was that boy?' Nan asked, as they drove off.

'He's in my class,' Josh answered, looking out the back window.

'Oh, lovely, a new school friend for you,' said Nan. 'Speaking of your friends, how is Baxter doing?'

'He should be back at school next week,' Josh answered absently, still looking out the back window.

'Good, good,' said Nan. 'He's such a nice, smart boy.'

'Josh,' said Maddie, whispering. She looked up at him with a sheepish expression on her face. 'I oopsed.'

Josh frowned. 'What do you mean?'

'I told Kelvin about the blue dragon,' she said, wincing. 'Oops!'

Josh gave his sister a reassuring smile. 'Don't worry, he's too dumb to know what you meant. But you have to keep quiet about it from now on, Maddie. Cross your heart and hope to die.'

Maddie nodded. 'I will. I promise. Cross my heart and hope to die.'

'Nobody can know.'

'I know. It's the toppest top secret.'

'What are you two whispering about back there?' Nan called from behind the wheel.

'If I told you, Nan, I'd die,' Maddie replied seriously.

'Ah, well then,' Nan said, breaking into a wide smile. 'We can't have that, dear. So, did anything interesting happen to either of you today?'

Josh looked at Maddie. 'No, just an average day, Nan.'

CHAPTER 9

In the dark of night, two twin-engine Chinook CH-47 helicopters lifted off from the Tarin Kowt airfield and, without lights, wheeled toward the south. Once the Chinooks were well away from the city, flying over open country, they turned west and made for the Hindu Kush mountains. This had been done to ensure that no Taliban agent in Tarin Kowt would see them flying toward Bamiyan Province.

Ben and Caesar were riding in the second heelo, along with Charlie, Lucky, Baz and several of the foreign members of Strike Force Blue Dragon. Duke Hazard and the Americans were in the leading Chinook, accompanied by the rest of the foreign Special Forces troops. On his usual metal leash, Caesar sat between Ben's legs, tongue hanging out, looking around at the soldiers sitting on either side of Ben along the wall of the cabin. Caesar recognised his fellow Australians, and among friends, he was feeling right at home.

Bending down to Caesar, Ben ruffled his neck and, to be heard above the din of the helicopter's engines, yelled into his right ear. 'We've got an important job ahead of us, mate. You might even be doing a bit of swimming.'

At the mention of swimming, Caesar looked around at Ben, his tail wagging with excitement. Ben knew how much Caesar loved to play in the sea. Occasionally, the pair went swimming at the beach when they had time off. Like all labradors, Caesar's feet were naturally webbed, which made swimming easier for him. Ben knew the origins of the labrador retriever breed went back to water dogs in Newfoundland, Canada, where they were used to retrieve nets and fish as well as waterfowl shot by their masters.

Seeing Caesar's wagging tail, Ben grinned. 'I thought you'd like that. You'd enjoy a swim, wouldn't you, mate?'

In response, Caesar's tongue snaked out and he licked the side of Ben's face.

🐾🐾

The US Naval Base San Diego in southern California is the largest naval installation on the west coast of the United States, with 20,000 military personnel and 6000 civilian employees. Scores of grey warships call San Diego home, including two massive nuclear aircraft carriers, cruisers, destroyers, frigates and support vessels. But Commander Dave Renzo and his deputy, Lieutenant Brad Ellerman, weren't interested in any of them. They were looking for one of the smallest vessels in the US Navy.

Round-faced Renzo was greying at the temples and had a stomach that bulged over his belt. Renzo had spent all his adult life in the US Navy's submarine service. After graduating from the Annapolis Naval Academy, he'd served as an officer in some of the US Navy's largest nuclear submarines. But Renzo had an independent streak, and in later years he'd specialised in captaining small research subs.

Short, slim and movie-star handsome, Lieutenant Ellerman looked young enough to be Renzo's son. Ellerman had a background as a US Navy clearance diver before he joined Renzo as co-pilot of deep-sea research vessels three years ago. Their regular research sub, the *Davy Jones*, had been undergoing repairs for months, leaving the pair without a posting and kicking their heels around the San Diego base. That is, until their commanding admiral had given them an unusual, dangerous and top-secret assignment.

A huge dockside shed door slid open noisily and the two white-uniformed officers followed a tubby, white-haired chief petty officer inside.

'Can we have some light, Chief?' asked Commander Renzo.

'Yeah, it's black as night in here,' said Lieutenant Ellerman beside him.

'Hold on,' said the chief petty officer, whose name was Brogan. Finding a bank of light switches, he flicked them all up. 'There you go.'

Fluorescent light flooded the shed's interior, revealing a motley collection of old grey boats. None was more than twenty metres long, most were metal and some were stacked on top of others. Barges, tenders and admiral's launches, they had all once led active lives around the base, or had been aboard warships that had since been sent to the scrap merchants or sunk as diving wrecks.

'What a junk heap,' Ellerman exclaimed.

'Oh, not so fast there, Lieutenant,' Brogan said a little defensively. 'I know the history of every single boat, and they have some life left in them yet.' He began to make his way through the maze of small craft, heading toward the rear of the shed. 'Follow me. *Your* baby is over here.'

With the sound of their footsteps reverberating around the metal walls, the chief petty officer led his superiors to a far corner, where a long, narrow shape lay covered with tarpaulins. Renzo and Ellerman helped Brogan drag the tarps away to reveal a long, slender black shape sitting on a metal cradle. The shape's symmetry was interrupted by a bump toward the rear of its narrow deck.

'Behold the *Pencil*,' said Brogan cheerily. 'Better known as the DSRV-801X. It's a criminal waste, if you ask me, letting a perfectly serviceable craft like this sit gathering dust.'

'So, she's good to go?' Renzo asked, walking around the mini-sub and studying it with a professional eye.

'Oh, no, I didn't say that, sir,' said Brogan. 'She needs work done on her before she goes into the water again. For one thing, all the electrics have been stripped out and will have to be replaced. Then there's a mandatory maintenance check of her engines, ballast tanks and controls to make sure everything's in good working order.'

Ellerman frowned. 'How long will that take?'

'Oh . . .' The chief petty officer screwed up his face as he gave it some thought. 'A month. Two at the outside.'

'We don't have two months,' said Renzo. 'We don't even have a month!'

Brogan chuckled. 'Don't tell me you want the *Pencil* all ship-shape in a few weeks, sir?'

'No, Chief,' Renzo replied. 'We don't even have weeks. This vessel has to be ready for sea in *days*.'

The chief petty officer's mouth dropped open. 'You're kidding me,' he said, once he'd recovered his composure. 'This is a joke, right? It's impossible to get this vessel ready for sea in just a few days.'

Renzo shook his head. 'No joke, I'm afraid.' Reaching into his tunic pocket, he took out a folded letter and held it out. 'Read the signature on that,' he instructed.

Taking the letter, Brogan unfolded it. Seeing the signature at the bottom, he stiffened. 'The President of the United States!' he exclaimed, almost in disbelief.

'Our commander-in-chief says we have to have this vessel ready for operations in a few days, Chief. So, here's what's got to happen – you're going to ship this vessel over to the air station on North Island. Then Lieutenant Ellerman and I are going to take it where no submarine has ever gone before. Is that clear?'

Brogan gulped. 'Clear, sir.'

'Whatever you need – men, equipment – you've got the President's authority to bring it in. Drop whatever else you're working on and you get this baby seaworthy.'

'Aye, aye, sir.' Brogan sounded less than convinced that he could do the job in the time allowed. But orders were orders.

'Carry on, Chief.'

The chief petty officer saluted, then almost ran from the shed to round up the men and equipment he needed. As he departed, Renzo and Ellerman surveyed the craft.

'A little rust around the rudder,' Ellerman observed, squatting to look at the slender stern, 'but, otherwise, she looks pretty sound to me.'

'Let's take a look inside,' Renzo suggested.

The pair climbed a narrow ladder to the deck of the little submarine. Then, kneeling on the deck, they opened the circular forward hatch. As the hatch cover swung up and open, stale air came wafting out.

Renzo looked at his deputy. 'So, Brad, you and I have to operate this thing.'

'Can't be much different from the other deep submersibles we've piloted, Commander,' said Ellerman, peering down into the dark interior.

'Here, use my flashlight,' said Renzo, taking a torch from his trouser pocket and handing it to Ellerman. 'Lead the way. Let's see what we've got to work with.'

Flicking it on, Ellerman clambered down through the narrow, round hatchway and entered the *Pencil*'s forward compartment. 'Don't get stuck in the hatchway, sir,' he called back jokingly.

'Ha-de-ha!' Renzo retorted as he reached the hatchway. 'I might have put on a few pounds since the last time we worked together, pal, but it's just stored-up muscle.'

As Renzo and Ellerman were inspecting the *Pencil* in San Diego, Dr Park was sitting deep inside a dark, dank cave in Afghanistan.

'Our ordeal will not last much longer, my friends,' he assured his companions.

Secretary-General Park was doing his best to keep the spirits of his fellow hostages raised, despite their difficult situation. He and his six companions had each been given a single blanket by their Taliban captors. Their lavatory was a stinking bucket which their captors exchanged daily for an empty one. The captives were being kept on a dry ledge beside a large freshwater pool, so were able to drink when they were thirsty by scooping water with cupped hands. But food was in shorter supply. They were fed just once a day, in the evening – a little cooked chicken or goat with a small bucket of rice and a few cooked vegetables.

Their new diet was hardest on the only female member of the hostage party, Liberty Lee, who was a Buddhist and a vegetarian. Yet Liberty endured their primitive conditions without a word of complaint or any sign of discomfort. She was, after all, Dr Park's personal bodyguard and a martial arts expert highly trained in how to use her mind as well as her body. She faced their tough situation with blank-faced fortitude.

The same could not be said of some of her male companions. Lieutenant Frankel, their German co-pilot, had fallen and broken both an ankle and a wrist while being marched through the mountains by their Taliban captors. Liberty, who was trained in first aid, had strapped Frankel's ankle and wrist with the help of their pilot, Captain Rix. But without painkillers, it was clear that Lieutenant Frankel was in great discomfort. And although he didn't complain, he groaned throughout the night, keeping the others awake.

Fader, a Danish member of the secretary-general's staff, had developed a fever with a dangerously high temperature. But he also bravely made no complaint. Loubet, the French transport officer on Dr Park's staff, had jolted his back when the helicopter went down. But, while in obvious pain, he assured the others he was fine. It was Mikashi, the secretary-general's press officer, who was faring worst of all. Though highly intelligent and a whizz with words, Mikashi was a delicate man. Not only was he taking their deprivations badly, he was convinced the Taliban were going to kill them. Every now and then, he would burst into tears and wail, 'We're all going to die! We're all going to die!'

When he did so again, for the seventh time that day, Dr Park tried to calm and comfort him. 'It is all right, Mikashi,' he said soothingly. 'Do not worry, we are all going to get out of this.'

'Yes, do buck up, Mikashi, there's a good chap,' said Jeremy Brown, Dr Park's secretary, trying to hide his impatience with the man. 'Of course we'll get out of this.'

'Yes, without doubt,' Loubet concurred, wincing as he shifted his position to try to get comfortable.

'How can you be so sure?' Mikashi snivelled. 'The coalition forces are not going to leave Afghanistan in a week. The Taliban will start shooting us one at a time, just as they have threatened.'

'It will not come to that,' Dr Park assured him. He lowered his voice. 'We will be rescued before that time arrives. I am confident of that.'

'How so?' Mikashi looked at the secretary-general beseechingly. 'The ISAF troops don't even know where to look for us. They cannot know that we are here. How would they find us?'

Dr Park took Mikashi's hand and patted it reassuringly. 'I can assure you, Mikashi, that the ISAF generals know where we are and that a rescue mission will be mounted.'

Mikashi looked unconvinced, then his eyes widened. 'Is there a homing device on one of us?'

'Something like that,' said the secretary-general. 'It is best that I do not reveal the source of my confidence.'

Mikashi brightened considerably. 'Ah, of course.'

So that they would not get their hopes up too high, or let something slip to their captors, Dr Park had told none of his companions that he had tried to alert friendly governments to where they were being held via the video the Taliban had forced him to shoot. He had not even let on how he'd worked out where they were being held. Prior to coming to Afghanistan, Dr Park had taken a crash course to improve the basic Pashto that he already spoke in order to converse with local leaders in their own tongue, without the use of interpreters. The Taliban commander who had captured the UN party was unaware that Dr Park could speak their language, and while marching the hostages to this place, the commander had spoken to his men about 'the large cave' and 'the blue lake of the dragon'.

'But when you spoke on the video,' said Mikashi, 'you told the world that you did not want any attempt made to rescue us.'

Dr Park shook his head. 'No, I said that I did not wish any lives put at risk on my account. I was telling my friends and colleagues to devise a method of rescuing us that minimised the potential for loss of life.'

'Oh. Then, you think that they are going to rescue us?' Mikashi sounded even more hopeful now.

'Yes. And soon.'

'Secretary-General, someone is coming,' whispered Liberty Lee.

A faint light could be seen in the distance, coming through the cave toward them. Before long, five bearded Taliban fighters with round caps on their heads appeared, with a few of them carrying gas lanterns. All were armed. Their leader had not yet introduced himself to his hostages, but his name was Commander Baradar and he was the most senior Taliban commander in Uruzgan Province. After taking Dr Park and his party captive, Baradar had brought them across the mountains to this hiding place in the neighbouring province.

Baradar was a solid man with deep-set eyes and a black beard flecked with grey. He wore loose, dark clothes. With an AK-47 automatic rifle slung casually over his shoulder, Commander Baradar came to a halt in front of the hostages. In the light of the lanterns carried by his men, he studied the hostages in silence.

'Food,' moaned Mikashi. 'Give us food!'

'Too early for food,' Baradar replied in halting English. It was only midmorning, and their rations would be delivered in the evening. 'UN Chief, come,' barked Baradar.

Two of Baradar's men hurried in and took the secretary-general beneath the arms, hauling him to his feet.

'Stop!' Liberty Lee yelled, jumping up. 'You will not harm him!'

Baradar quickly unshouldered his AK-47 and pointed it at her. 'Sit!' he snapped. 'Or I shoot you!'

'Yes, please sit down, Miss Lee,' said Dr Park. 'That is an order.'

Glowering at their captors, Liberty sank back to the ground.

Baradar turned and walked further into the cave, followed by the two insurgents escorting Dr Park.

'Abdul, set it up facing that rock,' Commander Baradar ordered in Pashto.

The slovenly Abdul Razah, one of Baradar's longest-serving fighters, set up a tripod with a video camera facing the spot designated by his leader. Abdul had been one of the Taliban fighters under Baradar's command who had ambushed the joint Australian–American Special Forces patrol involving Ben, Caesar, Charlie and Duke Hazard. After Caesar had been handed over to the Taliban by the Haidari family, Baradar had put the cruel Abdul in charge of guarding Caesar.

The secretary-general sat on a rock facing the camera, the same place that he had filmed the video three days before. 'Please, Commander,' said Dr Park, 'can you bring painkillers for Lieutenant Frankel? And Mr Fader is very unwell. He needs a doctor.'

'Not my concern,' Baradar answered with a dismissive wave of the hand. 'You will make new video. Days are passing and, the infidel armies, they do not make to prepare for leaving my country. You must tell them that you will die if they ignore warning.'

Baradar gave Abdul an instruction in Pashto, and Abdul came around from behind the camera to hand Dr Park a sheet of paper. Two other insurgents strung up a green curtain behind the secretary-general, fixing it to the rocky wall with duct tape. The two men then stood either side of Dr Park, holding their lanterns high to light the scene.

'Start the camera,' Baradar ordered.

'Yes, Commander.' Abdul scurried behind the camera and pressed the 'record' button. Frowning quizzically, he bent down to examine the camera.

'What is wrong, Abdul Razah?' Baradar demanded irritably.

Abdul looked up, bewildered. 'The camera, it will not work, Commander.'

'You have put batteries in the camera?'

'Yes, Commander, of course I have put batteries in the camera.' Abdul was looking at it from all angles, trying to work out what was wrong.

'You have put the video cassette in the camera?'

'Yes, Commander, of c–' Abdul stopped in mid-sentence and fumbled in the cloth bag slung over his shoulder. Sheepishly, he took out a cassette and slotted it into the camera. He pressed 'record' again and, this time, a red light came on. 'The camera is recording now, Commander,' he announced with relief.

'Idiot!' Baradar growled under his breath. He turned to the waiting secretary-general. 'UN Chief, read statement to camera. Begin! Now!'

Dr Park lifted the statement and, straining to read it in the poor light, followed Baradar's order. 'This is Dr Park. I am instructed to tell you that my captors are very angry,' he recited. 'They wish me to say they are not fools. They can see that foreign forces occupying Afghanistan are making no attempt to leave the country.

The last time that I spoke to you, I said that the infidel governments had seven days before they would start killing my colleagues and myself. By the time you see this, those days will have almost run out. You have until the fourteenth of this month of July. No longer. And if you have not obeyed my captors by that time, we will all die.'

Commander Baradar then had Dr Park taken back to join the other hostages.

As the secretary-general was hustled away, Abdul removed the cassette from the camera. 'What do you want me to do with this, Commander?' Abdul asked, holding up the cassette.

'You will personally take the cassette to our contacts in Bamiyan at once. Tell them to arrange for it to be uploaded to YouTube without delay.'

'Yes, Commander.'

'Do not lose it or damage it.'

'No, Commander. I mean, yes, I will not lose or damage it.'

Commander Baradar glowered at Abdul. 'Well, what are you waiting for? Go! One of the others will pack up the camera. Go!'

'Yes, Commander.' Stuffing the cassette into his bag, Abdul hurried away to fulfil his orders.

CHAPTER 10

FOB Nero, a small forward operating base several kilometres to the south of the city of Bamiyan, sat on a rise in a valley surrounded by dry, barren hills. From here, a detachment from the Afghan National Army made routine patrols through the hills, looking for Taliban and other insurgents. It was here that Strike Force Blue Dragon had snuck in under the cover of night. FOB Nero would be their base for now, while the bears back at HQ worked to confirm that the secretary-general was indeed being held in Deep Cave.

Ben, Caesar and their comrades grabbed a few hours of sleep on their first night in Bamiyan Province. Back in Australia, Caesar usually slept at the army kennels at Holsworthy Army Barracks, or, when he was at home with Ben at 3 Kokoda Crescent, in a backyard kennel. Here at FOB Nero, Caesar slept beside Ben inside one of the shipping containers, snuggling up to him and sharing body warmth through the chilly night. In the same container, Charlie, Lucky and Baz stretched out in sleeping bags around them.

When the sun rose over the base on their first morning there, Ben and Caesar were greeted by the sight of a rectangular fort with high outer walls made from concrete blocks, overlooked by guard towers that sat on tall, spindly iron legs. The FOB's headquarters had a tall, ugly metal mast on its roof, bearing an array of radio, TV and mobile phone antennae, and dishes that kept the troops in touch with the outside world. In the centre of the base was a large open space where helicopters set down and took off.

Many of FOB Nero's buildings around the perimeter were former shipping containers that had originally been flown to the base, dangling from US Army Chinooks. Other buildings were just temporary shelters made from corrugated iron and dirt-filled sandbags. Beyond the walls of the base, there were no signs of life. As far as the eye could see, the yellow-white hills all around were without trees, shrubs or animals. The only signs of life were within the camp walls.

Here, on the heelo pad, Ben now took Caesar for an exercise jog, letting him off the leash to trot free alongside him, all the while keeping the folded leash in his hand in case he needed to secure Caesar in a hurry. As always, Caesar enjoyed his exercise run, loping alongside Ben and taking in the sights and sounds of the base with his tail wagging.

Wearing green T-shirts and camouflage trousers, with their holstered Browning pistols strapped to their thighs, Charlie, Baz and Lucky were doing push-ups beside the landing pad as Ben and Caesar trotted by, doing their circuits. Wearing Zoomers made no difference to Charlie's ability to do push-ups and other exercises. All his physical strength was in his arms and upper body. Up and down he went like a well-oiled machine, sometimes on just one arm.

'Why would anyone want to live in desolate country like this?' Baz wondered aloud as he pumped up and down without a puff.

'By the same token, Baz, why would anyone want to live in Bendigo?' said Lucky, with a wink at Charlie.

'Mate, Bendigo is paradise!' Baz returned.

'Well, the locals probably think the same about this place,' Charlie remarked.

'Then they need their eyes seen to,' Baz grumbled. 'Looks like hell to me.'

'Bendigo? Paradise?' said Charlie, smiling and shaking his head.

'It is to me, cobber,' Baz came back. 'And to a lot of other Bendigoers. Where are you from originally? I know that you and Ben went to school together in Sydney.'

'I was born on an island,' Charlie replied. 'Moved to Sydney after my parents died. I had an uncle there.'

'Which island?' Baz persisted.

Charlie grinned. 'You are an inquisitive bloke, aren't you, Baz?'

'Only asking, mate,' said Baz. 'What about you, Lucky? Where were you born?'

'New Zealand, mate. Bay of Islands.'

Baz paused mid push-up. 'You're a Kiwi? Crikey! All these years we've been serving together, and I never knew that.'

'You never asked before, Baz.'

'I suppose I didn't. One thing I always meant to ask you – where'd you get the nickname "Lucky"? I don't reckon you're any luckier than the next bloke.'

Lucky chuckled. 'It's my name, Baz.'

'Yeah. A nickname.'

'No, not a nickname,' corrected Lucky. 'It's the name my parents gave me.'

'Crikey! Why? Is it some wacko Bay of Islands tradition?'

'Nope. A family tradition. My dad's name is Happy Mertz. And I'm Lucky Mertz. Simple as that.'

The two high iron gates at the main entrance of the base opened. An old, grey battered van drove in and pulled up in a cloud of dust. As the gates closed behind the van, two young Afghan men jumped down from its cab and headed straight to the rear doors. Swinging the doors open, the pair began to unload equipment.

Ali Moon, the strike force's interpreter, was sitting on an empty crate nearby, in conversation with two ANA soldiers on guard. Charlie, suspicious of the newcomers, stopped what he was doing and called out to the interpreter. 'Ali, who are those two blokes? They don't look military to me.'

Ali put Charlie's question to the two ANA men, then called back their answer. 'These two men are Afghan performers, Sergeant Charlie. They go around the FOBs, entertaining the foreign ISAF troops for tips. They are known to the men here. Foreign troops, such as the Americans, like them.'

'They're like buskers,' Bendigo Baz observed.

Ali, who had no idea what a busker was, said, 'These men juggle and do acrobatics. They are of no threat to us.'

'Okay.' Charlie nodded, then returned his gaze to the two young men. They looked alike. Probably brothers, Charlie thought. The elder of the two had a neat beard, while the other was clean-shaven. They appeared to be urging a black goat to jump down to the ground from the back of the van. What part a goat could possibly play in the entertainers' act, Charlie struggled to imagine.

Out on the helicopter pad, Ben, still jogging, looked back to see that Caesar had come to a sudden halt. The chocolate-brown labrador was standing still and looking at the grey van. Ben stopped and retraced his steps, dropping to one knee beside Caesar and ruffling his neck. 'What's up, mate?'

Caesar glanced at Ben for a moment before returning his focus to the van, staring at it. He could only see the bottom half of the legs of the two young Afghan men behind the van. But when one of the entertainers, the younger of the two, came out from behind the van and into full view, leading the black goat, Caesar's tail began to wag.

Ben wasn't sure what Caesar's interest in the two men signalled. 'What is it, Caesar?' he queried, hoping for a clue from the labrador. 'You want to say hello to the goat? Is that it?'

Over the years that he had been working with war dogs, Ben had seen dogs befriend cats, pigs and even horses. Thinking that Caesar wanted to make a friend of the newly arrived goat, the only other animal on the base apart from Alabama, Ben fixed the metal leash to Caesar's collar and came to his feet. 'Come on then, let's introduce ourselves.'

Caesar's tail wagged even more vigorously as Ben led him toward the van. When the young Afghan saw Ben and Caesar approaching, he suddenly looked frightened.

'Nothing to worry about, mate,' Ben said with a smile.

But the young man began to back away. 'Go away, dog!' he said in English.

'He won't hurt you,' Ben assured him.

'I never see this dog before,' said the young man.

Ben frowned. 'What do you mean?' He looked down at Caesar, who was straining at the leash. Ben relented and gave Caesar enough leeway to approach the goat. But it was soon clear that Caesar wasn't interested in the goat at all. Instead, Caesar made his way toward the clean-shaven young man.

'No, no! Go away, Intelligent Dog,' said the young man. Looking horrified, he reeled back and held up his hands. 'Ibrahim, help me! Intelligent Dog has returned!'

This call for help brought the other young man around from the back of the van. 'Did you say Intelligent Dog, brother?' he said, before stopping in his tracks.

Caesar, whining in frustration, then strained at the leash in the direction of the other Afghan man.

The bearded man looked at Ben in fear. 'We did not steal your dog, sir,' he said.

'What?' Ben returned, confused. 'What are you talking about?'

'My brother, Ahmad, and myself, we did not steal your dog.' He spoke rapidly, and sweat had broken out on his brow. 'This animal came to us. We only looked after it for a time. But we did not steal it.'

'Caesar, sit!' commanded Ben, determined to get to the bottom of this mystery.

Caesar promptly obeyed Ben's command, sitting and looking up at the bearded Afghan, his tail thumping on the ground.

Unable to hide an affectionate smile, Ibrahim reached down and patted the brown labrador. 'Hello, Intelligent Dog. You found us again.'

'Let me get this straight,' said a befuddled Ben. 'You know Caesar? He spent time with you?'

'Indeed, sir,' said Ibrahim. 'But please do not arrest us for stealing your dog. It was lost, and it found us out in the wilderness.'

Ben smiled. 'I understand. Don't worry, no one will be arresting you. On the contrary. I want to thank you for looking after Caesar when he was lost.' He reached out and shook Ibrahim's hand.

'Caesar?' said Ahmad, the younger brother, who was looking less alarmed now. 'Is that the name you have for this animal? To us, he is Intelligent Dog.'

'His name is Caesar,' said Ben, giving Caesar a solid pat on the side. Caesar turned and tried to lick him on the mouth. 'But you're right, he's a very intelligent dog.'

'A wonderful dog, sir,' said Ibrahim. 'We were able to teach your Caesar some very entertaining tricks. He came with us to many bases such as this and performed.'

'Is that right?' Ben marvelled. Most of what had happened to Caesar in those thirteen months that he was lost in Afghanistan had remained a mystery to Ben and the Fulton family. They had heard that a local boy had taken him in immediately following the Taliban ambush that had separated Ben and his beloved EDD.

Ben now knew who that boy was – Haji, the boy they'd encountered in the Tarin Kowt bazaar the previous day. Ben was also aware that Caesar had been in the hands of the Taliban for many months before escaping. What had happened to Caesar in the six months prior to Sergeant Tim McHenry identifying him with two Afghan performers at an FOB like this one had been a mystery. Only now did Ben put two and two together and realise that these were those very same performers.

As if to confirm this, Sergeant McHenry now came walking toward the van. He was in the company of Duke Hazard, and both were in full combat equipment.

'Hey, Fulton!' called McHenry. 'Those are the same two guys who had your dog. I had to wrangle Caesar back from them!'

'I know,' said Ben. 'And I've just been thanking them for looking after him. He was heavier when I got him back than when I lost him, so they fed him well.'

'They didn't want to give him up, I can tell you,' McHenry said in his Texan drawl. 'They'd taught him all these circus tricks. Real impressive. Caesar was making a mint for them.' He looked at Ahmad and Ibrahim. 'I guess your act took a beating after I took Caesar back from you?'

'It is true, sir,' Ahmad agreed with a sad sigh. 'Making a living from our profession was never easy, but especially so since losing Intelligent Dog. We replaced him with this goat.' He nodded to the black goat, and the goat bleated, as if on cue. 'Goats are very nimble of foot,' Ahmad went on, 'but not as intelligent as a dog.'

'And much less obedient,' Ibrahim added.

'Yes, a goat can be very stubborn,' Ahmad sadly agreed. 'I wonder if Intelligent Dog remembers any of the tricks we taught him?'

'Caesar forgets nothing and no one,' Ben assured him.

'Then, for the sake of times that are old,' said Ibrahim, 'would you allow your intelligent dog to do one of his old tricks with us, sir?'

'Yeah, let them give it a whirl, Fulton,' Sergeant Hazard piped up.

'I'd like to see that,' said McHenry. 'Let them try something with Caesar, Fulton.'

Ben looked down at Caesar, who seemed to be taking in the conversation. 'How about it, mate? Want to do a trick with the brothers?'

Tongue hanging out, Caesar looked up at him, as if to say, *You're in charge, boss.*

'Look, Intelligent Dog,' said Ibrahim, taking several green rubber balls from the back of the van.

Caesar's tail began to wag furiously. Mention of the word 'trick' had caught his attention, and now the sight of the balls awoke his play instinct. Even though he had missed Ben desperately while they were separated, and had never ceased looking for him in Afghanistan, he'd enjoyed performing with the brothers. Caesar looked at Ben and whimpered, as if to say, *Can I play with them, boss? Please!*

'Is it permissible, sir?' Ibrahim asked.

Ben smiled. 'Why not? Go ahead.'

Ahmad looked at Ibrahim. 'Shall we try a trampoline trick with Intelligent Dog, brother?'

Ibrahim nodded excitedly. 'A most excellent idea.'

Once Ahmad had tethered the black goat to one of the van's doorhandles, the brothers brought out a small folding trampoline from the back of the van and proceeded to set it up. As they did, a crowd of Rangers and men of the strike force gathered around to watch, with Charlie, Lucky and Baz abandoning their exercise to join them. The Afghan soldiers at the base, in contrast, seemed not to be the slightest bit interested.

Ibrahim instructed Ben on precisely where Caesar should sit, then Ahmad began to bounce on the trampoline. On the far side of the trampoline, Ibrahim commenced juggling three green rubber balls. With his tongue hanging out the side of his mouth, Caesar's tail wagged furiously and his front legs trembled with anticipation. But he held his position, waiting for his cue from the brothers. Up and down bounced Ahmad. Up and down went the rubber balls.

'It is all to do with timing, dear sirs,' Ibrahim told

his small audience as he juggled the balls with skill. He glanced at his younger brother on the trampoline. 'Ahmad, tell me when you are ready.'

'I am almost at the right height, Ibrahim.' Several bounces later, he announced, 'I am ready.'

'Very good,' said Ibrahim. 'Intelligent Dog, you jump when I say "go".'

Caesar's head rose and fell in time with his bouncing brother, never once taking his eyes off the juggling balls.

'Intelligent Dog . . . go!'

Caesar rose up and sprang toward the trampoline. Flying through the air and over the trampoline, he slid beneath Ahmad. The jumping brother, at the top of a bounce as the labrador passed beneath him, drew up his legs to create more clearance. Caesar's jump was spectacular, but that was not the end of the trick. As soon as he hit the ground, Caesar jumped up and snatched one of the green balls as it came down while Ibrahim caught the other two. The watching soldiers burst into applause as Ahmad dismounted from the trampoline. He and Ibrahim stood in front of their small audience and, smiling wide, took a bow.

Caesar stood beside the brothers with a green ball in his mouth, his tail wagging back and forth. Back when Caesar had travelled with the brothers, their performances had generated applause, cheers and whistles, followed by friendly pats galore as the labrador helped collect donations from the ISAF soldiers. Caesar had loved all the attention.

'Thank you, sirs,' said Ibrahim, sounding a little sad. 'This was how it was when we were The Three Brothers, the finest travelling performers in all of Afghanistan – my brother Ahmad, Intelligent Dog and myself.'

Ben patted his thigh, and Caesar immediately came trotting over to him, dropping the green ball at his feet. Caesar then looked up at Ben, as if to say, *Go on, throw the ball!*

Ben smiled and ruffled Caesar's ears. 'You would chase a rubber ball all day if I let you, wouldn't you, mate? No wonder you took to circus life.'

'He's one heck of a clever animal, Fulton,' said Hazard, smiling down at Caesar. 'But I'm afraid we got business to attend to.' He looked around at Charlie, who was standing close by. 'Grover, me and my people, we're going out with this morning's ANA foot patrol. I want to get a feel for this place. I need you and your Diggers to go out with the afternoon patrol. You got that?'

'Roger to that,' said Charlie, smiling to himself. The morning patrol would go out during the coolest part of the day, while the Australians were being sent out on the afternoon patrol when temperatures soared into the high thirties. As strike force commander, Hazard could pick and choose what he did and when, and he was choosing the more comfortable patrol time for himself.

'If the bad guys are watching this FOB,' Hazard went on, 'they're used to seeing foreign troops go out on patrol with the ANA, so we won't look out of place.'

Charlie nodded. 'Makes sense.'

'And take your EDD along,' said Hazard. 'They don't have much of a problem with IEDs around here but you never know. We'll take Alabama with us.'

Charlie looked to Ben and Caesar. 'Looks like you and Caesar will join Lucky, Baz and me on the afternoon patrol.'

'Copy that,' Ben acknowledged. 'We're both ready and raring to go.'

But there was something he had to do first. Ben walked toward Ibrahim and Ahmad. The brothers were surrounded by American Rangers and men of Strike Force Blue Dragon, who were giving them praise and wads of dollar notes for their impromptu performance. The brothers enjoyed the praise, but they needed the cash more. Ben, reaching into a tunic pocket, took out some Afghan money, the equivalent of fifty dollars. Handing it to Ibrahim, he said, 'Thanks, mate. From both Caesar and me.'

CHAPTER 11

Apart from the fifteen members of Strike Force Blue Dragon, there were a hundred members of the Afghan National Army at FOB Nero, plus twenty men from a US Rangers battalion. Each day, some of those Rangers went out with ANA men on the morning and afternoon patrols. This particular morning, Duke Hazard and his three American comrades from the strike force took the place of the Rangers on the patrol. Toward noon, as the day was heating up, the patrol returned to base. Their sweep along the district's few roads and through lonely, silent hills had been uneventful. They hadn't seen a single soul.

Later in the day, the Australians and Ali Moon joined forty Afghan soldiers for the afternoon patrol. The base's deputy commander, an ANA lieutenant named Karzan, was leading the patrol. A handsome man with a neat moustache, Karzan was from the Hazara community. This was his home province, so he knew his way around. When the forty-five men going on the patrol had assembled, one of the base's two iron gates opened a metre or so, and everyone stood aside to allow Ben and Caesar to go first. It was Caesar's job to check for IEDs and mines buried beside the road and beneath the surface of the road itself.

'Seek on, Caesar,' Ben instructed, and with Caesar on a long metal leash, handler and EDD walked on.

Keeping his nose close to the ground, Caesar wagged his tail contentedly as they made their way down the road. To him, EDD work was like a big game – a game of 'find the parcel' that he could play all day if need be. Although Alabama and Corporal Lazar had checked this route during the morning patrol, it didn't necessarily mean it was safe now. Insurgents could have snuck in to hide IEDs after Alabama and his handler had moved on.

Lieutenant Karzan came next in line, followed by an Afghan radioman carrying a heavy military radio on his back, with Charlie, Lucky, Baz and Ali close behind. ANA soldiers brought up the rear in a long, strung-out line as the patrol moved down the single dirt road that led to FOB Nero. All the soldiers were well armed, although mostly with light weapons. Ben carried a standard Australian Steyr 9 mm automatic rifle, a compact weapon that allowed him plenty of freedom of movement when working with Caesar. Charlie's weapon of choice was an M4 carbine fitted with a grenade launcher. Lucky Mertz, an expert marksman, shouldered a SIG SAUER long-range sniper rifle and had a rocket-launcher slung on his back. Baz carried his regular F89 Minimi light machinegun, a weapon that was almost as long as he was tall.

Before long, they came to another road running through the swelteringly hot valley to the city of Bamiyan, which lay out of sight beyond the hills. As Ben paused to look to Lieutenant Karzan for directions, perspiration ran down his face. Karzan pointed east toward Bamiyan. Ben nodded in acknowledgement and quickly wiped away the perspiration with the back of his gloved hand.

After ten minutes, the road intersected with a more substantial sealed highway that ran southeast, linking Bamiyan with the Dragon Lake region. A heat haze shimmered from the roadway's baking asphalt ahead. Deliberately walking away from Dragon Lake to conceal their interest in it, the patrol headed toward Bamiyan. So far, they hadn't encountered so much as a bird in the sky, but they knew there was a chance they were being watched from the hills.

The patrol rounded the corner of a rocky bluff. They could now see the city of Bamiyan in the distance with a smoky haze hanging over it. A single traveller could be seen walking up the road toward them. When he spotted the patrol, the traveller stopped in his tracks.

'If he runs,' said Lucky, reaching for his sniper rifle, 'I could drop him with a single round.'

'Not so fast, Lucky,' said Charlie. 'If we draw a bead on him, we'll scare him into running for it anyway. We keep walking toward him with our weapons low.'

'Okay, you're the boss, Charlie.' Lucky lowered his weapon and slipped it back over his shoulder.

As the patrol continued along the road, the traveller also resumed his progress at a leisurely pace. Before long, patrol and traveller met on the road. The traveller, wearing dark clothes and a round Afghan cap, had a scarf covering the lower part of his face and a cloth bag slung over his right shoulder.

'Show us your face, friend,' Lieutenant Karzan said, pointing to the man's scarf. 'And tell me, where are you going on this deserted road?'

The man removed his scarf, revealing a long face and a thick, shaggy black beard common to Pashtun people and to members of the Taliban. 'What is the problem? I am going to visit a friend,' he replied in Pashto.

'Where?' Ali demanded.

'At the lake,' said the traveller. 'My friend fishes there.'

Ali was sceptical. 'What kind of fish does he catch?'

The traveller shrugged and smiled slyly. 'Small ones.'

Ali translated the conversation into English for the Australians.

Lieutenant Karzan, who could speak Pashto, was

suspicious. 'Raise your hands,' he instructed, pointing his automatic rifle at the man. Still smiling, the traveller complied. Karzan searched him and his bag for weapons, but found none.

'I can go now?' said the traveller.

Ben had brought Caesar to the seated position on a tight leash when they had first approached the stranger. But he now noticed that Caesar had come to his feet and was looking at the traveller intently. A low growl began to rumble deep in the labrador's throat.

Ben dropped down to one knee beside him. 'You don't like this bloke, Caesar, do you?'

Caesar, refusing to take his eyes off the traveller, continued to growl. He knew this man very well. This was Abdul Razah, his former Taliban jailer. But Caesar had no way of telling Ben exactly who this man was.

Ben stood up again and loosened the leash. 'Seek on, Caesar,' he instructed.

Caesar trotted straight up to Abdul and sat down in front of him, looking up at him without flinching. This was Caesar's typical signature which indicated that he'd picked up the scent of explosives.

'This bloke is explosives positive,' Ben declared, bringing his rifle to bear on the Afghan. 'He's been in contact with explosives recently. And Caesar seems to know him from previous contact. I think he's a hostile.'

'Arrest him,' Lieutenant Karzan commanded coldly.

Charlie, Lucky and Baz immediately moved forward to surround Abdul, whose smile quickly disappeared. They tied his hands behind his back. Abdul glared at Caesar, angry that the labrador had pointed him out. In response, Caesar let out another low growl. The prisoner was handed over to a group of Lieutenant Karzan's men, who would take him back to FOB Nero for questioning. The rest of the patrol, including Caesar and the Australians, resumed their course. No one apart from Caesar knew that this was Abdul Razah. And not even Caesar was aware that Abdul knew precisely where Secretary-General Park and his party were being held.

When Ben, Caesar and the others returned to FOB Nero after dark, it was to receive several pieces of interesting news. As the traveller cooled his heels in the FOB's jail – another shipping container – the fifteen men of Strike Force Blue Dragon assembled at the base's briefing room, an area formed by a tarpaulin stretched between half-a-dozen posts, to hear the results of his questioning.

'The prisoner is a Pashtun,' Karzan began. 'He says that his name is Mohammad Derz and that he is from a village in western Uruzgan. But he has no papers on him to confirm that. He has what appear to be old bullet wound scars. We suspect he is Taliban, though he denies it. Apart from a story about visiting a friend who fishes in Band-e-Azhdahar, he has no good reason to be in this region.'

'Okay, thanks, Lieutenant,' said Sergeant Hazard. He turned to Charlie and his companions. 'While you Aussies were out on patrol this afternoon, we got a link from General McAvoy in Tarin Kowt. Gather round.' Hazard opened a laptop, then faced the screen toward the men.

'We've had a drone watching the only landward entrance to Deep Cave,' said McAvoy, looking stern. 'At dawn this morning we picked up a single man leaving that entrance. This is the highest resolution image of him we can get off the video from the drone. We have a tentative ID of this guy from the CIA's visual-recognition database. We think he could be Abdul Razah, a low-level operative in the Taliban's Uruzgan brigade, a unit commanded by our old friend Commander Baradar.'

The screen now filled with the blurry picture, shot from above, of a single figure emerging from white rocks and making his way toward a rough road. He had a cloth bag slung over one shoulder.

'That's our man!' Charlie remarked with certainty. 'That's the bloke we picked up this morning on the road.'

Hazard nodded. 'Now we know that this guy, Derz, or Abdul Razah, or whoever he is, was spotted leaving Deep Cave. And he was coming from the direction of Bamiyan when you found him. That tells me he went into Bamiyan to deliver something – a message, maybe – and was on his way back to the cave. This guy knows where the Big Cheese is. I'd bet my pension plan on it!'

'Do we try to force him to tell us where the Big Cheese is?' said McHenry.

Charlie shook his head. 'He wouldn't talk. And we don't have the luxury of time for the bears to interrogate him back at Tarin Kowt.'

There was a frustrated silence before Ben spoke up. 'What if we let him escape?' he suggested.

Hazard looked at Ben as if he were mad. 'Are you nuts, Fulton?'

'Think about it. He could lead us straight to the Big Cheese,' said Ben.

Hazard stroked his bearded chin and chewed a little harder on the gum in his mouth. 'What if we do release him and he doesn't lead us there?'

'Chances are he will,' said Charlie, coming around to Ben's way of thinking. 'I think we should give it a try.'

Hazard shook his head, troubled by the proposal. 'I don't like the idea of letting a Taliban prisoner go free.'

'Do you have a better idea?' said Ben, growing impatient. 'Time's running out for the hostages.'

'And if the prisoner does lead us to the Big Cheese we'll recapture this guy in the process,' Charlie added.

Still Hazard hesitated as he tried to decide whether or not he should release their prisoner.

🐾🐾

Later that evening, Lieutenant Karzan and several Afghan soldiers entered the shipping container that was being used as the FOB's makeshift jail cell. They found their prisoner, Abdul Razah, on his knees facing east, completing his last prayer session of the day.

Lieutenant Karzan handed Abdul a white robe. 'You must take off the clothes you are wearing and put this on,' he ordered. When Abdul glared defiantly at him, making no move to comply, Karzan added, 'If you do not take off the clothes, we will remove them from you.'

Reluctantly, Abdul undressed and exchanged his own dusty, grimy garments for the white robe.

'Your headgear as well,' said Karzan, holding out his right hand and clicking his fingers impatiently.

With a scowl, Abdul took off his cap and handed it to Lieutenant Karzan.

As the soldiers departed from the cell, Ali Moon turned back to the prisoner and said in a low, conspiratorial voice, 'It is all right, my friend, they are only searching your clothes for anything suspicious that may be sewn into them. They will be returned to you shortly.'

Half an hour later, Abdul's clothes were indeed

returned to him. Nothing had been found on or inside them. As Ali handed him the clothes through the cell's open door, bright lights lit up the helicopter landing pad a little distance behind him.

Abdul frowned at the sight of the lights. 'What is happening out there? Is a helicopter expected?' Abdul would not admit it to his captors, but he was fearful of being placed in a helicopter and taken to the government prison at Tarin Kowt. Abdul had heard rumours about the treatment of Taliban prisoners, and Commander Baradar's own father had died there.

'No helicopters are expected,' Ali advised. 'The foreigners are preparing for a show.'

'A show?'

Ali waved a hand. 'There are two travelling Afghan jugglers and acrobats here. They are going to entertain the foreign troops tonight.'

'Jugglers and acrobats? Humph!' Abdul snorted. 'All entertainments are the work of the Devil.'

'I agree,' Ali whispered, leaning closer to the prisoner. 'But I cannot say that to the foreigners. There is much I cannot say if I wish to keep my job with ISAF.'

Ali withdrew, the door clanging shut behind him, and Abdul put on his own clothes. Disdainfully tossing aside the white robe that he had been forced to wear, Abdul spat on it – for the humiliation of being made to undress and put it on. 'Death to all infidels!' he cursed.

All thirty-five foreign troops at FOB Nero gathered to watch Ahmad and Ibrahim put on their regular show. Some of the local Afghan soldiers were on duty, manning the guard towers and peering out into the black night. Most of the other Afghan soldiers at the base went to their beds, uninterested in the brothers' entertainment. Of the local troops, only Lieutenant Karzan joined the ISAF audience.

A large bedsheet had been strung across the side of the van. On it the words 'The Three Brothers' were painted in red. Tonight, in front of the backdrop, Ahmad and Ibrahim began their show by juggling balls, batons and knives.

Caesar was also in the audience, watching the performance with Ben. A smile creased Ben's lips as he noticed that Caesar's front legs were quivering. How Caesar would love to be up there with Ahmad and Ibrahim, jumping and catching balls.

Everyone watched on as the brothers progressed to acrobatics, with Ibrahim lifting Ahmad into the air using only one arm and then launching him into somersaults. At one point, Ahmad balanced on Ibrahim's shoulders while juggling three balls, four balls and finally, five balls.

The trampoline featured in the brothers' next tricks. Without Caesar's participation this time, the brothers' trampoline tricks were all about juggling. Ahmad juggled as he bounced, receiving the balls thrown to him by Ibrahim. Then both juggled, one on the ground and one bouncing on the trampoline, before they exchanged balls mid-juggle without dropping a single one. It was all very impressive, with the onlookers clapping and whistling, appreciative of any distraction from the tedium of FOB life.

Next, an ordinary ladder was placed horizontally between the two stepladders. Encouraged by Ahmad, the black goat quickly climbed one stepladder and stood on the top. It nimbly walked across the ordinary ladder's rungs to the second stepladder. This brought plenty of smiles and applause from the audience.

The goat, however, had had enough. Refusing to come down the second stepladder, it looked at the brothers and the audience, bleating. As Ahmad and Ibrahim had said earlier, goats can be very stubborn. There was nothing the brothers could do to entice their goat to come down. The more they tried, the more the audience laughed, with some young US Rangers rolling about in hysterics.

The door to Abdul's cell opened slightly.

'Come, my friend, quickly!' urged a voice from outside.

Abdul, who had been lying on a mattress on the floor, sat up. 'Who is it?' he asked warily.

'Come, while the infidels are enjoying their entertainment,' Ali whispered. 'I will help you escape. But we must not delay.'

Abdul hesitated.

'Hurry, while the foreigners are distracted,' Ali called impatiently. 'I will let you out the gate. Or do you wish to be sent to the government prison at Tarin Kowt?'

Now that Ali had voiced his greatest fear, Abdul leapt to action. Coming to his feet, he hurried to the partly open door. The opening was just wide enough for him to squeeze through.

'Follow me, my friend,' said Ali, leading the way.

Around the well-lit landing pad to their right, the audience of soldiers was transfixed on Ahmad and Ibrahim's act. In the darkness along the camp wall, Ali led Abdul to the base's main gateway. A smaller pedestrian gate the size of a house door stood beside the large metal gates. Producing a key, Ali unlocked the padlock on the smaller entranceway.

'From where did you get the key?' Abdul whispered.

A sly smile came over Ali's face. 'For money, anything can be had in a camp where there are Afghan soldiers,' he replied. Being careful not to make a sound, he slowly drew back the bolt and opened the door. 'Hurry!' he urged. 'And may Allah protect you.'

Without a word of thanks, Abdul passed through the opening and disappeared into the night. Ali, smiling to himself, closed the door and locked it once more.

Back at the landing pad, Sergeant Hazard looked down at an electronic device on the ground in front of him. On the device's small screen was a map, and on the map was a tiny green dot blinking on and off. Grinning broadly, Hazard leaned over to Charlie and Ben and whispered, 'Our mouse has taken the bait. He's on the move, guys. I just hope to hell he's heading to the Big Cheese!'

'Fingers crossed,' said Ben.

'If he doesn't lead us to the target, it'll be you two answering to General McAvoy.' Hazard produced a wry smile. 'I don't mind giving you two the blame for letting a valuable Taliban prisoner go free.'

CHAPTER 12

In a vast aircraft hangar at San Diego's Naval Air Station North Island, Commander Renzo and Lieutenant Ellerman stood looking at the long, thin black shape on which all the hopes of Operation Blue Dragon were focused.

'She looks fine to me,' said Ellerman, running an admiring eye over mini-submarine DSRV-801X. 'Nice job, Chief. You've got rid of the rust around the rudder.'

A tired Chief Petty Officer Brogan was shaking his head. 'A rusty rudder has been the least of our problems. With respect, sir, this whole deal has been too rushed. The *Pencil* is not ready for sea. People could die if you use this thing before it's ready!'

'And people *will* die if we don't, Chief,' Renzo shot back. 'So, what are the outstanding problems that you still have to deal with? We could be called into action any time now.'

The chief petty officer let out a long, deep sigh. 'Commander, if I reeled off the full list, we'd be here for hours.'

'Try me!' Renzo glared at Brogan, clearly irritated by his attitude. 'Give us the major items that still need to be done so we can put this vessel in the water and give her a trial run.'

'Sir, as things stand right now, there's no way I could let you put this sub in the water. The electrics are still a shemozzle. The ballast tanks are about as sound as a balloon with a pinprick in it. The diesel engine is running as rough as a hundred-year-old steam engine and could stop without warning.'

'I'm still waiting for the bad news, Chief,' said Renzo, which produced an ironic laugh from Ellerman.

Brogan looked flabbergasted. 'Sir, if you take this thing out, you could go straight to the bottom of the ocean – and stay there! It'd be your coffin.'

'We're prepared to take that risk,' said Ellerman. 'Frankly, Chief, we have no choice.'

'I say again,' Renzo reiterated, 'this craft has to be ready for sea – and fast! Forget about the diesel motor. We won't be travelling far. We'll run the sub exclusively on the electric motor. It's quieter, anyway. Just make sure that it's in running order and the batteries are charged.'

'You won't be travelling far?' Brogan scratched his head. 'Sir, can I ask what the heck this mission is? What could be so important that you're prepared to put your life on the line in this sub?'

'Sorry, can't tell you a thing about our mission, Chief,' Renzo replied, moving to the *Pencil* and running a hand along its smooth, rubberised outer coating. 'Just know that it's of vital international importance.'

'Where are the men who've been working on the *Pencil*?' Ellerman asked.

'Sleeping, sir,' Brogan answered, trying to mask a weary yawn. 'I've had them working twelve hours a day.'

Renzo swung around with a fierce look on his face. 'No wonder it's not ready yet! You don't want to send this sub out, is that it?'

'Er . . . no, sir!' Brogan protested.

'Bring in a second work crew to take over when the first finishes. Focus on the "must do" jobs, and work on this baby around the clock. You got that? Around the clock! No questions, no arguments.'

'Aye, aye, sir,' said Brogan through clenched teeth. 'Around the clock.'

In the command bunker at FOB Nero, Caesar yawned as he lay watching four sergeants huddled around a laptop computer. As this was a joint Australian–American-led op, Ben, Charlie, McHenry and Hazard were the four most senior members of Strike Force Blue Dragon, and it was up to them to decide what the next step of the op should be. A map of the Dragon Lake area filled the screen, and a lone green dot glowed at a location beside the lake.

'That's it,' said Charlie, tapping the green dot on the screen. 'Deep Cave. Abdul Razah has gone straight to it.'

'I gotta admit,' said Sergeant Hazard, 'you guys had me worried. But you're right, he's made a beeline for the cave. No doubt about it.'

The Taliban's Abdul Razah had been tricked into thinking that Ali Moon, a part Pashtun, sympathised with him and the Taliban. But Ali had been in on Ben and Charlie's plan all along, only pretending to be Abdul's accomplice. It had been a classic set-up. After Abdul's clothes were confiscated, a small electronic tracking device had been inserted into the lining of his cap by Duke Hazard. Abdul hadn't suspected a thing. After he'd made his escape, Abdul had been tracked every step of the way as he scurried through the night. And as the tracking device in his cap had revealed, those steps led directly to Deep Cave.

Sergeant Hazard had signaller Cisco send a radio message to Special Ops HQ at Tarin Kowt. 'Target location confirmed. Request permission to proceed with extraction.'

Five minutes passed before a reply was received from Lieutenant General McAvoy. 'Permission granted. Heelo en route to collect Sky Team. Good luck, blue dragons.'

Chewing his gum, Sergeant Hazard turned to Charlie with a victorious grin on his face. 'We got the green light, buddy. All we gotta do now is work out who's on Sky Team and who's on Land Team.'

They had previously been instructed to split into two teams once the operation went forward. Sky Team was to parachute into Dragon Lake to link up with the *Pencil* for the journey through the underwater entry into Deep Cave. Land Team, meanwhile, was responsible for attacking the cave's only land entrance in order to keep the Taliban busy.

'Should we toss for it?' Charlie suggested. 'Seems the fairest way to decide as far as I'm concerned.'

Hazard shrugged. 'Sure, why not? Heads, my people go with Sky Team. Tails, you Aussies do. Agreed?'

Charlie nodded. 'Agreed.'

'It just so happens I got me a lucky dime,' said Sergeant McHenry, reaching into a tunic pocket and pulling out a small silver coin.

'How many heads does it have?' Ben asked with a grin.

McHenry laughed. 'Ben, buddy, you think I'd have a two-headed coin? Come on, do I look like a cheater?'

'Let's have a look at it, just the same,' said Charlie.

'Suit yourself.' McHenry passed the coin over to him.

Once Charlie had satisfied himself that just one side of the American ten cent coin had the head of a US President on it, he said, 'Okay, I'll toss it.'

'Go right ahead,' Hazard replied with a shrug.

'Here goes.' Charlie flipped the coin into the air. It flew up, spinning all the way, with all eyes, including Caesar's, following it. With a faint *chink*, it hit the concrete floor. The dime spun there for a few seconds before falling flat. All four men bent to look closely at it. So, too, did Caesar.

'Tails,' Ben announced.

'We go with Sky Team,' said Charlie matter-of-factly.

'Want to make it best out of three?' Hazard suggested. He clearly wanted to be with Sky Team because it had the best chance of rescuing Secretary-General Park and his colleagues. Both teams had equally important roles, but if all went to plan with the mini-sub, Sky Team would be the group that got to the hostages first.

Charlie pursed his lips. 'You know what, Hazard? I think we'll go with the one toss.'

'Thought you might say that,' Hazard said resignedly. 'Okay, we had a deal. Let's figure out who's on which team. It'll be seven men and an EDD to each. The interpreter goes with Land Team, so, in addition to you four guys and Caesar, you can choose three more people for Sky Team. Who do you want?'

'Men with experience in a water environment,' Charlie stressed.

'Okay, I guess that's a no-brainer. So, you take Banner, the Special Boats guy, Mortenson, the Danish diver, and . . .' Sergeant Hazard screwed up his face as he thought through the specialities of each foreign member of the force.

'Angus Bruce, the Royal Marine Commando,' Charlie suggested.

Hazard nodded. 'That would be your third guy. A pity you can't take Wolf the combat medic along. Those hostages could be in a bad way.'

Charlie nodded grimly. 'Wolf will still be close by, with you and the rest of Land Team. And you may need his firepower if there's a fight at the entrance.'

Hazard nodded. 'You got that right.'

'And if Sky Team has to bring out the hostages the same way we go in, aboard the mini-sub,' continued Charlie, 'there won't be any room for extra passengers. The *Pencil* will take sixteen bodies max. That's my seven men, plus Caesar and seven hostages.'

At the mention of his name, Caesar quickly sat up and looked at Ben and Charlie with an expression on his face that seemed to say, *Ready for work when you are, guys.*

'There would be room for one more man,' said Hazard. 'You want to take the medic? I think you should.'

'Our equipment will take up the extra space,' said Charlie, running a hand through his hair. He was tired of having to argue with Hazard over every decision. Charlie wondered whether the American was just difficult by nature or if it was personal.

'We all have medical training,' Ben added. 'Enough to stabilise injured hostages until Wolf gets to them.'

Charlie folded his arms, signalling that he was done talking. 'I'm happy with the team I've got.'

Hazard shrugged. 'Okay. Let's wrap this up. The heelo's on its way. You and your team should get your gear ready. Zero Hour will depend on when the fly boys get the sub over here from California. The way I figure, they're gonna have to get that mini-sub into the air in the next couple of hours or we'll miss the deadline.'

'Let's get it done,' said Charlie.

He and Ben were just walking away when Hazard called after them. 'What the heck do we do if they don't get that sub over here? What's our Plan B, Grover?'

'There is no workable Plan B,' Charlie said over his shoulder.

'They *have* to get the sub over here,' said Ben. 'Or Dr Park is toast.'

The telephone beside Commander Renzo's bed let out a shrill ring. Sitting up and noting from the glowing face of his digital clock that it was just past three in the morning, he groaned and answered the phone. 'Renzo.'

'Commander,' came an unfamiliar voice, 'this is

General Mitch McAvoy calling you from Tarin Kowt, Afghanistan.'

Rubbing the sleep from his eyes, Renzo sat a little straighter. 'Yes, sir.'

'You know who I am?'

'Yes, sir. You're in charge of Operation Blue Dragon. Naval Intelligence filled me in, sir.'

'How's that *Pencil* coming along?'

'Er, it's just fine, sir. Just fine.' Renzo tried to sound upbeat, hoping that his dissatisfaction with the pace of the work on the mini-sub didn't show in his voice.

'Outstanding. I'm calling to tell you to get that fish in the air.'

'Really? When, sir?' A jolt of alarm ran through Renzo's body.

'Now, Commander. An Air Force C-17 is standing by at North Island air station.'

'Oh.'

'Is there a problem, *Commander* Renzo?' said McAvoy, making sure to stress that McAvoy was his subordinate by a long way.

'A problem? No, sir. No problem at all.'

'Excellent. I wanted to make this call to personally wish you and Lieutenant Ellerman the best of luck. There's a heck of a lot riding on this mission.'

'I'm aware of that, sir. But don't worry, we can pull this off.'

'I know you can, and so does the President. Good luck and good hunting. I look forward to talking to you again in a few days' time to congratulate you on a mission accomplished.'

'Thank you, sir.'

After he hung up the call, Commander Renzo sat in pensive silence, thinking about the dangerous mission that lay ahead and the enormous responsibility that now rested on his shoulders. Never in his career had the stakes been so high. He must rescue the secretary-general of the United Nations, captaining a craft that was technically not ready for sea. He'd never baulked at difficult or dangerous missions before and wasn't about to start now. Besides, he was under orders.

Snapping out of his leaden thoughts, he dialled his co-pilot's number. A drowsy Lieutenant Ellerman answered the phone. 'Wake up, sleepyhead,' Renzo said cheerfully. 'We got a sub to fly.'

'Really?' Ellerman yawned loudly. 'When?'

'Now.'

Ellerman didn't even end the call. He just dropped the phone and ran.

CHAPTER 13

A giant C-17 Globemaster of the US Air Force's Air Mobility Command stood in darkness to one side of the North Island air station's runway, well away from the normal US Navy and Marine Corps aircraft traffic so that its top-secret cargo was out of sight of curious eyes. Renzo and Ellerman, now in blue US Navy combat fatigues, were driven out to the massive aircraft in a Humvee. When they climbed out, they found Chief Petty Officer Brogan waiting for them at the C-17's lowered rear ramp.

'Your baby's loaded aboard the aircraft, Commander,' said Brogan, after exchanging salutes with the officers. 'I can't guarantee it'll do all you want it to do but my team and me have done our best . . .'

'Don't worry about it, Chief,' said Renzo, patting Brogan on the back. 'The *Pencil* is our concern now. Go and get some rest. We'll take it from here.'

'Okay, sir.' Brogan sounded relieved. 'Good luck to

you both. Oh, and watch the reverse thrust control. It proved a bit tricky last time I tried it.'

'We only intend on going forward, anyways,' joked Lieutenant Ellerman.

As Brogan disappeared into the darkness Renzo and Ellerman walked up the metal ramp. The vast curved interiors of a C-17 could accommodate several M1 Abrams tanks, a Black Hawk helicopter, or hundreds of paratroopers sitting in four long rows from the plane's nose to its tail. But on this early morning, eerily lit by the glow of green lamps along the fuselage walls, this particular C-17 was carrying just a single unusual payload – a long, thin black mini-submarine. The *Pencil*.

A team of USAF cargo handlers was busy strapping dozens of parachute packs to the craft as Renzo and Ellerman came to a halt beside it. The two men looked at it and then at each other.

'Our new command, Brad,' Renzo said apprehensively.

'For better or for worse, I guess, sir,' replied Ellerman.

'There's no time to put the *Pencil* in the water and run her through her paces. It's not too late for you to drop out, you know, buddy. Me, I'm just hankering to be the first sailor to pilot a US Navy sub in an Afghan lake. That's a first! But you –'

'What? Drop out and leave you on your own in this

sardine tin?' Ellerman returned with a grin. 'Hell, sir, I want to be in the history books for making the deepest submarine dive in a landlocked country.'

'Okay, that's settled then,' Renzo responded with a chuckle.

Appearing from the front of the cabin, a female Staff Sergeant joined them with a salute. 'Welcome aboard, Commander, Lieutenant. I'm Staff Sergeant Barbra Kramer, and I'll be your loadmaster for this mission.'

'Thank you, Sergeant Kramer,' Renzo returned. 'I'm guessing that you probably haven't had many submarines as cargo before today.'

'Commander, you'd be surprised what this C-17 has carried.' Tall, slim and short-haired, Kramer had the air of someone who knew their job inside out. 'Let me tell you, sir, this heavy-lifter has been assigned a lot of precious cargo over the last couple of years. For starters, it has flown the presidential limousine quite a few times. One time, we gave the President himself a ride.'

'You don't say,' said Renzo, impressed. 'The President on this aircraft?'

'Yes, sir. And for that one time, this C-17 carried the designation of Air Force One.'

'Interesting.' Keen to get down to the subject of their mission, Renzo asked, 'Tell me, just how do you plan to drop the submarine into the lake?'

'We'll just push her out at 7000 feet, sir,' Kramer

replied. 'Dragon Lake is already 3000 feet above sea level, so the sub will only have 4000 feet to drop. We've attached the largest cargo chutes we can get our hands on. We're kinda hoping that will be enough to slow the sub's fall so that it eases into the water like a hot knife going through butter. That's the theory. We don't have a lot of experience with submarine airdrops.'

'Have you *ever* parachuted a submarine from a C-17 before, Sergeant?' Ellerman asked.

'Er . . .' She produced an embarrassed smile. 'No, sir. Never. But don't worry, this aircrew is the best in Mobility Command. Covert insertion is our specialty. It's you two that I'm worried about. Ever made a parachute jump before now?'

'I did a bit of weekend skydiving when I was younger,' said Ellerman.

Sergeant Kramer nodded, then turned to Renzo. 'How about you, sir?'

'This will be my first time,' Renzo admitted.

Kramer raised her eyebrows. 'It must be a real emergency if there isn't time to give you jump training, sir.'

'It is an emergency, believe me, Sergeant,' Renzo assured her.

'Okay. The jumping part isn't so hard. Steering yourselves to the sub, that's another story.'

'So, we don't jump at the same time as the submarine goes out the back?' Renzo queried.

'No, sir. That would be too risky. You two will jump immediately after the sub drop.'

'We'll have to swim to the vessel once we're in the water?' said Ellerman.

Sergeant Kramer nodded. 'Correct, sir. We'll send you both out with inflatable dinghies. Once you are in the water, you will use them to get to the sub.'

'What will the light conditions be at the time of the drop?' Renzo asked.

'It will be early morning, Afghanistan time, sir. With no moon.'

'No moon?' said Ellerman, sounding a little worried. 'Pitch-black?'

'Yes, sir. You won't be able to see the sub once you are in the water, unless you come down right on top of it, and that's about as likely as me scoring a Super Bowl touchdown. So, we've fixed a transmitter to the sub's conning tower, and you'll both have GPS homing devices on your belts. Just follow the beeps and you'll find the sub.' Staff Sergeant Kramer glanced at the luminous dial on her wristwatch. 'If you have any more questions, sirs, can I ask you to hold them until we're in the air? We need to take off. We'll only just make it to the lake while it's still dark.'

Renzo nodded. 'We can't risk a daylight drop. The bad guys will see us coming.'

The three of them moved further into the bowels of the aircraft and strapped themselves to the webbed seat-ing running along the fuselage wall. As they did, the end of the C-17's rear ramp began to rise and the aircraft's four Pratt and Whitney jet engines began to whine into life. The initial air phase of Operation Blue Dragon was officially underway. Ellerman gave Renzo a smile and the thumbs up. Renzo nodded and smiled weakly, and reassured himself that, despite Chief Brogan's doubts about the *Pencil*'s readiness and his own lack of parachuting experience, this op was going to be as easy as a walk in the park.

Walking home from school, Josh and his best friend, Baxter Chung, were talking about the new computer game Baxter's parents had given him that was about soldiers and high-tech warfare. The pair was so wrapped up in their conversation, neither boy noticed that they were being followed.

'Hey, Dog Boy!' came a familiar voice.

'Oh, no,' Josh groaned. 'Not again.' Only the night before, Josh had received another bullying email from Kelvin Corbett. 'Speed up, Baxter!' he urged.

Baxter looked back over his shoulder as they walked. 'What do you want, Kelvin?' said Baxter.

'I wasn't talking to you, Baxter,' Kelvin retorted. 'I'm talking to your friend there, the one with the famous

blunder dog. Not a wonder dog, a blunder dog. Get it?'
He laughed hysterically at his own joke.

'Not funny, Kelvin,' said Josh, half to himself.

'Go away, Kelvin,' said Baxter, hurrying to keep up
with Josh. 'I wish I hadn't given you Josh's email address.'

Josh looked around at him in surprise. '*You* gave him
my email address?'

Baxter winced. 'Sorry, Josh. He gave me *Fight Master*
in exchange for it, and I've been wanting to play that
game for ages. It's really good.'

'You shouldn't have given away my email address
without my permission,' Josh said angrily. Ahead, a
police car had pulled up at the red light at the next intersection. The sight inspired Josh's next thought, which
he aired out loud. 'That should be a crime, giving away
someone's private information. The police should be
able to arrest people for that.'

'I said I was sorry, Josh,' Baxter said guiltily, lowering
his head.

When they reached the intersection, Josh dropped
his heavy backpack to the kerb to take some weight
off, and both boys looked around to check where their
tormentor was. To their joint relief, Kelvin was walking
away in the opposite direction.

Baxter smiled. 'The police car probably scared
him off.'

'Maybe.' Josh nodded glumly. He lifted his backpack

and walked on in silence, unable to shake the feeling of betrayal.

The pair parted without a word at the next intersection, each headed for his own home. Josh had just rounded another corner when Kelvin stepped out from behind a hedge, right in front of him. Kelvin was breathing hard as if he'd been running. Folding his arms and planting his feet, he blocked Josh's way.

Josh came to an abrupt halt, his heart pounding in his chest. 'Where'd you come from?'

'Around the back way,' Kelvin replied smugly.

'Will you just stop picking on me, Kelvin!' said Josh. Built-up frustration made him want to scream it. He just didn't know what to do to stop Kelvin bugging him.

'What'll you give me to leave you alone?' Kelvin sneered.

'I don't know! Just leave me alone!'

'Let's see what've you got in there.' Kelvin reached out and snatched the backpack from Josh's shoulder.

'Let go!' Josh cried, trying to retrieve his backpack.

But Kelvin, being taller, held it out of Josh's reach. 'I think I'll keep this, Dog Boy.'

'That's mine,' Josh protested. 'Give it back!'

Kelvin leered at him. 'Make me!'

'You're a thief,' Josh said, close to tears.

'If you say anything,' said Kelvin, walking away with Josh's backpack, 'I'll say you gave it to me. It'll be your word against mine, Dog Boy. Ha!'

In the cool of the dawn, Ben stood outside his shipping container quarters at FOB Nero with Caesar lying at his feet. He took out his mobile phone and dialled his Holsworthy home number. Getting the engaged signal, he rang Nan Fulton's mobile number instead.

'Hello, I can't take your call right now,' came Nan's recorded voice. Ben held the phone down to Caesar's ear as Nan went on. 'If you leave a message after the beep, I'll get back to you when I can. Bye, and thanks for calling.'

Hearing this, and recognising Nan's voice, Caesar let out a little whimper and put his feet up on Ben's chest, trying to get closer to the phone as Ben stood up again.

Grinning, Ben ruffled Caesar's neck, and left a message. 'Hi Josh. Hi Maddie. Hi Mum. It's Caesar and me. We both miss you heaps. We're about to go on an op, so we'll be out of contact for a while. Don't worry if you don't hear from us for a few days. We love you. See you soon.'

Ben slipped his phone into his pocket. Putting his rifle over his right shoulder and hoisting his heavy military backpack onto the left, Ben led Caesar to join Charlie and the other Sky Team members who were assembled beside the heelo pad. They all looked to the southeast where the black shape of a Chinook helicopter could be seen growing larger with each passing second, silhouetted by the rising sun. Sky Team's ride back to Tarin Kowt was about to land.

Putting his backpack on the ground and dropping to one knee, Ben pulled out Caesar's doggles and puppy Peltors. Caesar's tail began wagging vigorously with anticipation. The questioning look on his face seemed to say, *Time for work, boss*?

'Yes, we're off on a mission, mate,' Ben said with a smile, giving his partner a pat. 'There's lots of work for us ahead.'

As the noise of the Chinook's engines met his ears, Ben leapt to his feet and hoisted his backpack onto his shoulders.

Josh burst through the front door and headed straight for his bedroom. Maddie looked up from where she sat on the sofa watching TV. That was unlike him, she thought. Josh usually went into the kitchen to say hello to Nan when he arrived home from school. Frowning to herself, Maddie got up and followed after him. 'Joshie,' she called. She found Josh's bedroom door closed. 'Joshie, are you okay?'

'Go away!' he responded.

Maddie opened the door to find Josh sitting on his

bed with his head in his hands. 'Where's your backpack, Joshie? Is it outside?'

'Mind your own business,' Josh murmured into his hands.

'But where is it?'

'I lost it, okay!' Josh yelled. 'Go away!'

Not used to Josh shouting at her, Maddie's bottom lip trembled. Turning and running from the room, Maddie bellowed, 'Nan! Josh has lost his backpack!'

'No, don't tell Nan, Maddie!' Josh yelled after her.

But it was too late. Maddie had already reached the kitchen, where Nan was on the phone.

'What's that, Maddie?' said Nan. 'Josh has what?'

'Lost his backpack!' Maddie replied, wide-eyed. 'With all his things in it!'

Nan ended her call and, in a flash, was on her feet and headed for Josh's room. She found him where Maddie had left him, sitting disconsolately on his bed.

Nan softened at the sight of him so upset. 'Josh,' she said gently, 'what's this about your backpack?'

'I lost it,' he glumly answered.

Nan sat down beside him and placed a reassuring hand on his back. 'How?'

Josh looked up at her and shrugged. 'I just did.'

'Where did you lose it?' Nan prompted.

Josh paused. 'Um, on the way home from school.'

'And *how* did you lose it?' Nan asked.

'It just sort of vanished.' Josh smiled weakly.

Nan gave him a pointed look. 'Josh, I wasn't born yesterday.'

'I never said you were, Nan,' Josh replied sheepishly.

'You don't just lose things.'

'I do sometimes,' Maddie said quietly from the door-way.

Nan smiled at Maddie's attempt to support her brother, then turned back to Josh. 'Did someone take your back-pack from you? Other boys from school, maybe?'

Josh pulled a pained expression. He didn't want to admit that he, the son of a soldier, had allowed Kelvin to take his bag. And he didn't want Nan to cause a fuss at school either.

'Don't lie to me, Josh Fulton,' Nan said sternly. 'No matter what, I'd like to hear the truth.'

CHAPTER 14

Inside Deep Cave, Commander Baradar and his men had made a comfortable camp for themselves a hundred metres from the landward entrance. They had mattresses spread on the hard ground and a cooking fire from which smoke curled up into the rocky ceiling. At the mouth of the cave, around a bend from their encampment, the insurgents had heaped boulders to create a wall two metres high, where they could offer a defence if attacked.

Twenty-two fighters from the Taliban's Uruzgan brigade spent their days here. In rotating shifts, two men were constantly stationed on a hilltop several hundred metres away. They were responsible for keeping watch on the cave entrance and warning of any approaches – especially by government troops, Afghan police or ISAF soldiers. Commander Baradar would check in with this sentry outpost several times a day via walkie-talkie.

Baradar had just just received confirmation from the sentries that all was clear when something strange occurred. Sitting on his mattress, reading a copy of the Holy Koran by the light of a gas lantern, Abdul Razah removed his round cap to scratch his greasy head. As he did this, a small cylindrical object half the size of a cigarette tumbled from his hat and fell to the floor.

The small movement caught Baradar's eye. 'What is that?' he demanded. Moving closer, he picked up the piece of metal. Being an experienced insurgent and guerrilla fighter, Baradar knew at once what it was. 'A homing device!' he exclaimed with sudden anxiety. 'You had a homing device in your headwear, Abdul Razah!'

Abdul, open-mouthed, looked with disbelief at the device in his superior's hand. 'How did that get there?'

'That's what I'm asking *you*, you imbecile!' Baradar raged. 'What is the meaning of this?!'

Abdul had told no one of his arrest by ISAF troops on the road back from Bamiyan. Nor had he told them that he had been held at FOB Nero for a number of hours before he made his escape. He had lied to Baradar, blaming his extended absence on a delay in Bamiyan. With the discovery of the homing device, he had no choice but to admit what had taken place.

When Commander Baradar heard that Abdul had been in the hands of ISAF, he was furious. And concerned. 'You have led the infidels to us!' he stormed.

'They cannot know that we have the secretary-general here, Commander,' said Abdul Razah, trying to placate him. 'How do they know that it is not just myself here in these caves?'

Baradar dropped the tracking device to the rocky floor and ground the device flat with the heel of his boot, destroying it. 'I curse the infidels!' he raged.

Abdul cowered, afraid of what Commander Baradar might do.

After a moment Commander Baradar grew thoughtful. 'But do they know who we are guarding, or do they not?' he said slowly. 'This is the question.'

Perspiring heavily, Ben Fulton stood in the Special Forces hangar beside the Tarin Kowt runway. Though the night was cooling fast, it had been a fiercely hot day in Uruzgan Province. Ben was wearing a black balaclava over his head and polypropylene thermal underwear beneath black combat fatigues. That underwear, made from the same plastic material as Australia's world-first polymer banknotes, was designed to keep its wearer warm.

Ben would need the thermal underwear once Operation Blue Dragon was underway, first at high altitude, and later in the chilly waters of Dragon Lake. But at the moment it was downright uncomfortable. Caesar was beside him, busy eating a tasty steak dinner from a tin bowl. A camp cook had brought the food and bowl out to the hangar for him especially. Caesar didn't need thermal underwear. His thick, greasy fur would keep him warm no matter what the altitude, in and out of water.

Ben wore black from head to foot. A black flying helmet, the kind worn by combat pilots, complete with an oxygen mask. Black combat trousers. Black tunic. Bulging black equipment pouches on a black webbing belt. Black bulletproof vest. A black life preserver that could be inflated in water with the pull of a tab. And a small oxygen bottle in a black rectangular pack strapped to the front of his vest. A compact Heckler & Koch MP5 submachine gun was slung over his right shoulder.

Black was the colour that Special Forces troops universally wore on night missions in order to blend into the darkness. On his cheeks, Ben had smeared black Special Ops make-up, which looked like greasy charcoal, so they wouldn't be visible in the dark. Caesar also wore his own black combat gear. A made-to-fit Kevlar vest covered his back and chest while his black doggles sat on the top of his head.

Sergeant Bruce, the Scottish commando who was now a member of Sky Team, came over to chat with Ben. He, too, was dressed all in black. 'He's a fine looking laddie, your Caesar,' said Bruce. 'And he looks a hoot in those doggles! He reminds me of Brodie, the dog I had at home in Dundee when I was a wee boy.' He dropped to one knee beside Caesar.

'Don't try patting him while he's eating,' Ben cautioned. 'Never come between a dog and his tucker.'

Sergeant Bruce nodded. 'Aye, you're right – my terrier, Brodie, would nip at me, too, if there was food involved.' He stood up again. 'Your Caesar is a very smart dog, so they tell me, Ben.'

Looking down at Caesar as he ate, Ben smiled. 'Smarter than a lot of humans.'

'And yet labradors aren't rated the most intelligent of dogs, are they? Border collies from Scotland are the most intelligent of all the breeds, are they not?' The Scotsman smiled cheekily.

Ben nodded good-naturedly. 'Labs rate seventh most intelligent, but their loyalty, courage and tenacity under fire make them top military dogs.' Ben took a black laptop from his backpack and turned it on for testing.

'Why is it, I wonder,' said Bruce as he checked the equipment on his belt, 'that some dogs have those qualities while others, even of the same breed, will run for their lives at the first explosion?'

'You know,' said Ben, as he waited for his computer to boot, 'there was an experiment at the University of Sydney to test a theory of Professor Sally McShane's that some dogs, like some humans, have courage, loyalty and tenacity in their genes. Caesar took part in that experiment with a bunch of other dogs.'

'How did they test them?' asked Sergeant Bruce, slapping a full magazine into his rifle.

'It was all about the way they eat.'

Angus frowned. 'The way they eat?'

Ben nodded to the labrador. 'Look at Caesar now. Look at the way he's holding his bowl in place with his right paw.'

Sergeant Bruce looked down. Sure enough, Caesar was using his right paw to prevent the bowl from sliding over the concrete floor. 'Aye,' said Angus, 'what of it?'

Holding the laptop in one hand, Ben opened his operational program. 'Professor McShane worked out that dogs that use their right paw to hold the food container are left-brain oriented. And the left brain is all about courage and tenacity. She said that dogs that mostly use their left paws like that are right-brained and are more emotional and flighty.'

'Left-brained and right-brained dogs?' Sergeant Bruce pulled a face. 'Oh, I don't know about that,' he said. 'I think there are stupid dogs and clever dogs, just as there are stupid people and clever people.'

'The professor would disagree with you, mate,' Ben said, before turning his full attention to the laptop. When he was satisfied that it was good to go, he shut it down.

'You blokes set?' Charlie asked, walking across the hangar from where the other members of Sky Team had assembled. Charlie was accompanied by Major Jinko, who'd come to see the team off.

'Just about,' said Ben, returning the laptop to his backpack. 'Just waiting for Caesar to finish his dinner.'

Major Jinko was carrying a green canvas carry bag, which he held open in front of Ben and Sergeant Bruce. 'Mobile phones please, gentlemen.'

Without a word, Ben and Sergeant Bruce took their phones from their pockets and dropped them into the bag, which already contained the phones of other team members. For security reasons, they weren't permitted to take private phones on ops. They would collect them on their return from the mission.

'As soon as Caesar's fed, Ben,' said Charlie, 'we'll have our final briefing.'

Ben nodded. 'We're off soon, then?'

'The C-17 carrying the *Pencil* has picked up a tail-wind and is making good time,' said Major Jinko. 'It'll be over the target on schedule or even a little early. And the met people say the weather over Dragon Lake is perfect for insertion – clear skies and low wind. Operation Blue Dragon is "go".'

Ben smiled. 'The sooner the better, sir. Caesar loves parachute jumps.'

'Yeah, he's a HALO junkie,' Charlie agreed.

'Can Caesar swim?' asked Sergeant Bruce, half-jokingly. 'We're dropping into a lake, remember.'

'There's nothing Caesar likes better than a swim,' Ben replied. 'Apart from HALO jumps.'

Caesar looked up from his now-empty bowl and his tail began to wag. The mention of swimming and HALO jumps was music to his ears.

Sergeant Bruce grinned. 'A multi-talented mutt indeed.'

At that moment, Major Jinko's mobile phone rang. Duke Hazard was on the other end, calling from FOB Nero. Jinko answered, then said, 'Hold on, Sergeant, I'll put you onto Grover.' He handed the phone to Charlie.

Charlie held the phone to his ear. 'What's up, Hazard?'

'Grover,' Hazard said abruptly, 'be advised that the tracking device we had on Abdul Razah has just died.'

'Its battery's run out?'

'Unlikely. The tech guys say the battery should have lasted a month, minimum. There's a good chance the Taliban found the tracking device and destroyed it.'

'In which case, they could be on to us and our op.' Charlie looked grim.

'Maybe so. Maybe not. The possibility exists.'

'And if they *are* onto us? Where does that leave us and the hostages?'

'The Taliban could kill the hostages right away or they could vamoose from that cave and transfer the

prisoners someplace else. We'll know if they do move –
Special Ops HQ has drones watching the cave entrance
twenty-four hours a day.' Sergeant Hazard paused. 'But
there is a third alternative. The Taliban could just hunker
down and wait for us to come to them and fight it out.
You should be aware that there's a strong possibility the
hostiles are now expecting us. Do you copy?'

'Copy that. But they won't be expecting us to come in
via the second entrance.'

'That's the one ace up our sleeve, buddy. Without
that, this mission would be screwed.'

'So, it's all systems go?'

'Roger that. A second heelo has arrived to insert
Land Team. From this point on we will communicate
via secure comms.'

'Copy that, Hazard.'

'Excellent. Are you and your people good to go?'

'Roger to that,' Charlie responded.

'Then let's make this thing happen, my friend. Let's
go extract the Big Cheese from the mousetrap.'

In the pitch-black of Deep Cave, Liberty Lee crawled
over to Dr Park and nudged him awake.

'Secretary-General,' Liberty whispered, 'the Taliban
are coming.'

Pulling himself up, Dr Park peered into the darkness. Sure enough, he spotted lights in the distance, growing brighter as they got closer.

'It is not mealtime again – we ate only several hours ago,' Dr Park said, half to himself. 'Why are they coming now?'

'Commander Baradar's deadline must soon be expiring, sir,' said Liberty. Around them, the other members of the UN party began to stir.

'Are they bringing a doctor?' Fader asked weakly.

'Yes, a doctor and more food,' said Mikashi, softly. 'There is never enough food.'

'Do stop your complaining, Mikashi, there's a good fellow,' murmured Jeremy Brown.

'Sir,' said Liberty Lee, keeping her voice low so that only the secretary-general could hear her, 'I think I should try to escape and bring help. Before they start shooting us.'

Dr Park shook his head in concern. 'That would be dangerous.'

'I am trained to take care of myself, sir,' Liberty assured him. 'And I cannot continue to do nothing. Do I have your permission to attempt to escape?'

Dr Park thought for a moment. 'It would be best if you did not. Such an attempt might endanger the lives of the others. We must continue to hope that our friends outside are at this moment organising a rescue bid.'

'And what if they are not, sir?' she asked, sounding frustrated.

'I cannot believe that the world would abandon us, Miss Lee,' Dr Park said softly. He placed a hand on her arm, reassuringly. 'Have faith.'

Before long, Commander Baradar, Abdul Razah and four other Taliban fighters stood looking down at their prisoners.

'Do you wish me to make another video, Commander Baradar?' Dr Park asked.

'No,' Baradar replied. 'There is no more time for videos.' He motioned to those of his men who were not holding lanterns. 'Do it.'

'You won't kill us?' Mikashi wailed as two of Baradar's men advanced toward the prisoners.

The two insurgents roughly took hold of Jeremy Brown, pulling him to his feet and binding his arms behind his back.

'If I must be the first to die, sir,' Brown said bravely, looking over to the secretary-general, 'tell my family that my last thoughts were of them.'

'You will not die,' Baradar interrupted. 'Not yet.'

'Then why are you doing this?' asked Dr Park, as two of Baradar's men dragged Captain Rix, one of the German pilots, to his feet and bound his hands. 'Why are you tying up my colleagues?'

'The infidels might be coming,' Abdul Razah blurted

out in English, as he held his lantern high.

'Is that true?' Liberty asked. 'Foreign troops are nearby?'

'You are a fool, Abdul Razah,' Baradar said disparagingly in Pashto. 'A fool whose mouth is larger than his brain.'

'What harm is there in them knowing?' Abdul said with a shrug. 'They will all soon be dead anyway.'

The two insurgents who were tying up the hostages now turned to Liberty Lee, motioning for her to save them the trouble of hauling her to her feet. Liberty quickly obeyed, standing up. One took hold of her arm to swing her around so that her back was to him. As she turned, Liberty noted that Commander Baradar and Abdul were locked in a heated conversation, with the other lantern-bearers looking on. Seizing her chance, Liberty's right arm swung up and around like a whip, and her elbow crashed into the nearest insurgent's throat.

Clutching his throat and gasping for air, the man dropped to his knees. In another swift, fluid movement, Liberty brought her left leg up and around as she pivoted on her right foot, sending her left foot straight into the abdomen of the second insurgent. He doubled-up in pain and surprise. In another rapid movement, Liberty swept the edge of her hand into the man's neck and he, too, went down. In a blur that made Liberty's three martial arts moves appear as one single movement, the two Taliban fighters had been downed, allowing Liberty to sprint away into the darkness.

'Miss Lee!' Dr Park called after her with concern.

'Run!' Jeremy Brown urged her.

'Allez, vite!' Loubet concurred.

Liberty's actions had been instinctive. Even though she was disobeying the secretary-general's order to not attempt an escape, she knew that if she'd allowed the Taliban to tie her up, any future attempt to protect the secretary-general would have been impossible.

'Stop her!' bellowed Baradar.

With Liberty's two victims on the ground, Abdul and the other two lantern-bearers grabbed the AK-47s from their shoulders. This took precious seconds, and with the lanterns discarded, reducing the field of light, aided Liberty's escape. Baradar let off a furious burst of fire in her direction as Liberty dodged and weaved her way across the rocky cave floor and into the gloom. Bullets ricocheted off stone walls and sparks flew, but none hit their intended target.

Abdul and his two companions, meanwhile, had brought their guns to bear and they, too, opened fire in Liberty's direction. The sound was deafening, but their effect was zero. Liberty Lee dived into the waters of the pool, disappearing beneath its surface as a hail of bullets sprayed overhead.

'Get that she-devil!' Baradar yelled. 'Get her!'

Abdul, picking up his lantern with one hand and grasping his rifle in the other, hurried to the edge of the pool and surveyed the rippling surface as far as the low light would allow.

'The moment she surfaces, blast her,' Baradar commanded.

Minutes passed without any sign of Liberty Lee.

'We must have hit her,' said one insurgent.

Abdul nodded. 'Either that or she drowned. She is finished, Commander. We will not see her again.'

Baradar turned to his two shaken men lying on the ground, the pair so expertly floored by Liberty Lee. 'Get up! Get up!' he growled. 'What are you – *women*?'

Clutching their throats, the pair groggily came to their feet.

'Now,' Baradar ordered, 'fit the explosives to the secretary-general.'

Moving gingerly, the two men pulled a white canvas vest from a knapsack that one of them had brought. As the horrified hostages watched on, the vest, bulging with plastic explosives, was strapped around Secretary-General Park's torso.

'If infidel soldiers attempt to rescue you, Secretary-General,' Baradar said with a demonic smile, 'this vest will be detonated. Pray to your heathen gods that the infidels are not making such a great mistake.'

CHAPTER 15

It was early evening when Nan Fulton brought her little orange Ford Fiesta to a stop beside the kerb. Bending to look out the front passenger window, she surveyed the Tobruk Road building on her left. In the Fiesta's back seat sat a sullen Josh and an excited Maddie.

'Nan, you're not really going to go up to Kelvin's place, are you?' Josh asked hopefully.

'Yes, *we* are,' Nan replied, unfastening her seatbelt.

'Kelvin's going to get it now,' Maddie declared with relish.

'Oh, I shouldn't have told you that it was Kelvin who took my backpack,' moaned Josh. He feared it was just going to make things worse.

Nan turned around to face him. 'Of course you should have, darling,' she responded. 'If anything like this ever happens again – at school, online, anywhere – you let me or your father know straightaway, Josh. The same goes for you, Maddie.'

Maddie nodded seriously. 'Cross my heart, Nan.'

'Yeah, but I knew you'd go off and do something like this if I told,' Josh countered. He looked at the building where Kelvin lived, dread filling his stomach.

'That's the whole point, Josh,' said Nan. 'Young people are often too shy or afraid to stand up for themselves, or just don't want to cause trouble. Or they think they can handle it themselves – but often they can't, and things get out of hand. These things need to be nipped in the bud. But we can only help you if you speak up.' Nan waved a finger under his nose. 'Do you understand, Josh? You should speak up.'

'Yes, Nan,' Josh said with a sigh.

'Let's go. We have a stolen backpack to recover.'

The three of them emerged onto the footpath. Ahead of them stood a six-storey block of grey brick apartments. Modern and functional, each apartment had glass-fronted balconies. The building's front door opened into a large foyer. Tall glass windows at the far end of the foyer looked out over the greenery of Anzac Park. Nan ushered them into the lift.

As the doors closed and the lift began to glide up to the first floor, Josh looked up at Nan worriedly. 'What are you going to do?'

Nan squeezed his shoulder reassuringly. 'Don't worry, Josh, everything will be fine.

When the lift opened, Nan led them in search of the Corbett's apartment, coming to a stop at number 108.

Josh's heart was beating fast. Maddie had gone quiet, and she gripped Nan's left hand tightly as Nan used her right hand to ring the doorbell.

A woman in her forties opened the door. 'What do you want?' the woman demanded, glaring at Nan and the children.

'Mrs Corbett?' said Nan with a smile. 'The mother of Kelvin Corbett?'

The woman regarded Nan suspiciously. 'I might be. Who are you?'

'My grandson, Josh,' began Nan, gesturing at Josh, 'goes to school with Kelvin. This afternoon Kelvin took Josh's backpack, and we have come by to collect it.'

Mrs Corbett frowned. 'My Kelvin is a good boy,' she said defensively.

'Good boys don't bully or steal, Mrs Corbett,' Nan declared. She held out a hand. 'Josh's backpack, please.'

'Bella, who's at the door?' came a gruff adult male voice from within.

Kelvin's mother suddenly looked frightened. 'No one, sweetie,' she called back over her shoulder. She quickly turned back to Nan, lowering her voice. 'Please, go away. You don't want to annoy my husband.'

Moments later, Jerry Corbett was standing beside his wife. 'What's going on?' he demanded, scowling.

'I've come to ask your son Kelvin to stop bullying

my grandson and to return Josh's backpack, Mr Corbett,' Nan stated evenly.

Kelvin's father peered at Josh. 'Ah, Josh *Fulton*, is it?' His face lit up in a way that made Josh feel uneasy. 'The famous Dog Boy!'

'His name isn't Dog Boy,' Maddie spoke up.

'I reckon it is,' said Mr Corbett. 'With his trumped-up father with his medals and his blunder dog.'

'You're just jealous that you don't have a Caesar, mister,' Maddie said boldly.

'I'm still waiting, Mr Corbett,' Nan insisted, her hand outstretched.

Kelvin's father glared at her. 'For what?'

'For your son to return the backpack he took from my grandson,' replied Nan.

'He did no such thing!' growled Mr Corbett.

'Yes, he did!' Josh protested. 'He took it off me on the way home from school this afternoon.'

'Garbage!' Corbett declared.

'Mr Corbett,' Nan said calmly, 'I don't want to have to report this to –'

'Get lost!' barked Mr Corbett before slamming the door in their faces.

'Well!' Nan exclaimed indignantly. 'We'll have to see about that. Come along, children.' She guided them back toward the lifts.

'I could have told you that wouldn't work,' Josh

lamented. 'Kelvin's father is as nasty as he is.'

'That Mr Corbett isn't a humungatarian, that's for sure,' said Maddie.

🐾 🐾

Descending from a black sky, a US Army Chinook touched down on a clear patch of ground in an empty valley of the Hindu Kush, five kilometres from Dragon Lake. Within seconds, four heavily armed men and a dog emerged from the cabin's interior. Duke Hazard, Tim McHenry, Brian Cisco, Mars Lazar and EDD Alabama came down the rear ramp at a jog. All wore night-vision goggles that lit up the night for them in an eerie green. They went to ground in rocks nearby, then covered the LZ – the landing zone – with their weapons.

As soon as the first group was in position, Hazard waved to the Chinook, and four more men emptied out of the heelo – Willy Wolf, Jean-Claude Lyon, Toushi Harada and Ali Moon. As soon as they set foot on the rocky ground, the Chinook promptly lifted off and soared away into the night. It had been on the ground no more than a minute. Very quickly, the noise of its engines faded away and the silence of the mountain wilderness wrapped around the eight men and their EDD.

Lying flat on his stomach among the rocks, Duke Hazard checked his portable GPS and then pointed to the southwest to indicate the direction he and his team were to follow. 'Lazar, take point,' he called in a hoarse whisper. The night air was so chilly that his breath was visible as he spoke. 'Move out.'

Corporal Lazar rose up. With Alabama on a long leash – his nose down as he trotted along taking in all the aromas of the terrain – the pair commenced moving southwest, paving the way for the rest of Land Team. Lazar walked with a carbine cradled in his arms, ready for instant use. Sergeant Duke Hazard, still lying among the rocks near the LZ, unclipped the leather cover from the face of his watch and checked the time on its luminous dial. He nodded to himself. Operation Blue Dragon's Land Team was right on schedule.

In calculating the times for this mission, Hazard had allowed two hours for Land Team to cover the five overland kilometres to the vicinity of Dragon Lake. He knew that, normally, he and his men could cover between three and five kilometres in an hour when walking fast over reasonably flat ground. Conservatively, then, two hours was plenty of time to walk five kilometres across this barren landscape, despite their heavy weapons load. Once in sight of the lake, the team had another hour to move into position to assault the landward entrance to Deep Cave at Zero Hour before dawn.

Hazard came to his feet and, M-16 assault rifle at the ready, set off after Lazar. Hazard had designated their marching order before the team left FOB Nero. Without a word, Cisco was the next to rise up, and with the aerial from the big military radio on his back waving back and forth with every step, he took third position in the well-spaced line of men now traipsing over the moonlit landscape. After a pause, McHenry stood and set off after Cisco. Ali came next, followed by Wolf and then Harada. Sergeant Lyon brought up the rear, every now and then swinging around, Minimi machinegun at the ready, to study the country behind them and assure himself that the line of eight international Special Forces soldiers was not being followed.

Before long, Land Team had melted silently into the night.

Laura McMichaels, principal of Josh's Holsworthy school, looked up from her desk and, with a smile, removed her reading glasses. 'Mrs Fulton, come in, come in. What can I do for you today?'

'Thank you for seeing us right away, Mrs McMichaels,' Nan said, steering Josh and Maddie to a settee before taking a seat across from the principal. She had driven directly to the school from the Corbett apartment, catching the school principal before she went home for the day. 'We have a matter of theft and bullying to discuss with you.'

The principal's smile vanished, replaced by a look of concern. 'Theft? Bullying?' Mrs McMichaels turned to Josh and Maddie, both of them her students. 'Please, tell me all about it.'

With the deafening roar of its four propeller-driven engines, a hulking grey Hercules C-130 transport aircraft rolled through the night and drew to a shuddering halt outside the Special Forces hangar at Tarin Kowt. Inside the hangar, Charlie Grover, in the middle of his final briefing to his Sky Team comrades, was forced to wait for the plane to come to a halt and kill its engines before he could continue. As the engines of the Hercules died, its rear ramp came down.

'Looks like your ride has arrived, boys,' said Major Jinko.

Charlie nodded, before turning back to the whiteboard he'd been using. 'So, to recap, we'll be circling the DZ at 20,000 feet – out of hearing range of anyone on the ground – waiting for the C-17 carrying the sub to come over.' On the whiteboard Charlie had drawn a shape representing Dragon Lake, which was their DZ, or drop zone, plus winged shapes above it which represented the aircraft.

'As soon as we have AEW&C confirmation that the sub has splashed down,' Charlie went on, 'we hit the silk and do a HALO drop into the lake in darkness. Once we're in the water, we use the inflatable dinghy that's being dropped with us to make our way to the sub. After that, we're in the hands of the sub's crew, whose job it is to get us into Deep Cave through the underwater channel. Once we surface in the pool in the cave, we disembark and Ben will deploy EDD Caesar. At Zero Hour, while the Taliban are kept busy by Land Team at the cave's land entrance, we move in and free the hostages.' Charlie paused and looked at his team. 'Any questions?'

'How will the dog do in the water?' asked Corporal Mortenson, the Danish diver. He was the only member of Sky Team wearing a wetsuit – his usual outfit for a marine op.

'Dogs can swim, mate,' said Bendigo Baz. 'You do know that?'

Casper shrugged. 'I was worried that the dog might be a burden to us.'

'Mate,' said Charlie, 'Caesar won't be a burden. Believe me, the day will come when you'll be grateful to have Caesar around.'

'Caesar is a strong swimmer,' assured Ben. 'Just the same, once we're in the water, I'll get him and my gear into the dinghy with everyone else.'

'So, Caesar gets a water-taxi ride?' said Corporal Banner, smiling wide. 'Man, what a spoilt pooch.'

This generated a laugh from several of the others.

Hearing his name mentioned, Caesar began to wag his tail, his pink tongue hanging out the corner of his mouth. Caesar, now with a full belly, instinctively knew that he and Ben would soon be going on a mission. He had seen and heard the Hercules pull up outside, jogging memories of the parachute jumps that he and Ben had done together in the past. And as Ben had told Sergeant Bruce, Caesar loved making parachute jumps.

'What happens if something goes wrong with the mini-sub once it's in the lake and we can't use it?' Sergeant Bruce asked.

'If for any reason the sub can't be used,' said Major Jinko, 'the crew have orders to blow the explosive charges onboard and sink the sub to prevent the Taliban knowing it was ever in the lake. Secrecy is everything.'

'And what happens to us in that eventuality, man?' asked Corporal Banner. 'Is there a Plan B if we're in that lake without a sub?'

'Yep,' said Charlie. 'We would link up with Land Team. But that won't be happening. This op has to go off without a hitch if we're going to save the Big Cheese. So, think positively, everyone. Any more questions?'

'How do we locate the sub once we're in the water?'

Mortenson asked. 'It'll be as black as Hades out there.'

'With this homing device,' said Charlie, holding up a device about half the size of a paperback. 'You take charge of that, Mortenson.' He handed the device to the Dane. 'It'll lead us right to the *Pencil*.'

'What's Zero Hour?' Sergeant Bruce asked.

'Zero Hour is 0515 hours,' Major Jinko advised. 'Synchronise your watches now, all of you.'

Charlie checked the time on his watch, which he had previously synchronised with Duke Hazard's. 'The time now is 0245. Check?'

'Check,' the others confirmed in unison, adjusting the time on their watches to precisely match Charlie's.

'Okay, let's get our gear stowed aboard the Herc,' said Charlie.

'What's our ETD, Charlie?' Lucky Mertz asked, as he shouldered his parachute.

'ETD is 0330,' Charlie replied. 'We've got forty-five minutes to get cleared away. Let's do it, blokes. Let's bring the Big Cheese home.'

'Yeah!' yelled Bendigo Baz, punching the air. 'Time to sort the mice from the men!'

As the others picked up their gear and walked out onto the tarmac toward the waiting Hercules, Charlie stayed back with Major Jinko to help give Ben a hand with his equipment. Ben had the heaviest individual load of any of the members of Sky Team. In addition to being responsible for Caesar and donning a parachute large enough to support the pair of them, he carried his MP5 submachine gun, a weapon designed for anti-terrorist operations in confined spaces, spare 9 mm magazines, stun grenades, a sheathed commando knife, a torch, a full water bottle and several packs of MRE emergency rations for Caesar and himself. He also had a medical kit and spare Browning magazines in his trouser pockets. His Browning Hi Power 9 mm automatic pistol was holstered on his right thigh, and an altimeter strapped to his left wrist would tell him when it was time to deploy his parachute after he left the aircraft.

But that wasn't the end of Ben's load. A waterproof bag attached to Ben's belt contained flying gloves, combat gloves, night-vision equipment, his laptop computer, two radio transceivers and a video camera that could be clipped onto Caesar's Kevlar vest for forward reconaissance work. Under Ben's life preserver, a small personal radio for communication within Sky Team was attached to his bulletproof vest, and night-vision goggles were strapped to his helmet. And once it came time to jump from the Hercules, Caesar would also be strapped to him. Jumping into a lake from 20,000 feet carrying all of this would be, to say the least, a challenge. Not that Ben was concerned – he was trained and ready for it.

Charlie carried both Ben's parachute pack and his

own as well as a large black haversack that was strapped to his chest. 'This will be Caesar's first operational HALO jump, won't it?' Charlie asked Ben as they walked to the waiting Hercules.

'We've done it often enough in training,' Ben replied. Caesar trotted happily along beside him on his metal leash, tail wagging.

'Into water?'

Ben nodded. 'A couple of times into water. Caesar will be fine. How about you, mate? Will those Zoomers of yours be up to it?'

'Not a problem, cobber,' Charlie confidently replied.

'They won't slow you down in the water?'

'No way. These Zoomers are made from carbon fibre, remember? They're as light as a feather, and it's not as if they'll rust.'

None of the other members of the task force had mentioned Charlie's artificial legs. Ben assumed they hadn't even noticed his Zoomers. If they had, they'd apparently soon forgotten them, with Charlie proving to be as agile as any member of the team.

'Glad to be back on ops?' Ben asked.

'It's what I'm trained for, mate. And it's what I'm best at. God knows what I would've done with my life if Josh hadn't put me onto Zoomers. There aren't many options for legless soldiers. These things have given me a new lease on life.'

Major Jinko stood watching from the hangar door as the last of the eight to board, Charlie, Ben and an excited Caesar, walked up the lowered ramp and into the Hercules. Soon, Sky Team would be in the air.

CHAPTER 16

There was a tense silence in the Special Ops control room at Tarin Kowt. Lieutenant General McAvoy, Brigadier Quiggly and Major Jinko all eyed a bank of LCD screens that covered a wall in the room. In front of them, a team of Special Operations staff from Australia and the US sat at two rows of desks covered with computers and communications equipment. The entire Blue Dragon op was being controlled from this dark windowless room, and the lives of the secretary-general and his party were in the hands of these men and women.

'EITS in position above target,' announced one of the operators.

EITS, meaning 'Eye in the Sky', was the code-name for a Boeing Wedgetail aircraft from the Royal Australian Air Force's No. 2 Squadron. Wedgetails were specially built for the Australian Army by Boeing as an AEW&C (airborne early warning and control aircraft). Based on the airframe of the Boeing 737 passenger jet, each Wedgetail carries a massive radar array atop its fuselage, plus downward-pointing sensors and long-range cameras in its belly. The main cabin of each Wedgetail is designed to accommodate eight RAAF operators sitting at a line of consoles, each with a glowing screen depicting various aspects of a chosen target.

The Wedgetail slowly circled Dragon Lake and the entrance to Deep Cave at 35,000 feet. By the time the two US aircraft involved in this phase of the operation joined the Wedgetail over the target, Lieutenant General McAvoy would have three aircraft stacked one above the other at 13,000-foot and 15,000-foot intervals.

'Let's see what EITS can see,' said the general. 'Put its infrared image of the lake up on the main screen.'

An indecipherable pale green image filled the room's main screen. It looked like a green snowstorm.

'Clearly, there's no life down on the lake,' Brigadier Quiggly remarked.

'Bring up the area five clicks around the entrance to Deep Cave,' McAvoy ordered. 'Give it to us in infrared.'

Another pale green image replaced the first on the big screen. This time, there were two clusters of bright green dots in the lower left side of the image.

'Zoom in on the smaller group to the left,' McAvoy instructed.

The image blurred for a moment, then sharpened so

that it was possible to see two bright green men, stationary like statues, on a hilltop.

'Hostiles,' said Major Jinko. 'Looks like we have two Taliban fighters guarding the approach to Deep Cave.'

'Now let's see the larger group,' said McAvoy.

The image changed to show eight green men in a staggered line approaching the hilltop where the two Taliban sentinels were waiting. This was Land Team.

'What's that extra image with the man on point?' McAvoy asked with a puzzled frown.

'That's Alabama, the EDD, sir,' Jinko advised.

'Uhuh,' a relieved McAvoy returned. 'Okay, advise Land Team of the location of those two guards. They'll need to take them out before they can approach the cave entrance.'

As one of the operators radioed Corporal Cisco with the message, another operator announced, 'Sky Team advise they are in position for insertion, sir, and are standing by for "go".'

'And where is Cheese Cutter now?' McAvoy asked. 'Cheese Cutter' was the codename he had allocated to the gigantic C-17 bringing the *Pencil*, Renzo and Ellerman over from California.

'Cheese Cutter is fifteen minutes out from target, sir.'

'Very good. Advise Sky Team that they are twenty minutes from "go".'

'Roger that.' The operator flicked a radio switch, then

said, 'Cheese Board from Cheese Master. Are you receiving? Over.'

The voice of the pilot of the Hercules carrying Sky Team crackled in the operator's ears. 'Cheese Board receiving. Over.'

'Cheese Board, advise your cargo that they have twenty minutes until "go".'

'Copy that, Cheese Master. Twenty minutes. Will advise. Cheese Board out.'

Seated in the webbing seats along one side of the cavernous interior of the Hercules, the members of Sky Team were concentrating on breathing. Each of the seven men had an oxygen mask covering his nose and mouth. They were breathing 100 per cent pure oxygen supplied by the aircraft. This was necessary to flush nitrogen from their systems so that they didn't suffer from decompression sickness once they jumped out of the plane at 20,000 feet.

Just before the jump, Charlie was to give the signal to change over to the less-rich oxygen supply that each man carried in the bottles strapped to their chests. Once out of the aircraft, they would breathe that oxygen until they reached a lower altitude. If they didn't follow this procedure, the men could black out, in which case they wouldn't be able to pull their parachute ripcord and would plummet to their death.

In the changeover process from aircraft oxygen to their individual oxygen supply, each soldier had to hold his breath. Just taking a single breath in the atmosphere within the cabin could prove fatal. Caesar was a different story. He, too, needed to breathe 100 per cent oxygen before changing over to the less-rich variety for his jump with Ben. But as clever as Caesar and other Special Forces dogs are, they don't know how to hold their breath during this changeover, nor can they be trained to do it.

So, in addition to his usual doggles, Caesar was wearing an airtight oxygen mask that had been custom-made to fit him. It was attached to two black oxygen bottles that Ben had strapped to the bottom of Caesar's Kevlar vest. When the time came, Ben would turn a switch on a valve connected to both bottles, which would automatically change Caesar's oxygen supply over from 100 per cent to his less-rich oxygen.

Caesar had worn this oxygen mask before and was accustomed to it. Not all war dogs are as accepting of the oxygen mask, and some otherwise promising dogs fail the HALO phase of their training when they can't tolerate the mask. Trusting Ben implicitly, Caesar wore and tolerated it. He lay patiently at Ben's feet in doggles and oxygen mask, waiting for the parachute jump that he expected to come. Every now and then, Ben would bend to give him a comforting pat and ruffle of the neck, and Caesar would raise his head and attempt to lick him, only for his long tongue to hit the plastic side of his mask.

'Twenty minutes to DZ,' came the pilot's voice in Charlie's headset.

Charlie immediately relayed the message to his comrades via a show of ten fingers twice. They all nodded and checked their watches.

🐾🐾

Liberty Lee kept low as she carefully picked her way among the rocks, working toward lights shining in the distance. Contrary to Abdul Razah's expectations, she had not drowned. During her years of training in Korean martial arts, Liberty had learned many things other than hitting and kicking. She had learned how to slow her heart rate and how to sleep standing up. She had also learned to hold her breath for an extraordinary length of time.

While fleeing her Taliban captors, Liberty had remained underwater for six minutes, swimming away from the light of their lanterns. When she'd eventually surfaced, it had been in the darkness of the far side of the pool. Since emerging from the water, Liberty had been trying to find a way out of the cave. Confronted by solid stone walls in all directions, Liberty concluded that there must only be a single entrance – the one used by the Taliban beyond the area where her colleagues were being held. She would have to cross that area to get out. Hoping the Taliban had withdrawn from the hostage site as they usually did, she took the risk of returning to it.

As she crouched behind a rocky outcrop, Liberty could see that not only had Commander Baradar left glowing lanterns at the hostage site, he had left Abdul Razah and another heavily armed insurgent to guard them closely, now that there was a possibility of ISAF forces being in the area. Liberty could make out all six remaining hostages huddled in the dull light, their hands bound behind their backs. Worse, she could see that Secretary-General Park had been forced to wear a bulging white vest, a vest she was sure contained explosives. The Taliban could be expected to detonate those explosives if they felt threatened, even if it meant killing themselves.

Liberty pulled back into the darkness as she tried to figure out what to do next. Whatever she did, she dared not risk the Taliban detonating that vest.

Aboard the C-17 codenamed Cheese Cutter, Dave Renzo and Brad Ellerman were preparing to make their parachute jumps and to follow the *Pencil* down into Dragon Lake. Both men had donned navy-blue waterproof jumpsuits and life preservers. Around their waists they wore belts to which were attached knives, one-man dinghy packs and GPS tracking devices. They had been breathing oxygen from the aircraft's system on the long flight over the North Pacific and South-East Asia. Now, as the Cheese Cutter descended to 7000 feet, they donned their parachutes and jumping helmets with the help of loadmaster Sergeant Kramer and her crew.

Over the intercom and above the roar of the engines, Commander Renzo asked, 'Staff Sergeant Kramer, what will be the procedure for the airdrop? How will you people be able to push that sub out the back? It weighs seventy tonnes!'

Kramer smiled. 'Simple, sir. Standard procedure for airdrops of heavy loads. Once we're over the target, the pilot will put us into a steep climb. Your submarine will roll out the back all by itself. It's only sitting on those wheels, it's not bolted on. Once the sub is freefalling, the wheels will drop away, fall into the lake and sink without a trace.'

'Then the lieutenant and myself jump?' Renzo asked.

Kramer nodded. 'Yes, right after we lose the cargo, sir. I'm about to lower the ramp, so I'll need you both to come with me. I'll harness you up, so you don't go out too soon. We'll release you when it's time to follow the sub.'

'Sir,' said Ellerman, turning to Commander Renzo,

'I suggest that you jump first and I follow. I'm used to steering parachutes, you're not. I can follow you down. That way, we land close together.'

Renzo nodded. 'Good thinking, Brad.'

The three of them unhitched from the intercom and walked to the tail of the aircraft where several USAF crewmen harnessed them to the side and out of the way of the mini-sub. Should any of them lose their footing, these safety harnesses would prevent them from falling out the back of the aircraft. Kramer also hitched the two men's parachutes to a static line, which would automatically open their chutes as they left the ramp. Kramer then pressed a large red button, and the massive stern ramp slowly came down to the horizontal, creating a gaping opening in the rear of the plane.

Renzo and Ellerman stared out into the black void. Renzo had never jumped out of a plane, let alone parachuted into a mountain lake in hostile territory. He had butterflies in his stomach, a sensation he hadn't experienced since performing in a school play when he was ten. He wasn't afraid, he assured himself, just out of his comfort zone.

Staff Sergeant Kramer spoke into her headset microphone. 'Passengers ready to go, Cap,' she advised the pilot.

'G minus six,' the pilot replied. The 'G' stood for 'Go'.

'Copy that. G minus six.' Kramer held up six fingers

to Renzo and Ellerman, signifying they were six minutes from drop time.

The two sailors nodded in confirmation.

Thirteen thousand feet above the C-17, at 20,000 feet, the seven Special Forces men of Sky Team were on their feet, Caesar by Ben's side, and waiting as their Herc's tail slowly came down. It was bitterly cold at this altitude – well below zero. If they were up at 35,000 feet, like the Wedgetail way above them, it would be minus forty-five degrees Celsius inside the open cargo cabin, and they would have begun to feel the effects of frostbite on their skin within minutes.

The men had already disconnected from the Hercules' oxygen supply and switched over to their individual oxygen tanks. Ben had also flicked the switch that changed Caesar's oxygen intake from 'rich' to 'normal'. Caesar looked out at the night sky from the back of the plane, soaking up the camaraderie of the men around him. He sensed that he and Ben were about to play a really good game.

Charlie bent down and lifted Caesar up, allowing Ben to attach his EDD to the special harness he was wearing. Caesar, in doggles and oxygen mask, now hung sideways across Ben's stomach. It wasn't a pretty sight but it was practical. As no one had yet found a way to teach dogs to open their own parachutes and steer to a designated landing zone, Ben and Caesar would jump as one and use the same parachute.

Charlie ruffled one of Caesar's ears, gave Ben a thumbs up with a gloved hand, then moved to the front of the line of jumpers. They all stood watching a red light on the fuselage wall. Ben and Caesar were at the back of the line with Baz directly in front of them.

Baz had been forced to leave behind his favourite Minimi machinegun. Instead, he was equipped with a lighter MP5 and a flotation bag filled with lead weights. Charlie had given Baz the role of 'sweeper' on this op. His task was to clean up after the rest of the team, to ensure no trace was left of their unorthodox arrival at Dragon Lake – an arrival now just minutes away. The plane's Air Force jumpmaster, also in oxygen gear, raised two fingers to the waiting jumpers, indicating two minutes to go.

'Go! Go! Go!' the pilot of Cheese Cutter instructed over the intercom.

In the next moment, the C-17's four jet engines began to race. As the aircraft's nose rose sharply, Staff Sergeant Kramer signalled to two subordinates. The men nodded and, each swinging a mallet, dislodged the wooden chocks from either side of the wheels of the mini-submarine's undercarriage. As the floor of the C-17 began to slope, Renzo and Ellerman took a firm, steadying hold of the webbing beside them.

The *Pencil* began to move, rolling on its under-carriage toward the C-17's rear, slowly at first, then with increasing velocity. The submarine rushed past Renzo, Ellerman and Kramer with a rumble of its wheels on the aircraft's metal floor. Sliding over the ramp, sub and undercarriage dropped away into the night and disappeared from view.

As Kramer unclipped Renzo's safety harness, the commander looked at her blankly. She pointed to the black sky. A thousand images flashed through Renzo's mind of the last time he'd gone down into the watery depths in a mini-sub. It had been another DSRV that had become lodged in the wreckage of a sunken warship, 310 metres below the surface. Renzo had been trapped alone on the seabed for hours and had had to be rescued by another DSRV.

He'd received a medal for his courage during that episode, but had been plagued with nightmares from his experience ever since. Renzo had never told anyone, preferring to keep his nightmares and his fears to himself. As far as the Navy and the world were concerned, Commander Dave Renzo had come through unscathed by those scary hours trapped at the bottom of the sea and was the bravest DSRV skipper there was.

When Renzo hesitated, Sergeant Kramer took his arm and guided him along the ramp. They came to a halt on the tip of the open ramp and wavered there until Ellerman came barrelling into Renzo's right shoulder. The force of their connection knocked Renzo from the ramp. Seconds later, he was falling free. He felt his parachute open with a jerk just as, nearby, Ellerman's chute was also deploying.

In the Special Operations HQ, all eyes were glued to the screen. Pictures beamed back from EITS allowed Lieutenant General McAvoy and his team to watch the *Pencil* slowly descend 4000 feet with the aid of black parachutes that had automatically deployed once the sub was free of the C-17. The sets of wheels that it had been resting on inside the C-17 had long since tumbled into the lake.

'We have touchdown!' Major Jinko announced with delight, as the *Pencil* hit the lake nose first with an almighty splash.

Once the parachutes had settled around the sub and the froth from its landing had subsided, the *Pencil* appeared to be riding well in the water.

'Thank the Lord it didn't sink,' McAvoy remarked. 'Where's the sub's crew?'

'Some distance to the west,' said Brigadier Quiggly, pointing to an image on another screen. It showed Commander Renzo and Lieutenant Ellerman making contact with the lake, metres apart from one another.

'Good enough,' said McAvoy. 'They're down, that's what counts. You can give Sky Team the "go".'

The lamp above the Hercules' open ramp changed from red to green. The plane's jumpmaster looked at the parachutists, and dropped his arm, as if starting a race.

Without a word, Charlie ran along the ramp and threw himself out into the night. Behind him, Lucky Mertz, Angus Bruce, Chris Banner, Casper Mortenson and Bendigo Baz followed his example and exited the aircraft one after the other. All were carrying their weapons, with equipment bags strapped to them. In addition to his weapon and equipment bag, Lucky Mertz carried a large black package which sagged from his waist – the deflated dinghy they would inflate and use to reach the submarine. With the extra weight of Caesar, Ben couldn't run, but could only lumber along. In seconds EDD and handler, too, had leapt off the ramp.

Now began a freefall that would end only when

Ben's altimeter showed that they had reached 4000 feet. Ben fell in the crab position, not quite upright, leaning forward with his arms and legs splayed. Caesar, strapped to Ben's front, revelled in the rushing slipstream. After a few seconds, Ben reached behind him and yanked his ripcord. There was a flutter of black silk as a small guide chute flew out followed by the main chute, which opened above them with a sudden jerk. Ben and Caesar's rapid fall abruptly slowed to a gentle descent.

The black Special Ops chute, once deployed, took a rectangular shape and it was possible to steer it to glide to a desired landing spot with precision. Ben steered toward the splashes of the six men who had gone before him. When he and Caesar hit the water, with the force of their speed and weight, they went under. As they did, Ben held his breath and reached for the tab on his life preserver and pulled hard. *Hissssss!* The life preserver quickly began to fill.

When they finally broke the surface of the water, Ben filled his lungs with the crisp night air. He immediately tilted back to get Caesar's head above water, then reached down and removed Caesar's oxygen mask and doggles, slipping them both into an empty black canvas pouch attached to his belt. He squeezed a catch on Caesar's harness and it clicked open.

Caesar, suddenly freed, paddled beside his master. The water was cold but Ben's thermals would insulate him, while Caesar had his natural insulation to keep him warm. It helped that there was not a breath of wind.

Ben began to strip off his gear, his helmet the first item to be discarded. It sank immediately, and for a moment Ben imagined hearing Maddie and Josh scolding him for littering the beautiful, untarnished Dragon Lake. It *was* littering but it couldn't be helped. People's lives were in the balance. Next, Ben struggled out of his parachute harness and began dragging in the black chute, bundling it as it reeled in. He could see and hear other members of the team swimming nearby.

'Over here!' came the hoarse voice of Lucky Mertz. 'I've got the dinghy inflated.'

With Caesar swimming beside him, Ben made his way to Lucky, who was kneeling in the black ten-man dinghy and helping others into it. He reached down, took Caesar's front legs and hauled the labrador in. Ben followed after him. Soon, most of the team were in the dinghy. Charlie was one of the last to reach it. As he and Baz hung onto the side of the rubber boat, Casper reached down and offered Charlie a hand.

Once inside the dinghy, Charlie frowned. 'Casper, where's your equipment bag?'

Mortenson looked away guiltily. 'Sorry, Charlie, I lost it.'

'*Lost it?*' Charlie said, aghast.

'It came off when I hit the water, and sank like a stone.'

Casper shrugged a helpless shrug. 'What can I say? My harness broke.'

'You've got to be kidding!' said Charlie, shaking his head.

'Sorry, Charlie, but these things happen.'

'Was anything vital in Casper's bag?' Lucky asked, trying to gauge the damage.

Charlie looked at the Danish diver. 'Where's the homing device? Don't tell me it was in your bag.' When Casper didn't reply, Charlie again shook his head in disbelief. 'Casper, you're the most experienced water operative in this group! I gave the homing device to you for *safekeeping*.'

'Sorry, Charlie,' Casper said again, unable to look him in the eye.

'Jeez!' Bendigo Baz exclaimed. 'How are we going to find the sub now?'

In the pitch-black it was impossible to even see the shore, let alone the low-lying black shape of the *Pencil*.

'We can't be in this lake when the sun rises!' Charlie exclaimed, half to himself. He turned to the others. 'If we are, locals could tip off the Taliban and the hostages will be as good as dead. Anybody got any bright ideas about how we locate the *Pencil* now?'

CHAPTER 17

Using their GPS devices, the US Navy's Renzo and Ellerman located the *Pencil* drifting on the silky-smooth lake. Kneeling in their little one-man dinghies, the two US Navy officers used their hands as oars to make their way to the floating mini-submarine. Once there, they stabbed holes in their craft to sink them. Then, with backs aching from rowing, they clambered up onto the *Pencil*'s narrow, metre-wide deck.

After opening the forward hatch without difficulty, Renzo headed below to check that all was intact. Ellerman, on his knees on the deck, began cutting away the lines leading to the deflated parachutes that had given the craft a reasonably soft landing. Before long, Renzo re-emerged from the circular hatchway and, leaving the hatch open, joined his subordinate on deck.

'All shipshape below, as far as I can see,' Renzo said, as he drew his knife and joined Ellerman in slashing the parachute ropes. 'Seems the *Pencil* survived the drop without any damage.'

'We'll only really know once we submerge,' Ellerman commented as he continued cutting. 'Fingers crossed.'

'Fingers *and toes* crossed,' Renzo responded. He paused to gaze out into the darkness. 'So, where are our passengers?'

A breeze had begun to pick up, making the surface of the lake increasingly choppy. As water lapped around them, Charlie looked at the blackened faces of his companions in the rubber dinghy. 'Any ideas?' he asked. 'Without the homing device, how the heck do we find that sub now?'

'Apart from rowing blindly around Dragon Lake, hoping to bump into it before sunrise,' added Lucky.

'I might have a solution,' Ben spoke up. 'Caesar.'

Caesar had been lying with his head resting on the edge of the dinghy. At the mention of his name, his head immediately came up and he looked at Ben attentively.

'What do you mean?' Charlie responded. 'I don't think Caesar's got a GPS homing device on him.'

'Caesar *is* a GPS homing device,' said Ben.

Charlie frowned. 'Say again?'

'Didn't you say the sub's been fitted with explosive charges to destroy it if things go wrong?'

'Yeah, but –'

'If the sub's crew is onboard and have left a hatch

open, there's a good possibility Caesar could pick up the scent of the explosives from the sub – *if* we're close enough and *if* the wind's blowing in the right direction.'

'A lot of "ifs" there!' Casper remarked.

Baz, still in the water and busy dragging all their parachutes into a large waterlogged bundle, declared confidently, 'Caesar will do it. That dog's worth his weight in gold, mate.'

'Well, it's worth a try, Ben,' said Charlie. 'Go for it.'

Ben bent and whispered to Caesar. 'You're going to have to do some more swimming, boy.' He clipped on a long leash, gave Caesar a vigorous pat, then lifted the labrador up and eased him over the side, back into the water. 'Seek on, Caesar. Seek on!'

Caesar didn't hesitate. He began to paddle, keeping his nose high out of the water as he sniffed the crisp early morning breeze.

'Nice one, super-sniffer,' said Lucky.

The men in the dinghy, unclipping small paddles from its sides, knelt and began to paddle after the labrador, leaving Baz behind.

'It's all up to Caesar now,' said Charlie, half to himself, as he rowed.

Baz was left treading water in their wake as seven black parachutes wafted about him like seaweed. Methodically, Baz tied the parachute harnesses to the floating lead-filled device he'd been carrying. He then pulled a tab and the air quickly escaped from the device. It sank rapidly, taking the parachutes down with it. In an instant all evidence of their drop vanished. With the job done, Baz swam after the dinghy, and was pulled aboard.

One of the two bearded Taliban insurgents on guard atop a hill nudged his companion, who was almost asleep.

'What is it?' the second sentry asked with a yawn.

'Listen,' said the first insurgent, cocking his head. 'Can you not hear that? Jet engines. An aircraft.'

The other man listened. 'Yes, I hear it. What of it? We hear aircraft flying overhead all the time.'

'But here in these remote mountains? At this time of the morning?' said the first man suspiciously. 'Could it be bringing devil soldiers?'

What they could hear was the sound of the engines of the C-17 that had just dropped the *Pencil* and its two-man crew into Dragon Lake, as it now climbed away into the distance, bound for a refuelling stop in Kuwait before returning to California. As for the Hercules that had dropped Sky Team, and the circling Wedgetail above it, they were flying too high to be heard from the ground.

'It is probably nothing,' said the second insurgent, 'but you had better report it to Commander Baradar.'

The first man took up his walkie-talkie, but as he opened his mouth to speak he was hit from behind by a flying Duke Hazard. In the same instant the second Taliban fighter was tackled by Sergeant Tim McHenry. The walkie-talkie spiralled from the first man's hands. Within seconds the two surprised Taliban fighters had been wrestled to the ground and disarmed. Members of Land Team, who had silently climbed the hill to where the pair had been on guard, then bound and gagged them.

Hazard called to his radio operator, 'Cisco, advise the general that the sentry post has been neutralised and that we're moving up to the cheese factory door.'

'Copy that,' Cisco acknowledged, unhitching his radio.

Caesar had been swimming through the waters of Dragon Lake for fifteen minutes, with Sky Team rowing slowly behind him. Charlie and Lucky had put their night-vision goggles back on and were scanning the vicinity for signs of the *Pencil*.

'Poor wee Caesar,' said Sergeant Bruce. 'How long can he keep this up, Ben?'

'Caesar would swim all day if I let him,' Ben answered. 'He never gives up.' Just the same, Ben was worried about exhausting his dog and he could tell that Caesar hadn't yet picked up a scent.

'If anyone could lead us to the sub, it'd be Caesar,' Baz said confidently.

'Yes, but it is a long shot, after all,' said Mortenson. 'I don't think a dog could –'

'Wait a minute,' said Ben. 'Look.' He pointed ahead of them. 'Caesar's heading off in a new direction and he's swimming harder. I think he might be on to something, boys.'

'Follow that dog!' ordered Charlie, and they all rowed a little harder.

After Caesar had been swimming in this new direction for several minutes, Baz pointed into the night. 'There it is! There's the sub, dead ahead!'

'Caesar the super-sniffer does it again!' said Lucky.

They rowed on until the dinghy bumped against the side of the sub. Caesar hadn't allowed Ben or the others to haul him back into the dinghy. Squirming from their grasp, he'd been obsessively determined to swim to the sub and locate the explosives that he'd picked up with his amazing sense of smell.

With Commander Renzo below deck, Lieutenant Ellerman was on hand to help the troops. Reaching down from the narrow deck, he took the mooring rope handed up to him by Corporal Banner.

'Morning, guys,' Ellerman said in a hushed voice, clearly relieved. 'We were worried you weren't going to make it.'

'Held up by a small hitch, sir,' Charlie replied, 'but our EDD saved the day.'

Caesar came swimming up, and only now would he allow Ben to pull him into the dinghy. Once aboard, he stood and shook himself from head to tail, showering those around him with water.

'Steady on there, Caesar, boy,' laughed Sergeant Bruce as he got a face full of spray.

'Well done, mate,' said Ben, giving Caesar a cuddle and a vigorous pat. 'Good job, Caesar. Good boy!'

'Yes, well done, Caesar,' Charlie agreed, and his sentiments were echoed by the others.

Caesar's dripping tail wagged with delight. But his nose pointed toward the open hatch, via which the smell of explosives was reaching his nostrils.

'Everyone on board the sub, quick as you can,' Charlie urged. 'I'll deal with the dinghy.'

The other members of Sky Team tossed their black equipment bags up onto the sub's deck then scrambled after them. With Lucky leading the way, the men then entered the sub's interior through the open forward hatch. Ben waited with Charlie and Lieutenant Ellerman. Then, grasping Caesar under his front legs,

Ben lowered his EDD through the hatchway to Baz, below, then climbed down after him.

Charlie, still in the dinghy, unsheathed his stiletto-blade commando knife and stabbed holes in the inflatable's side. As water rushed in and the boat quickly began to sink under him, Charlie took Ellerman's hand and stepped up onto the deck of the *Pencil*. As the dinghy went under, Charlie clambered down the hatch's internal ladder. Ellerman followed him, pausing on the ladder's second last rung to reach up and grasp a handle on the round hatch cover. Pulling it shut above him, Ellerman gave its handle several twists, sealing them all in. 'Hatch secure,' he called to Commander Renzo.

'All aboard for Deep Cave,' said Baz, as he settled beside Ben on a bench that ran along the side of the sub's narrow forward compartment. Caesar, now sitting on the floor, was wedged between Ben's knees.

'Sky Team is now Sub Team,' Lucky Mertz remarked.

'Very cramped in here,' observed Mortenson.

'We prefer to think of it as cosy,' said Ellerman, as he brushed past them and stepped over Caesar, making his way to the control position.

The craft's two motors and batteries were located in the stern – a diesel motor for surface running, an electric motor for underwater. At the control position immediately forward of the engine compartment, Commander Renzo was in the pilot's seat. He had a computer screen and a periscope in front of him, and some of the boat's controls.

Lieutenant Ellerman slipped into the co-pilot's seat beside him. As the actual driver of the sub, he had a steering wheel, a sonar screen and a variety of gauges in front of him. In the low, green electric light of the sub's interior the passengers, crowded on benches forward of the control position, could only see the legs of the two pilots, though they could still hear their exchanges.

'All set, Brad?' said Renzo.

Ellerman consulted the gauges in front of him. 'All set, sir.'

'Commence pressurisation.'

Ellerman flicked a switch. 'Pressurisation commenced.'

'Now, let's see if we have any propulsion. Start electric motor.'

Ellerman pressed a button. The sub shuddered a little, and then there came a reassuring electric hum from the stern. 'We have "go" for electric motor.'

A relieved Renzo smiled to himself. 'Very good. Slow ahead.'

'Slow ahead it is, sir,' Ellerman acknowledged.

Ben, Charlie and the other passengers could feel the *Pencil* vibrate as the propeller began to drive the craft forward.

'Blow forward tanks,' Renzo commanded. 'Take her down to fifty metres.'

'Fifty metres. Blowing forward tanks.' Ellerman pressed a button and pulled a lever.

With a loud hissing sound, the sub's forward ballast tanks emptied air out into the lake, and filled with water from outside. The *Pencil* angled downward at the bow, and within moments, the little craft had slipped beneath the surface of Dragon Lake.

Through his night-vision field glasses, Duke Hazard studied the landward entrance to Deep Cave.

'Any sign of life?' Sergeant Tim McHenry asked beside him.

'Two, maybe three, guards behind a rock barrier just inside the entrance,' replied Hazard.

'There must be more Taliban further inside.'

'Uhuh.' Hazard checked his watch. 'We gotta move closer, across the open ground, ready to launch the frontal attack at Zero Hour.

'Roger that.'

'With luck, those guys at the entrance will be asleep and won't see us coming.'

Walking in a stealthy crouch and with all their senses on alert, the members of Land Team began a careful night approach to within a hundred metres of the entrance of Deep Cave.

Once the *Pencil* had glided down to fifty metres, it levelled out.

'So far so good,' said Ellerman. 'Pressurisation is complete. Do we go to a hundred metres now, sir?'

Commander Renzo didn't reply.

Ellerman glanced to his left. Renzo, white in the face with perspiration visible on his brow, sat staring blankly ahead. 'Sir? A hundred metres?'

'Er, sure, sure,' Renzo replied, shaking his head as if to clear it. 'Go to one hundred.'

The submarine eased down another fifty metres. Once it levelled off, Ellerman eyed his sonar screen. Sonar signals could be heard pinging away from the craft and bouncing off the rocks on the lake walls and floor. 'Lakeside cave entrance to Deep Cave two hundred metres ahead,' he announced. 'No major obstructions on sonar. Looks like we have an unob-structed opening a good twenty metres across. Okay to go in, sir?'

Again, Renzo didn't reply.

'Sir?'

'Yes, yes,' Renzo came back, sounding irritated. 'But take it easy. Slow ahead.'

'Slow ahead it is.' Watching the sonar screen intently, Ellerman steered the sub toward the underwater entrance to Deep Cave.

In the *Pencil*'s forward compartment, it had become hot and stuffy. Caesar began to grow uncomfortable and restless. Noticing this, Ben kept Caesar occupied by ruffling his neck and whispering soothingly in his ear. For all those aboard, apart from Ellerman, the only one with a sonar view of what lay ahead, it was just a matter of sitting and waiting.

'Entrance dead ahead,' Ellerman announced. 'Entering now.' Sonar beeps increased in intensity as the sub eased into the tunnel through the rock. 'We've cleared the entrance and are navigating the channel that leads to the pool in the cave.'

'Steady, steady,' said Renzo, sounding anxious.

'Cave wall twenty metres dead ahead,' Ellerman reported. 'Permission to reverse engine and stop the old girl, sir?'

'Yes! Yes! Reverse! Reverse!' Renzo cried, suddenly panicked.

Ellerman threw the engine lever to into reverse, but nothing happened.

'For God's sake, man! What's wrong?' Renzo demanded.

'Chief Brogan did warn us there was a problem with the reverse thrust,' Ellerman replied, calmly trying the lever again and again, without success.

'Hold on! We're going to hit the wall!' Commander Renzo shrieked, alarming the passengers.

Moments later, with a resounding thump, the *Pencil* came to an abrupt halt as the bow rammed against the wall of the channel. The impact almost threw everyone from their seats. The green lights inside the sub flickered then went out. For a few long seconds they sat in darkness.

Something inside Renzo snapped. 'We're going to be stuck down here!' he cried. Slipping from his seat, he threw himself into the passenger compartment. 'I can't take that again! I've got to get out! Got to get out!'

Charlie was the first to slip a torch from his belt and turn it on. In its beam, he saw the wild look on Commander Renzo's face as he scrambled over the passengers, making for the forward hatch.

'Stop!' Ellerman yelled from the control position. 'He's lost his marbles! Stop him! Before he opens the hatch!'

All the men onboard knew that, if the hatch was opened, water would pour into the sub and, a hundred metres down, they would all be done for. Those nearest to Renzo, who was already reaching up to the hatch handle, were Baz and Corporal Banner. As one, they jumped up and grabbed hold of him. The commander, with a crazed look in his eyes, tried to wrestle free. Ben was on his feet, too, and from a trouser pocket he took out a plastic cylinder the size of a toothbrush.

'Hold him still!' Ben said firmly, ripping a plastic cover off the cylinder which contained a one-shot, pre-filled syringe. All members of Sky Team and Land Team carried one of these for personal use in the event they were wounded. In the light of torches now focused on Renzo by Lucky and Sergeant Bruce, Ben jabbed the syringe into Renzo's arm. Pushing it through the man's sleeve, he depressed the top, injecting fluid into the commander's bloodstream. Within moments, Renzo's struggles slackened and he collapsed limply into Corporal Banner's arms.

'What've you given him?' Ellerman called.

'A very strong painkiller,' Ben replied as Banner eased Commander Renzo onto a bench. 'He'll be out for a while.'

'Can you run this thing on your own, sir?' Charlie called.

'Yes, pretty much. But I could do with a hand up here from one of you guys.'

'That will be me,' said Charlie, slipping into Renzo's vacated seat. 'What do you want me to do, sir?'

'Just sit tight for the time being,' Ellerman replied, 'while I get the old girl out of this tight spot.'

With the press of a button, Ellerman blew compressed air into the sub's tanks. Like a lift in a lift shaft, the *Pencil* slowly rose horizontally, the bow scraping lightly on projecting rock as it went. The craft soon emerged into the clear water at the bottom of Deep Cave's vast pool.

'Turns out the cave entrance is a pretty tight fit,' said Ellerman. 'Had we known that before, we mightn't have embarked on this mission! But we're in now – like coming up the drainpipe into a sink full of water. We'll go to periscope depth and take a look around.'

Again the *Pencil* ascended, this time stopping just metres below the surface. Following Ellerman's instructions, Charlie activated the periscope control and the sub's long, thin periscope rose with an electric hum and gently broke the pool's surface.

'Use the periscope's joystick to take a look around,' Ellerman instructed.

'Roger to that.'

As Charlie turned the scope, an image appeared on the screen in front of him. Despite the low light, it was possible to discern blurry human figures on a ledge beside the pool.

'Bingo!' said Charlie. 'Looks like our hostages. Hard to make them out, though.'

Ellerman reached over Charlie's arm and flicked a switch, changing to an infrared lens. 'Better?'

'Much,' Charlie said with a nod. The green image on the screen clearly showed eight human figures.

'Looks like we have two guards – one with an RPG and one with an AK-47 – and six hostages.' He sounded a little concerned. 'Should be seven. One hostage is missing.'

'Killed by the Taliban?' Ellerman pondered aloud.

'I hope not.' Charlie checked his watch. 'You'd better get us ashore, sir. It's thirty minutes to Zero Hour.'

With just a ripple on the surface of the water, the *Pencil* silently emerged from the depths, surfacing bow first. The sub levelled out on the darkened, far side of the pool, five hundred metres from the ledge where the hostages were being kept. The forward hatch opened slowly and silently. Casper Mortenson was the first to climb up on deck. Slipping over the side and into the water, he swam to the rocky shore without making a noise. Pulling himself from the water, Mortenson pointed an infrared torch back to the sub, signalling the all clear.

Ben and Caesar were next in the water. They, too, swam to the rocks. While the others came ashore, Ben set up his equipment. With Caesar standing patiently beside him, he attached the video camera and transceiver to Caesar's black vest, and booted his laptop. When Charlie joined him, dripping wet like the rest of them, Ben said, in a whisper, 'Caesar's good to go, Charlie.'

Charlie nodded. 'Okay, send him out.'

Ben bent low to Caesar's right ear and whispered, 'Seek on, Caesar. Seek on!'

With his tail wagging, Caesar trotted forward. Acting as Sky Team's pathfinder, he disappeared into the darkness. Before long, Charlie and the others had readied their equipment. Leaving Ellerman in the sub with the unconscious Renzo, and with Ben leading, the team shuffled forward, one man at a time.

Lying on her stomach a hundred metres from the glowing lamps of the hostage site, Liberty Lee suddenly felt something brush her leg. Spinning around, ready to fight, she was astounded to see a labrador looking at her with its tongue hanging out and tail wagging.

'A dog?' she said to herself. 'How did you get here?' Noticing the high-tech equipment on Caesar's back, Liberty realised that help must be nearby. She pulled the labrador in close. 'Hello, four-legged friend,' she said, smiling, as she patted him.

Caesar knew instinctively that Liberty was a friend. Recognising her from their meeting on the lawn of

Admiralty House back at home, he licked her face in greeting.

Several hundred metres away, Ben saw flashes of Liberty's face on his screen, captured by the camera on Caesar's back. He dropped to one knee. 'Caesar's found the missing hostage,' he whispered to Charlie. 'It's Liberty Lee and she seems to be okay.'

'Great. You and I will go forward to her,' said Charlie. 'Tell Caesar to keep going.'

Ben pressed the 'transmit' button on his radio. 'Caesar, advance. Seek on!' Ben said softly, his voice emerging from the speaker on Caesar's back. Caesar immediately pulled away from Liberty's grasp and padded on toward the hostages. When Ben judged that Caesar was as close as was safe, he instructed his EDD to stop. 'Caesar, halt. Caesar, down.'

Caesar promptly dropped onto his stomach.

While the other members of Sky Team lay low, Charlie and Ben wriggled their way to Liberty Lee.

'I knew you wouldn't abandon us,' Liberty whispered when they slithered in beside her.

'Are the other hostages okay?' Charlie asked.

Liberty nodded. 'But some are unwell, and the Taliban have placed an explosive vest on the secretary-general.'

On his laptop screen, Ben was looking at the blurry image of Dr Park transmitted from Caesar's camera. 'I can see the vest,' he whispered. 'How will it be detonated?'

'I think the one they call Abdul Razah has a detonation switch.'

'Then we have to take him out first,' said Charlie, before crawling back to brief Lucky, their marksman.

Ben checked his watch. It was almost Zero Hour.

CHAPTER 18

Duke Hazard's eyes were glued to the face of his watch. The moment it ticked to 0510 hours, Zero Hour, he rose from cover and called, hoarsely, 'Let's go, people!'

M-16 at the ready, Hazard ran forward, crouching, headed for the entrance to Deep Cave. From nearby, McHenry, Lyon, Wolf and Harada also ran forward. Meanwhile, from behind a cluster of rocks, Mars Lazar and Brian Cisco opened up with Minimi machine-guns, pouring covering fire in the direction of the cave entrance. Behind the same rocks, Ali Moon was left in charge of the two bound Taliban insurgents.

Answering fire came from the cave entrance. Bullets from AK-47s ripped through the air. A rocket propelled grenade exploded beside Lazar, and he ceased firing. Another RPG lanced through the air and detonated on the ground a few metres in front of Hazard, the blast knocking him off his feet. Lying on his back, he could feel blood flowing down his cheek from a shrapnel cut.

Cursing, he pulled himself to his feet and resumed the dash to the cave.

Sergeant Lyon fired a grenade on the run, spewing it from the launcher beneath the barrel of his M-16. He was the first to reach the rocks at the cave entrance. Seeing the barrel of an RPG poking out, he yanked the weapon from the hands of an astonished Taliban fighter. Sergeant McHenry appeared beside him and vaulted over the rocky barrier to find two Taliban fighters on the ground, wounded, while a third insurgent was trying to reload an AK-47. Using the butt of his carbine, McHenry collected the man on the jaw. The insurgent went down. Lyon, and then Hazard, Wolf and Harada, now scaled the rocks to join McHenry.

After surveying the scene in the gloom, Hazard pressed the 'transmit' button on his personal radio. 'Land entrance secured,' he announced. 'Lazar, bring up Alabama. We need him to penetrate this cave.'

'Negative to that, Sarge,' Lazar replied, sounding strained. 'I've got frag wounds to the legs. So has Alabama. I can't move!'

At that moment, more AK-47 rounds went whizzing by Hazard's head. Ahead, he saw muzzle flashes. Many more Taliban were rushing to the entrance from deeper inside the cave. 'Oh, crap!' Hazard exclaimed. 'Hit the dirt!' he yelled, dropping to the ground. 'Stun grenades! Give 'em stun grenades.'

At the Taliban encampment inside Deep Cave, Commander Baradar had been awoken by the sound of gunfire. He knew at once what this must mean – ISAF troops were on the attack. First dispatching his remaining men to the entrance, to hold it as long as possible, Commander Baradar took out his mobile and tried to call Abdul Razah inside the cave, to instruct him to detonate the explosive vest on Dr Park. But Baradar's phone wouldn't transmit.

'Work of the devil!' he cursed.

For the moment, the life of the secretary-general had been preserved by a failure of technology. Casting the phone aside with disgust, Baradar took up his AK-47 and hurried deeper into the cave.

'Stay still!' mumbled Lucky Mertz. Using the infrared sight on his long-barrelled sniper rifle, he tried to get a bead on Abdul Razah.

The sounds of firing at the cave's landward entrance could be heard faintly in the distance. Abdul Razah had tried to call Commander Baradar for instructions but without success. Panicking, Abdul dodged about, uncertain of what to do. Then he stopped. He took out the detonation switch from his trouser pocket. As Abdul hesitated, a voice called to him from the distance.

'Detonate the vest!' yelled Commander Baradar. 'Do it now!'

With his target now stationary, Lucky Mertz pulled the trigger. The sniper's bullet hit Abdul in the left shoulder, spun him around and knocked him off his feet. The detonation switch went flying from his grasp and landed on the cave floor.

'Let's go!' bellowed Charlie, as Razah went down.

The members of Sky Team leapt to their feet and charged forward, their weapons levelled. As they dashed past Caesar, he, too, jumped up and ran after Ben.

The remaining Taliban guard turned their way, loosing off his RPG. A fraction of a second later, another round from Lucky's sniper rifle hit this second Taliban fighter in the arm. The man went down, dropping his weapon. Meanwhile, the blast from the man's RPG had knocked both Charlie and Mortenson from their feet as the others continued to charge.

Secretary-General Park, seeing that his two Taliban guards had been neutralised, struggled to his feet with his hands still bound behind his back. 'Thank you, thank you,' he said gratefully as his rescuers came running up to him. 'Bless you.'

'Secretary-General, get down!' Liberty Lee ran

forward on the heels of the Special Forces men. 'It's not yet safe!'

In the distant darkness, Commander Baradar had his AK-47 aimed at the figure in the white vest, illuminated by the lanterns by his feet. Baradar's finger curled around the trigger. He knew he only had to hit one of the explosive charges in the vest to detonate it, destroying hostages and rescuers in one fell swoop. Telling himself that he couldn't miss, Baradar pulled the trigger.

In several bounds, Caesar had overtaken the soldiers. His nose leading him like an arrow to the explosive vest, he did something that Ben hadn't instructed him to do. Nor was it something Caesar had been trained to do. Instinctively knowing that the secretary-general was in danger, Caesar risked his own life in a bid to save Dr Park. In the fraction of a second before Baradar fired his AK-47, the bounding Caesar left the ground, taking a monumental leap toward the secretary-general.

Caesar collided with Dr Park's chest, knocking him to the ground just as Baradar's 7.62 mm bullet flew by, only to slam into the cave wall behind them. Meanwhile, the flash from Baradar's rifle had been spotted by Lucky, who, making an educated guess on the gunman's location, quickly fired. Baradar went down.

'Get that vest off Dr Park!' Charlie yelled. 'Now!'

CHAPTER 19

Toward the end of that same day, Ben, Caesar and a blonde woman walked into the military hospital at Tarin Kowt. All the participants of Strike Force Blue Dragon, and the freed hostages, had been rapidly airlifted back to Tarin Kowt by Chinook. The trio found Duke Hazard, Mars Lazar and Casper Mortenson in hospital beds, the first two with their heads swathed in bandages, and Mortenson with his right leg heavily bandaged. Charlie was there, too, sitting in a wheelchair and looking despondent.

'Cheer up, Charlie,' said Ben, as Caesar made a beeline for his old friend and licked his hand in greeting. 'Caesar and I have brought someone to see you.'

Charlie looked up from Caesar to see newspaper reporter Amanda Ritchie standing beside Ben and holding a large carry bag. 'Amanda Ritchie!' Charlie said with surprise. 'What are you doing here?'

'I'm covering the story of the secretary-general's rescue,' Amanda replied with a grin. 'You boys did a fabulous job – Dr Park and all his UN party freed unharmed, and Commander Baradar, Abdul Razah and their lot in prison hospital, under guard. It's a brilliant result, Charlie.'

'But you're not allowed to name any of us,' Charlie reminded her. 'Top-secret Special Forces business and all that.'

'I know. But I can still write about the incredible job done by our Special Forces, including one war dog whose name is not a secret,' said Amanda. A look of concern came over her face. 'Are you okay, Charlie? You, er, look a little flat.'

'Charlie's okay,' Ben assured her, as Caesar came to sit by his feet.

'Yes, *I'm* fine but my Zoomers aren't,' Charlie said unhappily. 'A Taliban RPG shredded them in Deep Cave. I lost my legs for a second time!'

'Ah.' Amanda smiled. 'Your SAS mates back home thought you might be able to use these sometime,' she said, handing the carry bag to him. 'Looks to me like you could use them right now.'

Puzzled, Charlie unzipped the bag. When he saw what was inside, a broad smile lit up his face. 'My spare pair of Zoomers!'

'Get your legs on, mate,' Ben said with a grin. 'We have an appointment with Secretary-General Park.'

Ben and the other members of Sky Team and Land Team had the opportunity to shower, change into fresh day uniforms and collect their personal items before their scheduled meeting with the secretary-general. Now, standing in Tarin Kowt's Special Forces control room, the unwounded soldiers of Strike Force Blue Dragon waited for the VIP to arrive. Charlie Grover was with them, once more mobile, courtesy of his new Zoomers.

Ben Fulton stood next to the US Navy's Lieutenant Brad Ellerman, with Caesar sitting at his side. 'How's Commander Renzo doing, sir?' whispered Ben.

'He's doing fine,' Ellerman whispered back. 'Right now he's on a flight to Frankfurt to receive specialist medical care.'

'I hope he ends up okay,' said Ben. 'And what about the *Pencil* itself, sir? What's happening to it?'

'It's still where we left it, Sergeant, in Deep Cave. I'm tipping it'll be donated to the Afghan Government, to be operated in Dragon Lake as a tourist attraction.'

'That's a terrific idea, sir,' said Ben approvingly.

'Ten-shun!' a voice barked from the door.

All conversation ended abruptly as the men in the room came to attention. UN Secretary-General Park, Lieutenant General McAvoy, Brigadier Quiggly and

Major Jinko walked into the room, followed by Liberty Lee and Amanda Ritchie.

'At ease,' said Lieutenant General McAvoy, as the group reached the front of the gathering. 'The sec-gen wants a word with you people.'

'Gentlemen,' Dr Park began, looking around the faces of the men of Strike Force Blue Dragon, 'as I will also be telling your three wounded comrades in hospital, you have the gratitude of my family and the families of all the members of my party, for saving our lives. I only wish the United Nations had a suitable medal to give you all.'

'We were just doing our job, sir,' Charlie responded humbly.

'And you did your job very well, Sergeant,' Dr Park said with a smile. Now, as you know, the UN does not have its own army. It is reliant on the nations of the world to contribute troops to UN peacekeeping missions. Operation Blue Dragon has taught me that there is a need for a small, specialised unit that can be rapidly deployed on missions such as the rescue you have just carried out. So, I want to inform you that my office is creating just such a unit. And, subject to approval by your governments, I would like to invite you all to join.'

'Including Caesar, sir?' Ben asked.

'Especially Caesar,' Dr Park replied with a smile.

'What will this special unit be called, sir?' Sergeant Bruce asked.

'The Global Rapid Reaction Responders,' the secretary-general advised. 'Or, G-R-R-R.'

'GRRR?' Bendigo Baz said out loud, before breaking into a grin. 'That's appropriate, sir, considering Caesar's involvement.'

'What do you think of my invitation?' Dr Park asked, his eyes sparkling.

The men in the room all looked at each other.

'Who would be in command of the unit, sir?' Sergeant McHenry enquired.

'Liberty Lee would be the commander of GRRR,' Dr Park replied.

McHenry frowned. 'Miss Lee in command?'

The secretary-general smiled and looked Liberty's way. '*Captain* Lee. When she is not serving as my body-guard, Liberty Lee is a captain in the army of the Republic of Korea. Captain Lee will make a fine commander of GRRR.'

'Where would we have to be based, Secretary-General?' Willy Wolf asked.

'You will continue to serve with your own armies, but would be called on for GRRR duty as and when emergencies arise.'

There was a long silence as the men took in the information.

'So, how many of you would want to be a part of GRRR?' Liberty Lee pressed.

'Well,' said Charlie, 'you'd better count me in. It would be an honour.'

'Me too,' said Ben. 'And the same goes for Caesar,' he added, giving his EDD a pat.

With his tail wagging, Caesar looked from Ben to Liberty, as if to say, *Yes, count me in.*

'What about the rest of you blokes?' Charlie asked, looking around the room. 'Who else is up for joining GRRR?'

'Wherever you go, I go, Charlie,' said Baz. 'I'm in.'

'I'm in, too,' Lucky added.

'Okay, what the heck,' McHenry said in his Texan drawl. 'I'm up for it.'

One after the other, the rest of the strike force accepted Dr Park's offer to be a part of GRRR.

The secretary-general's face lit up. 'Thank you. Thank you all.'

He then proceeded to move among the group, talking with each of the men and gratefully shaking their hands. Dr Park then took Ben, Charlie and Amanda aside.

'I would not like to leave Afghanistan before at least doing something to help the Afghan people, especially their youth,' he said, an earnest look on his face. 'You gentlemen have spent much time in this country. And, Miss Ritchie, you also know Afghanistan well. Have you any suggestions?'

'I may have one, sir,' said Ben. 'There are two young Afghan acrobats who travel between FOBs entertaining ISAF troops. Ibrahim and Ahmad are their names, and they're great examples to young people here.'

Dr Park raised his eyebrows in interest. 'Indeed?'

'Yes, sir. It occurred to me that if they had a training academy for acrobats a lot of Afghan boys and girls might be given scholarships to that academy, to get them away from war. It would not only teach them acrobatics but boost their physical and mental skills, improve their confidence and give them team-building skills.'

'That's a great idea, Ben,' Charlie said enthusiastically.

'It *is* a great idea,' agreed Amanda. 'And I could start a media campaign back home to raise funds for the academy.'

'An excellent idea indeed,' Dr Park enthused. 'I will make it a UNESCO project.'

'And, if I can nominate a couple of Afghan children for scholarships right off the bat, sir,' Ben continued, 'it would be a kid from Uruzgan Province named Hajera Haidari, and his sister Meena.'

Dr Park nodded. 'Of course, Sergeant Fulton. Send my secretary, Mr Brown, their details. But now I'm afraid I must go. I wish to visit the soldiers in hospital before my flight back to New York. Thank you again for everything.' Bending to Caesar, he held out a hand. 'And thank you, too, Caesar. Goodbye to you, also.'

As he had once before, Caesar lifted a paw to the secretary-general, who shook it with a chuckle.

The secretary-general went to leave, then paused, turning back to them. 'Do you remember the story I told your children in Sydney, Sergeant Fulton, about the Korean general of old?'

Ben nodded. 'Yes, sir. Vividly.'

The secretary-general went on with a wry smile. 'I think the activation code for members of GRRR should be "rice for water". Don't you? When you hear that, gentlemen, you will know that I – and the world – need your services again. Goodbye.'

'Yes, sir!' Ben and Charlie said in unison.

'Dr Park sure is a top bloke,' remarked Charlie, watching the secretary-general leave.

Ben was about to agree when his mobile phone began to ring. Noting that it was his mum calling, and that she rarely called him without setting up a time by email, he answered at once. 'Mum? Is everything all right at home?'

'Ben!' Nan sounded relieved to hear his voice. 'Have you finished what you had to do over there?'

'Yes, all wrapped up. Why?'

'Oh, wonderful. I hope it's good news for Dr Park,' said Nan.

'It is. But you never heard it from me, Mum.'

'Oh, good. Anyway, I thought I should let you know

that Josh has been going through something, and I think it would be good if his father were here to bed it all down.'

'Mum, what is it?' Ben said, suddenly alarmed, his mind running through all the possibilities. 'If it's an emergency I can get immediate compassionate leave and will be on the next plane out.'

Nan hesitated. 'It's not an emergency exactly, but . . .'

'Mum! Tell me what the problem is.'

CHAPTER 20

With his feet on the coffee table in front of him, Mr
Corbett sat in front of the television with the remote
in his hand. He was just about to change the channel
when the phone rang. Setting down the remote control,
Mr Corbett answered the call.

'Yeah?' he said gruffly.

'Jerry Corbett?' came an unfamiliar voice.

'Yeah. Who wants to know?'

'Come out onto your balcony.'

'Huh?' Mr Corbett glanced at his balcony in confu-
sion.

'Come out onto your balcony. We have a surprise for
you.' The caller hung up.

For a moment, Mr Corbett looked at the phone. 'The
balcony?'

Laying the phone aside, Mr Corbett pulled himself to
his feet and walked to the sliding glass door that fronted
the apartment's balcony. Unlocking the door, he slid it
open. Stepping out onto the balcony, he walked to the

railing and looked down. The lawns below were damp with dew. The street was quiet. Away in the distance, a dog barked.

'What surprise?' Mr Corbett mumbled. At that moment, he heard a sound behind him. Turning, he saw two ropes dangling from above. 'What the . . .?'

In an instant, and with a whir of metal on rope, two black shapes came rappelling down from the roof of the apartment block. Mr Corbett found himself confronted by two men in black, men whose faces were covered by balaclavas so only their eyes and mouths were visible.

'Your stepson will stop bullying Josh Fulton,' said one of the black-clad strangers, his face just centimetres away from Mr Corbett's. 'And you will stop giving your stepson a hard time.'

'Me?' Mr Corbett returned with a quaking voice. 'That Kelvin's a sissy.'

'Ease up, mate,' said one of the strangers. 'We'll be watching you.'

'Look up there,' said the second figure, pointing to the night sky.

Mr Corbett followed the man's pointing finger.

'See the brightest light up there? That's a spy satellite. And one of its hundred cameras will be on you every moment of every day. If you or Kelvin step out of line again, we will know about it.'

'And we'll be back. That's a promise! You behave yourself, and make sure your stepson does too!'

And as quickly and silently as they had arrived, the two men were gone.

Mr Corbett was left, shaken, and wondering what the heck had just happened.

At the breakfast table, Josh, Maddie and Nan were laughing fit to burst. Late the previous evening, Ben and Charlie had arrived at 3 Kokoda Crescent unexpectedly for an overnight stay, surprising Josh and Maddie when they woke in the morning.

'It's so good to have you home, Dad,' said Josh, beaming. 'Even if it isn't for long.' Josh never complained that he missed his father while Ben was away on missions, but he couldn't contain his joy at having him home, even if it were for a brief time.

'What was your secret mission here all about, Daddy?' Maddie asked as she sat on her father's lap, playing idly with the last of her cereal. 'Or was it another top, top topperest secret?'

'Afraid so, Princess,' Ben answered with a grin. He and Charlie had told Josh and Maddie that they'd come back home urgently for a secret mission on Australia's shores. What they didn't tell them was that the mission was of a personal nature. From Nan's information about the Corbetts, Ben had worked out that Kelvin's bullying behaviour had a lot to do with how he was treated at home by his stepfather. Even the taunts of 'Dog Boy' had sounded to Ben like the sort of thing that would have come out of Mr Corbett's mouth first. But Ben was determined that Josh not find out that he and Charlie had set out to correct Mr Corbett's behaviour.

'Top topperest secret,' Charlie added. He and Ben had another secret. The supposed satellite the pair had told Jerry Corbett was watching him around the clock was nothing more than Sirius, the brightest star in the sky. But Mr Corbett didn't know that.

At that moment, the front doorbell rang.

'I'll go,' Josh volunteered, jumping up. When he opened the door, Josh found Kelvin Corbett standing on the doorstep. Kelvin held a backpack out to Josh.

'My backpack!' Josh exclaimed, quickly taking it back.

'Yeah,' said Kelvin, looking embarrassed.

'When we were both called to the principal's office the other day,' said Josh, 'you told her that you didn't know where my backpack was!'

'I know.' Kelvin guiltily dropped his eyes to the ground. 'I forgot where it was. But I remembered again.'

'Did someone tell you to give it back?'

'No, it was my idea,' Kelvin said quietly. 'My mum said she was really disappointed in me, and I hate that. I'm sorry, Josh. Please, don't get me into any more trouble.'

Josh shook his head. 'You got yourself into trouble, Kelvin.'

'I know.' Kelvin backed away. 'I'll see you at school, then.'

'Okay.'

Josh closed the door and, carrying his backpack, returned to the kitchen with a smile on his face.

'Who was at the door, Josh?' asked Nan.

'Kelvin Corbett.' Josh held up his backpack for all to see. 'He brought this back.'

'Wonders will never cease!' Nan exclaimed.

Josh shrugged. 'I think he brought it back so he wouldn't get into any more trouble when we see Mrs McMichaels again today.'

'Well, that's a good sign,' Charlie remarked.

'Josh, I rang your principal about Kelvin's bullying,' confessed Ben. 'Nan told me all about it.'

'Really?' A look of concern came over Josh's face. First Nan had spoken to the principal about Kelvin, and now his father had, too? 'What'd you say to her, Dad?'

'I suggested that you and Kelvin attend a martial arts training course together with Sergeant "Iron Fist" Kasula at Holsworthy Barracks. Just you and Kelvin and Iron Fist. I think it'll be good for the pair of you.'

'That's an excellent idea, Ben,' said Nan. 'It might even turn Josh and Kelvin into friends.'

'What's a marshal artist?' Maddie queried.

'*Martial arts*, dear,' said Nan. 'The art of unarmed self-defence – judo, karate, that sort of thing.'

'Are you up for it, Josh?' Ben asked.

Josh, returning to his chair, shrugged. 'I guess so, Dad.' He wasn't sure how he would fare with the larger Kelvin, but he was prepared to give it a go if it meant that Kelvin didn't bully anyone any more.

'But will Kelvin do the course?' Nan asked.

Ben nodded. 'Oh, yes. The principal has phoned his mother. Kelvin is under instructions from home to agree to do the course when he and Josh see the principal today. In return, nothing more will be said about the stolen backpack and Kelvin's record will stay clean.'

'Let's hope the boy learns his lesson,' said Nan, beginning to clear the breakfast table.

'Oh, I think a few people in the Corbett household have learned a lesson or two,' said Ben, smiling at Charlie. 'Just remember, kids, if anyone bullies you in future, online or in person, you tell a grown-up right away – Nan or me or a teacher. Don't let it go on.'

'Roger to that,' Charlie concurred.

'Yes, Dad,' Josh agreed.

'I promise,' Maddie pledged seriously.

'Looks like our little family is back on an even keel,' Ben said, putting his arms affectionately around Josh and Maddie.

'I wish Caesar was here,' said Maddie, pushing her cereal bowl away. 'He's part of our family, too.'

'You know the quarantine regulations, Maddie,' said Charlie. 'Caesar has to stay in Tarin Kowt for now.'

'And I'll be back with Caesar soon,' Ben added.

'This GRRR thing,' said Josh, 'will it mean you'll only do special missions in Afghanistan?'

'No, mate,' Charlie answered. 'We could be sent anywhere in the world at any time.'

'Cool. Can I tell Hanna?' asked Josh. 'Or is it top-secret stuff?'

'Hanna?' Ben shot Nan a questioning glance.

Nan smiled. 'Josh and Hanna Park have become good friends while you've been away.'

'Ah.' Ben paused for a moment to think. 'I'll clear it with Dr Park first, but I'm sure he'll be okay with you telling Hanna about GRRR. I think both you and Maddie have proven that you can keep vital secrets.'

'Yes,' said Maddie, pleased with herself. 'I only oopsed once.'

Ben frowned. 'You what, Princess?'

Maddie looked guiltily to Josh for help.

'That's *our* vital secret, Dad,' said Josh, with a wink at Maddie.

'Okay,' Ben returned with a grin.

After just two days at home, Ben returned to Tarin Kowt to rejoin Caesar, who was so excited to see him that Ben let him sleep beside his bed on his first night back. The next morning, Ben and Caesar were out on their routine jog around the base's running track when Ben's mobile buzzed. Coming to a stop, he took out his phone. Caller unknown. Noticing Ben's absence, Caesar turned around and trotted over to him.

Curious, Ben put the phone to his ear. 'This is Ben Fulton.'

'Hello, Sergeant Fulton.' Ben recognised the voice as belonging to Liberty Lee. 'I have a message for you. The message is: Rice for water.'

Ben smiled and ended the call. GRRR had its first mission. Ben knelt down beside Caesar. 'Sounds like we're needed, mate.'

With his tail wagging, Caesar looked up at Ben with an expression that seemed to say, *Ready for action when you are, boss. Let's go!*

STRIKE FORCE BLUE DRAGON

SKY TEAM

Sergeant Charlie Grover VC, SASR, team commander

Sergeant Ben Fulton, SOER, deputy team commander and EDD handler

Sergeant Angus Bruce, British Royal Marine Commandos, explosives expert

Corporal Casper Mortenson, Danish Army Hunter Corps, expert underwater diver

Corporal Chris Banner, British Royal Navy Special Boat Service, small boats expert

Corporal Lucky Mertz, SASR

Trooper 'Bendigo Baz', SASR

EDD Caesar, SOER

LAND TEAM

Sergeant Duke Hazard, US Green Berets, team commander

Sergeant Tim McHenry, US Army Rangers, deputy team commander

Sergeant Jean-Claude Lyon, French Foreign Legion

Corporal Brian Cisco, US Green Berets, signaller

Corporal Mars Lazar, US Green Berets, EDD handler

Private Toushi Harada, Aki Haru, Japanese Self-Defence Force, technical warfare expert

Private Wilhelm 'Willy' Wolf, German Kommando
    Spezialkräfte, combat medic
EDD Alabama, US Green Berets
Ali Moon, civilian, interpreter

DSRV-801X, THE *PENCIL*
Commander Dave Renzo, US Navy
Lieutenant Brad Ellerman, US Navy

HOSTAGES

Dr Park Chun Ho, Secretary-General of the United Nations
Captain Liberty Lee, Republic of Korea Armed Forces, the
    secretary-general's bodyguard
Captain Rix, German Air Force, UN helicopter pilot
Lieutenant Frankel, German Air Force, UN helicopter
    co-pilot
Jeremy Brown, British, the secretary-general's principal
    private secretary
Mikashi, Japanese, the secretary-general's press officer
Fader, Danish, a UN official
Loubet, French, a UN official

LIST OF MILITARY TERMS

2IC	second-in-command
AEW&C	airborne early warning and control aircraft, such as the Wedgetail used by the RAAF's No. 2 Squadron
Air Force One	the US Air Force aircraft that carries the President of the United States of America
ANA	Afghan National Army
Apache, AH-64	twin-engine helicopter gunship
bears	military intelligence personnel
Black Hawk, S-70A	military helicopter used as a gunship as well as a cargo and troop carrier
Bushmaster	Australian-made troop-carrying vehicle, four-wheel drive; can carry eight troops plus a crew of two
carbine	rifle with a shorter barrel than an assault rifle
Chinook, CH-47	twin-rotor medium-lift military helicopter that carries cargo, vehicles and troops
CIA	Central Intelligence Agency; America's overseas spy agency
clicks	kilometres
copy that	'I have received' or 'I understand'

Diggers	nickname for Australian soldiers
doggles	protective goggles for war dogs
drone	unmanned military aircraft used for reconnaissance and bombing raids
DSRV	deep submersible research (or rescue) vessel
DZ	drop zone
EDD	explosive detection dog
ETD	estimated time of departure
extraction	pickup of troops from hostile territory by air, land or sea
fixed-wing aircraft	any aircraft that relies on wings for lift, as opposed to a helicopter
fly boys	aircrew
forward operating base (FOB)	a base in enemy territory
frag	shell fragments from an exploding artillery shell, grenade, bomb or missile
French Foreign Legion	French Army unit used for special operations. Traditionally accepts foreigners without asking questions
Galaxy, C-5	four-engine jet military aircraft, the largest in use within the US Air Force

Globemaster, C-17	four-engine jet heavy transport aircraft used to rapidly deploy troops, combat vehicles including tanks, heavy equipment and helicopters over long distances
Green Berets	unofficial name of the US Army Special Forces, because they all wear a green beret
HALO	high altitude low opening; parachute jump from high altitude followed by freefall, with the parachute opening at low altitude
heelo	helicopter, also written as 'helo'
Hercules, C-130	four-engine, propeller-driven military transport aircraft similar to but smaller than the Globemaster, pronounced 'Her-kew-leez' and often referred to as 'Herc'
hostiles	enemy fighters
Humvee	American military vehicle, four-wheel drive
Hunter Corps	the special forces unit of the Royal Danish Army
ID	identification
IED	improvised explosive device or homemade bomb

insertion	secret landing of troops behind enemy lines
insurgent	guerrilla fighter who does not use a regular military uniform or tactics and who blends in with the local population
intel	intelligence information
ISAF	International Security Assistance Force, in Afghanistan
jumpmaster	aircraft crew member who supervises parachutists
kal	an Afghan farm compound, pronounced 'karl' and also sometimes spelt 'qal'
Kommando Spezialkräfte (KSK)	elite German military special operations force
loadmaster	crew member in charge of cargo and passengers in military cargo aircraft and helicopters
LZ	landing zone
M-16	American-made 5.56 mm assault rifle
M1 Abrams tank	main battle tank of the US and Australian armies
malek	a neutral Afghan envoy trusted by both sides

mess, the	a place where troops gather to eat in a military camp
met	meteorological; weather
MP5	German-made compact Heckler & Koch MPF 9 mm submachine gun
MRE	meal, ready-to-eat; a sealed military ration pack of pre-cooked food
NCO	non-commissioned officer; a rank in the Australian Army between private and warrant officer, including sergeant, lance corporal and corporal
op(s)	military operation(s)
operator	Australian SAS Regiment soldier
point	the most forward position in a patrol
puppy Peltors	protective earmuffs for war dogs
RAAF	Royal Australian Air Force
roger	'yes' or 'I acknowledge'
round	bullet
Royal Marine Commandos	commando unit of the British Navy's Royal Marines
RPG	rocket-propelled grenade
secure comms	communications that can't be intercepted

seek on	a handler's instruction to an EDD to find explosives
Special Air Service Regiment (SASR)	elite Special Forces unit in the Australian Army
Special Boat Service (SBS)	a special operations unit of Britain's Royal Navy, specialising in small boat ops
Special Operations Engineer Regiment (SOER)	Australian Special Forces unit that specialises in military engineering and that trains and operates EDDs
special ops	special operations or secret missions
Spitfire	British World War Two fighter aircraft
trooper	lowest rank in the SASR, the equivalent of a private in other army units
USAF	United States Air Force
VC	Victoria Cross for Australia, the highest-ranking Australian military medal for gallantry
Zero Hour	the time set down by military for an operation to begin

FACT FILE

Notes from the Author

If you have read the first book in this series, *Caesar the War Dog*, you will know that a real war dog named Caesar served with Anzac troops during the First World War (1914–18). That Caesar, a New Zealand bulldog, searched for wounded men and carried water to them. Another war dog named Caesar, a black labrador–kelpie cross, served with Australian forces during the Vietnam War as an Australian Army tracker dog.

The fictional Caesar in this book is based on several real dogs of moden times – Sarbi, Endal and Cairo – and their exploits. Here are a few more facts about the real dogs, people, military units, places and equipment that appear in this book and inspired the stories in this series.

EXPLOSIVE DETECTION DOGS (EDDs)

The Australian Imperial Force used dogs during the First World War, primarily to carry messages. Sarbi was preceded by a long line of sniffer dogs used by the

Australian Army to detect land mines during the Korean War (1950–53) and, later, in the Vietnam War. In 1981, the current explosive detection dog program was introduced by the army's Royal Australian Engineer Corps, whose base is adjacent to Holsworthy Army Barracks in New South Wales. In 2005, Australian EDDs were sent to Afghanistan for the first time. A number have served there since and several have been killed or wounded in action.

SARBI

Sarbi, whose service number is EDD 436, is a black female labrador serving with the Australian Army. She began the EDD training program in June 2005 and graduated from the ninteen-week training course with Corporal D, joining the Australian Army's top-secret Incident Response Regiment (IRR) – now the Special Operations Engineer Regiment (SOER) – whose main job was to counter terrorist threats. In 2006, Sarbi and Corporal D were part of the security team at the Commonwealth Games in Melbourne. In April 2007, the pair was sent to Afghanistan for a seven-month deployment, returning to Afghanistan for their second tour of duty the following year.

On 2 September 2008, Sarbi and Corporal D were members of a Special Forces operation launched from a forward operating base a hundred kilometres northeast of Tarin Kowt. The operation went terribly wrong when five Humvees carrying Australian, American and Afghan troops were ambushed by a much larger Taliban force. In the ensuing battle, Corporal D was seriously wounded and became separated from Sarbi, who was also injured. Nine of the twelve Australians involved were wounded, as was their Afghan interpreter. Several American soldiers were also wounded in the battle. So began Sarbi's time lost in Taliban territory, a saga imagined in the first book of the Caesar the War Dog series.

After being 'missing in action' for thirteen months, Sarbi was wrangled back into friendly hands by a US Special Forces soldier. A month later, Sarbi and Corporal D were reunited at Tarin Kowt, in front of the Australian Prime Minister and the commanding US general in Afghanistan. Sarbi is the most decorated dog in the history of the Australian military, having been awarded all the medals that Caesar receives in *Caesar the War Dog*.

ENDAL

Endal was a sandy-coloured male labrador who was trained by the UK charity Canine Partners. He went on to qualify as a service dog and, in the late 1990s, was partnered with Allen Parton, a former Chief Petty Officer with Britain's Royal Navy. Confined to a wheelchair from injuries sustained during the Gulf War, initially Allen couldn't speak, so he taught Endal more than a hundred commands using hand signals.

In 2009, Endal suffered a stroke and had to be put down. During his lifetime, Endal became famous in Britain, receiving much media coverage and many awards for his dedicated and loyal service to his master. A young labrador named EJ (Endal Junior) took Endal's place as Allen Parton's care dog.

CAIRO

Cairo is a long-nosed Belgian Malinois shepherd with the United States Navy SEALs (Sea, Air and Land teams), a unit within the US Special Operations Command. He was trained for insertion by helicopter, and by parachute, strapped to his handler, just like Caesar is in this book. In, 2011, Cairo was part of SEAL Team 6, which landed by helicopter in a compound in Pakistan to deal with Osama bin Laden, the leader of the terrorist organisation Al Qaeda. Cairo's job was to go in first to locate explosives in the compound. Cairo and all members of his team returned safely from the successful mission.

AUSTRALIAN MILITARY INVOLVEMENT IN AFGHANISTAN

In 2001, the Australian Government sent SAS troops to participate in coalition operations in Afghanistan following Al Qaeda attacks in America. Although those Australian troops were withdrawn in 2002, Australia resumed its military involvement in Afghanistan as part of ISAF in 2005. By 2012, Australia had 1500 troops in Afghanistan, the largest military presence of any foreign nation other than members of the North Atlantic Treaty Organisation (NATO). Most of these Australian troops have been based in Uruzgan Province, and some in Kandahar Province, and have been involved in reconstruction programs, rebuilding destroyed or run-down infrastructure in Afghanistan, the training of the Afghan National Army, and logistical support to ISAF forces. In addition, 300 members of the Australian contingent have been SAS operators and commandos from 1 and 2 Commando Regiments, involved in special operations against the Taliban and other anti-government militias.

SPECIAL AIR SERVICE REGIMENT (SASR)

The original Special Air Service was created by the British Army during the Second World War for special operations behind enemy lines, with the motto of 'Who Dares Wins'. In 1957, the Australian Army created its own Special Air Service Regiment, commonly referred to as the Australian SAS, two years after the New Zealand Army founded its Special Air Service.

Australia's SAS is considered by many to be the finest Special Forces unit in the world, and its members help train Special Forces of other countries, including those of the United States of America.

The top-secret regiment is based at Campbell Barracks

at Swanbourne, in Perth, Western Australia. Because its men are often involved in covert anti-terrorist work, their names and faces cannot be revealed. The only exception to this rule is SAS members who receive the Victoria Cross. The unit is divided into three squadrons, with one squadron always on anti-terrorist duty and the others deployed on specific missions.

During the war in Afghanistan, Australian EDDs and their handlers have frequently worked with Australian SAS and commando units on special operations.

BAND-e-AZHDAHAR

Band-e-Azhdahar, or Dragon Lake, really exists in Afghanistan's Bamiyan Province, although Deep Cave was my invention.

THE TALIBAN

The Taliban is an armed political movement that originated in southeast Afghanistan and is confined to Afghan tribes that speak the Pashto language. In late 2001, foreign coalition troops joined Afghan Northern Alliance forces in driving Taliban and Al Qaeda fighters out of Afghanistan, after which an elected Afghan Government was established in the country.

Since then, Taliban forces, reinforced by other anti-ISAF militias and extremist Muslim fighters from many countries, and operating from mountainous regions of eastern

Afghanistan and western Pakistan, have waged a fierce insurgent war against the Afghan Government and ISAF forces.

THE *PENCIL*

The *Pencil* is based on a real mini-submarine built for the US Navy SEALs. Originally, it was intended to build twelve of these, but only the prototype was constructed, launched and tested. Due to its exorbitant cost, no more were built. The prototype was damaged in a fire, and retired. Just like the *Pencil*, this mini-sub had a crew of two, could carry sixteen passengers, and its hull was four times as strong as that of an ordinary submarine.

ZOOMERS

Charlie's high-tech Zoomers are based on real prosthetic 'blades' used by athletes.

THE UNITED NATIONS (UN)

The United Nations was founded in 1945 and its head-quarters is situated in New York City, USA. To date it has 193 member states, including Australia, which fund its worldwide humanitarian and peacekeeping operations. The secretary-general, who is elected by its members, is the organisation's most senior officer.

Member states provide the UN's peacekeeping forces. UN humanitarian agencies include the United

Nations Educational, Scientific and Cultural Organisation (UNESCO), the World Health Organisation (WHO), the World Food Programme (WFP), the International Court of Justice (ICJ or World Court), and the United Nations Children's Fund (UNICEF). Australia is currently a member of the UN Security Council, a body tasked with maintaining international peace and security.

About the Author

Stephen Dando-Collins is the award-winning author of more than thirty books, many of which have been translated into numerous languages. Most of Stephen's books are about military history and include subjects such as ancient Rome, the American West, colonial Australia and the First World War. *Pasteur's Gambit* was shortlisted for the science prize in the Victorian Premier's Literary Awards and won the Queensland Premier's Science Award. *Crack Hardy*, his most personal history, received wide acclaim. He has also written several titles for children, including *Chance in a Million* and *Caesar the War Dog*. Stephen and his wife, Louise, live and write in a former nunnery in Tasmania's Tamar Valley.

You can learn more about Stephen's other books at www.stephendandocollins.com. For updates about the adventures of Caesar, in print and on the screen, go to www.caesarthewardog.com.

Available now

Read on for the first chapter

CHAPTER 1

The first time that Corporal Ben Fulton saw Caesar, he didn't think much of him. In fact, he walked by him twice without a second glance. When he finally came to a stop in front of Caesar, on his third inspection of the line of dogs, Ben had a perplexed look on his face. 'That has got to be ugliest labrador retriever I have ever seen,' he said.

Corporal Ben had come to Huntingdon Kennels to look for a new dog, one that he could train to become an Australian Army sniffer dog. Huntingdon Kennels raised dogs for use by the police, emergency services and military, and Ben had asked to see the kennels' labrador retrievers. In his experience, labradors made the best sniffer dogs. So, the kennels lined up a dozen young labradors for Ben to inspect. Some were sandy coloured, some were black, and some, like Caesar, were brown. They were all aged between eighteen months and three years, and they sat in a line like soldiers, facing Ben. All had been given obedience training by the kennels.

As a result, they sat still and quiet as Ben walked up and down the line accompanied by Jan, a young woman who helped run the kennels.

Ben was looking for a dog with something special. The animal he ended up choosing would spend the rest of his working days with Ben, and there would be times when Ben's life, and the lives of other soldiers around them, would depend on that dog. So, Ben had to be sure that he and the dog would get on well, and that the animal had what it took to be a war dog. Just as every man doesn't always make a good soldier, not every dog has the courage, strength and loyalty to be a good war dog. None of the dogs Ben had viewed that morning stood out. Except for Caesar – and he stood out for all the wrong reasons – with his snout puffed up like a balloon on one side, he was not a pretty sight.

'That's Caesar,' said Jan. 'He's always getting into mischief. He went and stuck his nose into a beehive and got stung on the nose three or four times. The swelling will go down in a day or two. It doesn't seem to have bothered him much.'

As the corporal studied him, the labrador returned his gaze, taking in this well-built soldier of average height with a round, open face and dark, short-cropped hair. Then Caesar lowered his head, almost as if he was embarrassed by his puffy nose.

Ben smiled broadly. 'Poor Caesar,' he said, kneeling

beside the sitting dog and rubbing him behind the ear, which dogs love. 'Those nasty bee stings would have hurt like hell. Didn't they, mate?'

Caesar, immediately taking a liking to him, responded by wagging his tail and trying to lick Ben's face.

The manager of the kennels now joined them. 'You're not thinking of taking Caesar, are you, Corporal?' he said. 'That would be the worst dog in the kennels. We were considering getting rid of him.'

'Why?' Ben asked, turning to look at him.

'Caesar's always sticking his nose where he shouldn't,' said the manager. 'And he's a digger, too. Some dogs love to dig holes, but labrador retrievers aren't usually that interested in digging. This labrador would dig all day if you let him, just to see what he could dig up. That's not good for a working dog. You want his full attention.'

Ben patted Caesar's shining chocolate-brown coat, then stood up. He looked down at Caesar, and Caesar looked back up at him with a wagging tail and gleaming eyes that seemed to say, *Take me!*

'You know what?' said Ben. 'I'll take him, I'll take Caesar. I like him.'

'Really? Why him, of all dogs?' the surprised manager responded.

'Curiosity,' said Ben. 'A dog that puts his nose into a beehive and digs to see what he can find has loads of curiosity. And in my job, that's just the sort of dog

I need. He's got to be curious enough to find out what's hidden in a package, or to locate explosives hidden in a culvert beside the road. A dog like that can save lives.'

The manager shook his head. 'Well, good luck with him, Corporal. But I don't think you'll find Caesar will be much use to the army.'

'What's his ancestry?' Ben asked.

'His father and mother are labradors,' said Jan. 'But his grandfather was a German shepherd.'

'A German shepherd?' said Ben, nodding approvingly. 'I thought I could see a hint of another breed in his long snout. German shepherds are even more intelligent than labradors. If this dog has the best qualities of the curious labrador and the smart German shepherd, we could make quite a team.'

'Please yourself,' said the manager, unconvinced. 'But don't blame me if he disappoints you and lets you down one day.'

Despite the manager's lack of confidence in this brown labrador, Corporal Ben had been working with military dogs for ten years, and he considered himself the best judge. Signing the necessary papers, Ben officially made Caesar a recruit of the Australian Army, and made him his new trainee war dog.

Loved the book?

There's so much more
stuff to check out online

AUSTRALIAN READERS:

randomhouse.com.au/kids

NEW ZEALAND READERS:

randomhouse.co.nz/kids